BLADESTAY

BLADESTAY

JACKIE JOHNSON

CamCat
Books

Content Warning: This novel touches upon sexual assault and domestic violence and may be disturbing to some readers.

CamCat Publishing, LLC
Ft. Collins, Colorado 80524
camcatpublishing.com

This is a work of fiction. Names, characters, places, and incidents are either products of the author's imagination or are used fictitiously.

Hardcover ISBN 9780744306941
Paperback ISBN 9780744306958
Large-Print Paperback ISBN 9780744306972
eBook ISBN 9780744306989
Audiobook ISBN 9780744307122

Library of Congress Control Number: 2023936037

Book and cover design by Maryann Appel

5   3   1   2   4

*TO ALL THE KIDS WHO HAVE EVER
FELT POWERLESS.*

I

YOUNGBLOOD

THERE'S A SMALL GAP BETWEEN THEOLOGICAL FANATICISM
AND SOCIAL DISORDER; THEREIN LIES CHARISMA.

CHAPTER

1

It was two in the morning when the coyotes started hollering at each other, but by then Brody Boone had already slipped into wool trousers, a matching vest, and a buckskin jacket with copper rivets down the sleeve hems. The coyotes were a common nuisance; the crack of gunfire was not.

Relying on the silvery light of a fat moon, Brody strapped a ream of ammo over his hips and shoved pistols into the holsters hanging at his thighs. He thumbed shells into a wide-barreled shotgun as he quietly heeled the door shut on his way out.

Both his parents were heavy sleepers, but his little brother, Billy, was not. Brody's feet had hardly left the porch when he heard padding footsteps behind him. He wheeled around, shotgun snug in the hollow of his shoulder, finger off the trigger.

He dropped his aim to the ground as soon as he saw his little brother at the end of the barrel.

Brody smiled calmly as he reached out and tapped a finger against Billy's narrow chest, and when Billy looked down, Brody lightly flicked Billy's nose. Billy swatted at him, but Brody danced away from the slower reflexes, grinning.

"Cabron," Billy said.

"If you're gonna curse, do it in English."

Billy looked past Brody, hugging himself. "Adónde vas?"

"*English*, Bill."

Billy crossed his arms. "No estoy usando grocerias."

"Just you wait till your stubbornness costs your life."

Billy repeated the question in exaggerated aristocratic English.

"Burro," Brody said with a chuckle. "Hear the cows?"

They were lowing mournfully, and Billy nodded. "Wolves?"

"Coyotes," Brody said. "I'm just gonna go give them a scare, okay?"

"Be careful."

"Careful is for city folk and dandelions." Brody winked. "Go back to bed."

Billy began to protest, but Brody said, "How does coyote stew sound for breakfast?"

Billy wrinkled his nose. "Can't be worse than the rattler Pa insisted would taste like chicken."

Brody grinned again. "Go on now."

Brody made his way to the southern gate, ducked between the wood panels, and crossed a large, vacant prairie. At the edge of the patch of grassland, the terrain grew jagged with granite as the slope steeped to the west, a conglomerate of ponderosa tightening together the higher he climbed. Rays of pearl seeped through the branches, guiding Brody's steps to the plateau, hillsides he could likely hike blindfolded.

He stilled.

A breeze whispered from the east, tinged with the indication of campfire. Their homestead was too far from Ruidoso for this to come from town—this was coming from somewhere on their property. Catching his breath from the quick ascent, Brody scanned the valley and the accompanying hillsides for the glow of fire. Finding nothing, he continued eastbound and up, maintaining the advantage of high ground.

He followed a familiar deer trail, stopping again about a mile down the path. He lowered himself beside a pair of boulders pressed closely together, a landmark he called dicelegs—dice, because of how oddly square the outcropping had shaped and eroded; legs, because of how the bottom portion stretched almost like pillars down the steep slope of the hillside.

Swallowing, Brody found his mouth uncomfortably dry. He cursed himself for not bringing a canteen. He should know better, being a product of both the desert and the mountains, a child of survival and lawlessness.

Around and below the bend of the widely berthed outcropping was the orange glow he'd been after.

The thing about Brody was that he was fiercely protective, un-flinchingly loyal, and above all, an ego safely in check by his wits. At nineteen years old, he was already acutely discerning when it came to battles he could win and battles he could not.

Crouching, he stepped around the dicelegs and crept toward the glow, shotgun held steady at the orange as he kept a constant eye for movement. Brody spotted the chestnut mare before he saw the tips of flame, yellow and orange flicking into his vantage above the lip of the outcropping like the forked tongue of a diamondback tasting the air for prey.

The lip of the outcropping stood about six feet from the firepit be-low, and as Brody went flat on his belly to crawl to the edge, he noticed a pair of boots crossed at the ankle lounged stolidly.

Heart pounding, Brody appraised the wilderness for others. The noises of night chirped and howled and echoed a familiar cacophony, both distant and near. Mentally bouncing two ideas—of going back or confronting the lone stranger—he weighed the level of threat against his options. Plenty of travelers had seen themselves through these hills, a common connecting route between Texas and California, but rarely did anyone come this close to home. The Boone ranch was several hundred acres of staked land from his father's father, a hold that precariously survived the Mexican-American War. The validity of the family's claim to the land wasn't so much tolerated as it was overlooked in a time when thousands of other Mexican families were displaced in America's ubiquitous annexation of southern territories, a destiny of manifest proportions that would soon segue into a far bloodier conflict.

After long observation, Brody concluded the man by the fire was sleeping, and better still, that he was alone. Pushing off his stomach, he held the shotgun in one hand, a groove in the rough stone with the other, and gracefully lowered himself to the mild slope of the clearing below. He landed with a soft thud and immediately set the butt of the shotgun against his shoulder.

The boots belonged to an imposing figure with a barrel chest and a frontier-hardened girth to his limbs. The duster of the slumbering man encased him, his hands interlocked behind his head, hat purposefully askew across his forehead to darken his eyes from the blaze.

Without a twitch or stir, the slumbering man spoke. His voice was as callous as his skin, the same way a thundercloud commands respect when it rumbles, not because it is cruel, but because one does not negotiate with forces of nature. One endures them.

"You belong to these parts?" the man drawled, shadows dancing menacingly across the exposed, lower half of his face in the firelight.

"These parts belong to me. Family by right," Brody said, a defense in the statement that was as much genetic as it was tangible. "Who are you?"

"August Gaines."

Brody waited for the man to expand, but after a few moments of nothing but the sound of wood popping and hissing, he presumed—correctly—the man lacked verbosity.

Brody took a step closer, finger now on the trigger. "Don't you want to know my name?"

August poked a finger on the underside of the brim and lifted the hat from his face, showing the deep lines of many miles and long years. He gave the young man a slow appraisal as if considering a piece of livestock, then said, "I ain't decided yet if that's pertinent."

A bead of sweat fell down the back of Brody's neck, making him feel feverishly cold for a moment regardless of the waves of heat he stood next to.

"What's your business on my land, mister?"

"*Yours*," August echoed.

Brody stole a glance around. Somehow, the trees felt closer. The horse seemed larger. The fire, hotter. Swallowing past the feeling of cotton in his throat, Brody regripped his weapon.

Before Brody could respond, August spoke again. "Sit down, boy."

Brody was itching to do the opposite, felt the mistake of his choices before the vaporous reasons turned solid. From the corner of his eye, he thought he saw movement. He swept the shotgun in that direction, took a step back to angle himself better between a possible threat in the woods and the potential one on the ground.

"Good Lord, boy. You're making me nervous." August sat up and leaned his back against a propped saddle. He pulled out a pipe. "Sit down a beat, would you? I gather I'm not going back to sleep anytime soon, so I'd like to talk at you for a minute." He reached into the saddle pack, paused to make purposeful eye contact with the boy as to convey his nonnefarious intents, and once he received a single nod of consent from Brody, he pulled out a moccasin water bag. Without taking so much as a sip for himself, August lifted the water in the boy's direction.

Brody glanced at it but made no move for it.

August tossed it at Brody's feet.

Brody had every intention of hightailing it back home, but soon he found himself sitting fireside. Lulled by the stranger's pervasive calm, compelled by the dull ache in the man's deep voice, Brody never felt himself being coaxed out of his armor until he was no longer wearing any. The more August spoke, the heavier felt the weight in Brody's body. Soon, the shotgun lay forgotten beside him. A glass bottle surreptitiously replaced the moccasin. Furrows were traded for laugh lines. Brody had never met a man like August. A man who smiled only when it was earned, a man whose convictions seemed to blanket surrounding ones, a man who was a force of nature in every availing sense.

In the span of a few hours, Brody had developed a fondness for the patriarch, and although it never occurred to him why, the base reason was blatant: August seemed to buck society at every turn, but it didn't seem that society had punished him one bit for it.

CHAPTER

2

P atrick Holmes had been picking on Theo Creed since she turned
thirteen, which, she was told, meant that he had feelings for her.
As the years progressed, the teasing was beginning to border on
harassment, so when Theo saw Patrick sulking down the street, head
cocked toward the dirt road, hands shoved in his pockets, Theo pulled
her bonnet down, curled her shoulders, and cut across Main Street. They,
like everyone else in the small town of Bladestay, Colorado, had known
each other since they were infants, and Theo was intimately aware of
Patrick's mannerisms and moods, so as soon as she recognized the
scowl on his face, the way it contorted even at inanimate objects as if
everything was a burden or annoyance, the way he kicked at anything
in the vicinity of his toes, Theo knew to keep her distance.

"Theodora!"

Theo cringed but didn't slow.

"Theodora Creed!" Patrick called.

She heard his trot catch up to her, his well-worn boots creating dull thuds in the clay.

"Morning, Mr. Holmes," Theo said as his shoulder bumped into her, an overeager attempt to match her stride.

"Why you always needlin' me, girl?" Patrick said, jutting his elbow toward her as if he actually expected her to take hold.

She actively ignored the gesture. "I'm sure I have no idea what you're talking about, Mr. Holmes." Theo found out that the only way to truly get under his skin was to affront formality. She hadn't called him by his first name in over a year; she hadn't looked him in the eye since last week.

Patrick jogged a few steps ahead and blocked her path, leaning downward into her line of sight as to coax her into looking at him.

Like a creek around a stone, Theo slipped indifferently by him.

He snatched her arm, his fingers digging in the tender flesh just beneath her armpit. His palm was damp with sweat, and the way it moved against her skin made her stomach turn.

Sweetly, she said, "Aren't you strong." It was another thing Theo had discovered about Patrick: offer him compliments in such a way that he could never tell whether they're jocular or genuine. She tried to continue walking and Patrick squeezed harder. Patrick didn't used to get physical, but as he got older, taller, and stronger, he began to see the benefit of the bully's currency.

Finally, Theo lifted her face to look Patrick in the eye. She could smell the sour trace of stale whiskey that saturated his tongue, his clothes, his household.

Her stomach did another turn. Clenching her own fist, her voice changed from airy and innocent to heady and menacing. "Get your hands off me or I swear to God, I will give you a scar that will follow you six feet under."

Patrick's eyes toggled between hers, revealing an internal recoil at the harsh side that Theo never showed to anybody, much less Patrick.

"Hey, Patty," a voice called from atop the raised deck of the general store

Immediately, Patrick's grip loosened as his head darted over his shoulder. "Hiya, Mr. Blacksmith." He angled himself to be at Theo's side, quickly looping his arm so Theo's hand was forced into the crook of his elbow.

Bram Blacksmith was a towering, immaculately dressed man with many brightly colored waistcoats and an impeccably clean jaw. Pushing fifty, the man looked ten years his junior with tenaciously brown hair and limber athleticism. He wore a boastful gold ring on his left pinky finger, two wedding bands on a chain around his neck, and an equally polished gold chain at his breast. All the eligible women (and some not so eligible) in Bladestay would marry him in a heartbeat, but Blacksmith hadn't had eyes for anyone but a woman named Maureen, and that didn't change even after she'd moved to the cemetery.

Blacksmith leaned casually against the support pillar, arms crossed, a lump of chew in his lip and a six-shooter on his hip. "What're you up to, young man?"

Theo subtly tried to pull away, but Patrick grabbed her hand and kept hers in place.

At that time, a boy with auburn hair came out of the general store holding a broom in both his hands like he was wielding a sword.

"Cool it, Elliot," Blacksmith said to the boy without a glance in his son's direction.

Elliot was fifteen, two years Theo's junior and small for his age, but he was scrappy and stronger than he looked and as protective of Theo, if not more so, than her own siblings.

"Just escorting my girlfriend, sir." Patrick could be a mean kid, but rarely was he an idiot. He knew when to play nice and when he could get away with not doing so, and with Bram Blacksmith, nobody got away with anything. Patrick didn't much like to do things that he couldn't get away with.

"I have your things for your mother set aside, Theo," Blacksmith said without taking his glare from Patrick. Jamming a thumb over his shoulder to the entrance, he added, "Go on, hon. Elliot'll help you. I need a word with . . ." His eyes scanned the street lazily as he spat into it. Letting his eyes land back on Patrick, he added, ". . . your boyfriend."

She tried again to pull her hand free, but Patrick wasn't yet ready to give, even with the ice-blue gaze of Blacksmith falling upon him.

Fed up, Theo rose to the tips of her toes, her own fingers digging into Patrick's arm, and hissed something into his ear that would drastically change not only the course of Theo's day, but of her life. Then she ripped her hand free and began to stalk away.

Blacksmith hadn't heard what Theo said, and what nobody else heard that day was the very thing that made Patrick publicly snap. He snatched her arm again, yanked her backward, and clawed the green bonnet from her head. Hairpins tore free from the elaborate updo that had taken her mother an hour that morning, her towhead hair tumbling partially free in lopsided curls.

What happened next happened very fast.

Patrick grabbed a thick handful of her nearly white blond hair, yanked a four-inch blade from his belt, and sliced a huge chunk of hair from her head, scraping so close that the knife nicked her scalp.

Blacksmith was yelling something as Elliot leaped from the deck.

Theo shrieked when the blade sliced for her head, which quickly turned to a snarl when she realized what Patrick was doing wasn't deadly, just cruelty.

Her world rapidly narrowed.

She tried to rip free of his grip, and when she couldn't, she instead stepped close, angled her body, and kneed Patrick hard between the legs.

Patrick let out a horribly choked cry as the knife tumbled from his hand. As Patrick fell to his knees, doubled over and holding his crotch, Theo swept the knife from the red clay and plunged it into his shoulder. The first swing of the blade was reflexive; the second one was born of rage.

Theo was shocked at the ease in which the blade slipped deeply through skin and muscle, even more shocked in the aftermath, when she realized she had yanked the blade back out and was about to sink it back in. If it hadn't been for Elliot grabbing her wrist and twisting the knife from her grip, Theo wasn't sure how many times she would have watched the blade disappear into his skin. Later, when she would recall the moment, she would be disturbed to find that her memory was largely black and scattered, that adrenaline had erased logic and scrambled memory.

She wouldn't remember the specifics of Blacksmith intervening, wrapping his arm around her waist and physically dragging her away. She wouldn't remember how she fought to keep the knife, the curses she was yelling at the boy bleeding in the dirt. She wouldn't remember the scene she made for the gathering townspeople. But what she would remember is how the encounter she'd been thwarting for so long had finally and categorically derailed her life. But just as every shift in trajectory is not by choice, not all derailments are adverse, for the things disguised as mistakes often set us on the paths we were meant to travel all along.

CHAPTER

3

ifty-three miles outside Bladestay, August Gaines approached the town of Clayton Creek. His mare was short-striding with the ache of the weary, tripping over rocks she was usually sure-footed around. With over two hundred miles covered in the past two weeks, both horse and rider yearned for the relief of civilization.

August swung a leg over the silver-plated saddle and slid down, his feet hitting the dirt road with wavering legs. Adjusting himself, August swept a calloused palm down the mare's neck, once, in a brief, rare expression of affection. He slipped the headstall over the mare's ears, and she dipped her head in compliance, working her jaw to slide the bit from the corners of her mouth. Hooking the bridle on the saddle horn, August swung the lead line over his shoulder and began walking. As sturdiness returned to the man's legs, his stride grew hungrier as did the ache in his belly. Already, he could smell the roasting of pig on a spit through the persistent aroma of pine cones and evergreens.

Clayton Creek had boomed into existence at the discovery of gold in the nearby hills, a town that, like so many others in the rush, exploded into establishment, burned brightly, but extinguished quickly, leaving nothing behind but brick bones and silent ghosts. Often, the extinguishment was a self-consummation as the promise of wealth far outreached the reality, but sometimes towns like Clayton Creek were snuffed by the likes of August Gaines.

The entrance to the town welcomed newcomers with a stucco arch that had the name of the town painted in a metallic gilt across the crest.

August paused under the archway, running dirt-grimed fingers across the brailled plaster, considering the craftsmanship like a work of art. He resumed his walk. Knob spurs were silent on oiled boots. Thoroughly broken leather chaps hugged muscular thighs. His calf-length duster cloaked him like an entity.

Everything about August Gaines was quiet, contemplative even. He was a silent terror, the kind that slipped through the window without the latch clicking, without the glass breaking, without anybody knowing. He deeply craved grand entrances but appreciated more the power of tacit ones.

The sheriff and his deputy met August and his mare no more than twenty yards past the stucco entrance. No dust rose from the shod hooves of their horses; spring showers kept the paths muted.

The wide brim of August Gaines's white Staker hat shadowed his sharp features, and the high noon sun obliged.

It was the sheriff who spoke first.

"Welcome to Clayton Creek, partner. You sure look like you could use a hot meal and a warm bed, and why, we have—"

"Take my horse," August said. It wasn't his intention to be rude, but he was tired, and something irked him about an officer young enough to be his offspring.

Deputy and sheriff exchanged a glance.

"Excuse me?" the sheriff said.

August noticed the swell in his voice, the apprehension that leaked in as hospitality deflated. Although the sheriff was the older one, he didn't appear to be the wiser one. It was the deputy whom August focused on. The deputy was a young man, early twenties, but he had a seriousness to him that made August hone. He'd been through enough towns to know which trigger fingers would hesitate and which ones wouldn't.

"What's your business here?" the deputy asked.

When August began walking toward them, the deputy's hand slid conspicuously to the grip at his hip.

"Just passing through," August said to the deputy as he placed the mare's lead line into the sheriff's hand. He reached under his cloak at his breast—making the deputy's fingers tighten around the revolver at his hip—and pulled out a fistful of gold coins. August littered the coins at the sheriff's feet and said, "I won't be repeating myself," then sliced between them like a light breeze.

August headed for the mercantile, leaving the law of Clayton Creek to make what they would of his arrival.

Later that night, after a hot bath, a clean shave, purchased sex, and a large meal, August strolled down the lamplit alley behind the saloon, listening to the sound of expert fingers tormenting the keys of a finely tuned piano. Some patrons were singing haphazardly, some were laughing, and those who were doing neither were shouting conversations over the others.

August lit his pipe and rounded the corner, heading for the main boulevard. When he reached it, he crossed it, ignoring more propositions from those loitering in the darkness.

The roads were relatively quiet, but up and down the interconnecting streets, oil blazed warmly inside. Even on a mild spring day, Colorado sheds its warmth when the sun disappears, chasing most indoors when night sinks its cold fangs into domesticated flesh. With six cells, Clayton Creek's jailhouse was larger than most towns, but not a single one was currently incarcerating. That bothered August for reasons beyond his ability to put into words, which had nothing to do with his preference for saying nothing at all. It made him feel itchy and uncomfortable to know that either the law was lax or that the town simply didn't have a dark side.

He would be willing to make a bet that plenty of people in this town deserved to be locked up. But that was neither here nor there—he wasn't in the business of recruitment.

The sheriff was across the street in the saloon, fooling around with someone who wasn't his wife, leaving the deputy alone to chain smoke cigarettes and read weeks-old newspapers.

The deputy's body was quiet, but his eyes were manic when August entered the jailhouse.

"Evening," August said as he pointed at the chair on the opposite side of the desk. "Mind?" But August didn't wait to see if he did.

The deputy shook his head, rebounded the greeting, and gestured at the chair on the opposite side of the desk as August Gaines sank into it.

August tapped his spent tobacco onto the desk.

The deputy frowned lightly as he made his own tap of his cigarette into the crystal ashtray somewhat theatrically as to demonstrate where the other man should have dumped his.

August began to pack his pipe, intentionally stretching the silence. Patience, August understood, wasn't a virtue so much as it was a weapon.

But the deputy wasn't taking the bait.

August puffed, gesturing loosely with it at the jailhouse, smoke swirling. "No evildoers in Clayton Creek, I reckon."

"I reckon I don't give a flying flute what you reckon." The deputy stamped out his cigarette.

When the deputy perpetuated the silence, August nodded as if they had reached some kind of understanding.

He pointed the mouth of his pipe at the deputy and said, "I like you."

"Can't say there's much mutuality to that statement." The deputy lit another.

August echoed the deputy, reigniting his pipe. "Well now. Nobody cares much for their reckoning." He lit another match, stoking the embers gently.

"Is that what you are?" The deputy coldly held his gaze. "Some right hand o' God?" He snorted, smoke shooting from his nostrils. "I've seen plenty of your type before. Drifters who loot, drifters who steal, drifters who say they're the second coming of Christ. Which are you?"

August lazily picked something from his teeth, appreciating the deputy's condescending tone while delighting over how nervously tense he was.

"I've got business with a man who goes by the name of Lucas Haas. He been through these parts?" August asked.

"What kind of business?"

"Propitiation."

"Well, friend. That business sounds personal."

August reached back into his coat, making the deputy go for his gun, which August allowed.

Unflinching, August set a canvas-bound book on the table between them. Puffing on his pipe, August gestured loosely to the ledger, said, "Open to the third page." Then he retrieved a single piece of waxy paper, unfolded it carefully, and smoothed it out next to the book. It was a deed to thirty-thousand acres near Santa Fe.

The deputy's curiosity seemed to be growing alongside his apprehension, but as curiosity often did, it proved to be a stronger force than preservation. Keeping the barrel of the revolver resting atop the desk yet steady on August, the deputy thumbed to page three of the ledger.

"What am I looking for?" the deputy asked, his eyes scanning the page as they darted sporadically to keep an eye on his guest.

August stoked his pipe with a freshly lit match. "Bottom of the page. Look closely."

Frowning, the deputy picked up the weathered deed and gave it a closer inspection. Then he put his focus on the bottom of page three from the Clayton Creek Inn guest ledger.

August leaned forward, the chair groaning softly, and pressed a finger above the second-to-last moniker. Tapping it, he said, "What do you see?"

The deputy shrugged. "That an Alabama man by the name of Heath Mansford had a brief soiree in our here great town . . . six years ago." He emphasized the last part slightly, as to underline its unimportance this matter had on his life.

"Heath Mansford is Lucas Haas. See the way he do his *A*s? And the *H*? Dollars to buttons, kid."

"What are you after, Mr. Gaines?"

August regarded the deputy calmly, then said, "I'd like your outfit to find Lucas Haas and secure his neck in a noose."

"Whatever happened—"

"He took something from me."

The deputy heaved a sigh as if disappointed at himself for asking, "What'd he take?"

"A diamond"—August held up his fist—"as big as your fist."

The deputy's eyes widened, but not in an impressed way, in an unbelieving *I'm sure* sort of way.

"Be that as it may," the deputy said as he slid the deed across the desk back toward August, "you're following a trail so cold it's grown ice. How do you expect to find a thief that's been in the wind for this long?"

"Bit young to be so cynical, ain't you?"

"Bit old to be so entitled, ain't you?"

August took a slow glance across the jailhouse. "If you won't provide your services, you will provide fresh horses and as many supplies as I require."

"That's between your coin purse and our proprietors," the deputy said.

"I do believe," August puffed on his pipe, "you missed the part where this is a holdup, kid."

The deputy pulled back the hammer. "It's time for you to leave."

"Understandable." He stoked his pipe.

The deputy slapped the ledger shut. "How did you even come by this?"

"You ain't noticed the influx of guests as of late? Nah, I reckon people don't mind much when money comes into town; it's when it leaves that it starts to raise alarms. Clayton Creek, deputy? It belongs to me now."

The deputy stood, leveling the gun at August's face. "Get out of my town."

"Yours?" August said.

"I *will* shoot you."

August nodded, puffed. "Prudent."

The gunshot was deafening.

The deputy's mouth was frozen in an open grimace, his hand clutched over the blooming crimson across his chest. He collapsed back into his chair, his index finger constricting weakly, desperately trying to gather the strength to pull the trigger.

August scooted to his right, the legs of the chair scraping against the sanded wood floorboards.

The deputy's body slipped, slumping from his chair as if strings tugged him from the floor. His finger worked on the trigger, until finally, he managed to squeeze off one shot.

August was safely out of aim, and the deputy didn't have any more in him.

His body hit the floorboards with a heavy thump.

From behind the deputy, the door to a floor-to-ceiling armoire swung open with a subtle creak.

A short, skinny man with a black patch over his left eye stepped out of it, holstering a revolver.

"I do not need melodrama in my life, Flea," August said.

"My angle was bad," Flea said. He glanced down at the body. "Didn't want to hit ya, now."

August pocketed his pipe. "Have we found him?"

Flea grinned, showing his collection of gold. "Perchance."

August didn't like Flea. He had a flair for drama and a knack for getting under August's skin. But Flea was valuable. Flea was the best shot this side of the country. Not the quickest draw, no, but easily the best one.

"Okay so earlier I was sidling right close to this plummy honey and she was goin' on and on bout this tall 'n' handsome who got all the women hot 'n' bothered seven-bout years ago and get this, he had this accent she ain't been able to nail down—"

August held up his hand, closing his eyes. "Just tell me what you found out."

"Apparently, he went east."

August frowned. "Central City?"

Flea wagged his head back and forth slowly. "There's this tiny shantyville that was so little that it didn't show up on many maps. That is, until a sudden influx of money showed up about—"

"Six years ago."

"You got it."

August tapped the ash from his pipe. "Does this shantyville have a name?"

CHAPTER

4

Bladestay had a population of approximately three hundred souls, and its account for crime was relatively accurate: those who found themselves incarcerated were generally those who needed to sleep off a heavy night of drinking.

The events that led to the confinement of Theo and Patrick were a fluke the town had never seen in its thirty years of existence. It was all the town had been talking about since the morning, and although the travel of word is highly efficient in small towns, Theo and Patrick didn't see a familial face until supper.

As Theo sat on the edge of the cot, glaring at Patrick as if her gaze could burn holes through his flesh, she fantasized about how she would feel right now if she'd just had the chance to keep sinking the blade into his skin. She slid her fingers together, slowly rubbing her hands back and forth with fingers interlocked, savoring the feeling of Patrick's dried blood on her hands.

"Sheriff Macklin," Patrick said as he dodged Theo's glare. "I ain't do nothin' wrong, I don't know why ˮ

Theo said, "You went for my head with a knife, you yellow-bellied, steaming pile of—"

"I did *not*!" Patrick said.

"Patty—" The sheriff was cut off by a voice who'd been hiding just out of sight beyond the threshold.

"I saw everything!" When Elliot stepped into view, he pointed at Patrick. "So did my dad. We were *right there*."

Deputy Briggs made himself a blockade between Elliot and Patrick.

"Are you really going to try and deny it?" Elliot snapped, darting his eyes briefly to Theo, who was watching the interaction with aggravated calm. "Call me a liar? Call *my dad* a liar?"

Patrick said, "I don't care what you think you saw, you ain't hear what that little snake be mutterin' underneath her breath—"

"God, shut *up*," Theo said.

"Why's she get to talk to me like that, huh?" Patrick said.

As Deputy Briggs placed a hand on Elliot's chest, pushing him back out the way he came, Sheriff Macklin seconded Theo and Elliot: "*Do* quit yammerin', Patty-boy, or I'm gon' let Theo loose in your cell with your sad ass and sell tickets to the show."

Deputy Briggs laughed but kept a firm hand on Elliot. "She kicked your butt, you stupid goat. She'd done killed you if it weren't for this scrawny kid." Then to Elliot as he directed him back out the door: "What'd I tell you, huh? You can't be here right now. See how riled you be makin' things? Git, son."

Elliot chewed on a lip angrily, leaned into the deputy's palm challengingly, pointed at Patrick again, but said nothing, only looked once more at Theo before turning to march his exit.

It was about that time that Mr. and Mrs. Creed walked in the door, a basket of home-cooked supper hooked onto Rose's arm. With her head held high, Rose walked over to the desk between the two cells, dropped the basket on top of the desktop array, ripped off her leather gloves with an air of frustration, and jabbed a finger toward Patrick.

"You so much as look at my daughter again, and I will scoop your eyeballs out with a rusty spoon, you understand me?"

Deputy Briggs laughed again. "You hear that? The spoon will be rusty."

"I will have a word with your pa, young man," Theo's father said.

"Simmer down, folks," Sheriff Macklin said.

Patrick shrank deeper and deeper into a cower until his back was in the corner of the cell, his legs drawn to his chest atop his cot.

Theo had come over to the bars to be as close to her mother as the prison allowed, and her mother quickly shuffled over, sweeping the basket of food into her arms as she did.

"Open this door," Rose said.

"Your daughter acted in extreme violence, ma'am. I can't release—"

"We ain't askin' you to release her," Harrison said.

"Let me just fix her hair and give her something decent to eat, for heaven's sake," Rose snapped.

"You think I'm go'n' let you in with a pair of sheers now, Mrs. Creed?"

"I don't care if you shackle me, Sheriff," Theo said. "Please don't make me go about any more of my day with half a head of hair."

Sheriff Macklin leaned back into his chair deeply, bouncing his eyes from each present member of the Creed family, then finally gave a nod, hefted himself out of the chair with some trouble, then approached the bars where Theo and Rose were standing.

"Hands through the bars, sweetheart," Sheriff Macklin said, and Theo noticed for the first time how uncomfortable this whole scenario was making him.

Theo complied, sticking her hands through the bars for Sheriff Macklin to cuff her wrists with a bar between them.

Rose took the opportunity to fetch the chair that Sheriff Macklin had been lounging in. She dragged it into her daughter's cell after the Sheriff had unlocked the door and placed it carefully behind Theo's knees.

"Thanks, Mama," Theo said, lowering herself onto the chair with far more dignity than she felt.

Rose set the basket down next to Theo's feet and ran her long fingers through her daughter's jaggedly short hair on the left side of her head. "It's just hair, baby girl." But Theo could hear the sadness in her voice.

"I know, Mama."

"This time next year," Rose said, taking out a pair of sheers, "won't nobody know the difference."

The jailhouse was quiet except for the sound of metal slicing through hair. Theo's tears slid silently down her face, and try as she might, she couldn't find the gall to look Patrick in the face as her mother took off the rest of her hair.

"I think it's only fair," Theo's father said sourly, his gaze on Patrick.

"You can't be serious. Sheriff!" Patrick yelled out when it dawned on him what Theo's father had meant, and that the Sheriff wasn't going to stop them.

When Sheriff Macklin and Deputy Briggs finally managed to herd Mr. and Mrs. Creed out of the jailhouse, Patrick's father slipped in. Theo was certain he had been waiting for her parents to leave, a cowardice that apparently ran in the family. Patrick's father kept his head down, refused to look at Theo or speak above a mumble, said something about this all being unfair and, even more upset than her parents had been about the loss of Theo's hair, he seemed to be angrier at the haircut they'd given his son. Theo's father had been the one to sheer Patrick's head, and his craftsmanship was intentionally shoddy.

Patrick's father left after dropping his son a few fresh pairs of denim overalls and wool trousers, a beige waistcoat, and two heavily wrinkled, cotton long sleeve shirts. Theo had two changes of tartan skirts and matching blouses, but no sleepwear. She had expected to sleep fully clothed, anyhow.

She hardly slept that night, and by first light, she was achy from the stiff cot and cranky at her new reality. She didn't know what came next, didn't want to ask as she wasn't ready for the answer, but she suspected that the law of the town was just as much at a loss of what was the best way to move forward. These people knew her. They knew she wasn't a danger to the public, but the Sheriff did have precedent to consider. She figured they would let her out after a few days, Patrick after a few weeks, with just enough to scare them with the weight of consequence and the threat of heavier punishments in the future. She also figured that was about fair.

But Theo wouldn't find out what their ultimate choices would be, for a tall, broad-shouldered man in a white Staker hat and black duster rode into town that morning and shot the Sheriff and his deputy dead right out on the jailhouse patio over their morning coffee as if it weren't nothing but a thing.

CHAPTER

5

The sky was a soft, faint pink when the first gunshot jolted Theo and Patrick from their cots. Hands clutching to the bars of their cell, they pressed their faces to their prisons to try to catch a glimpse of what had happened—*was* happening—right outside. Patrick had the better vantage, Theo's angle difficult, but she saw it clear enough.

The blood from Deputy Briggs painted the street-facing window, a murder she didn't witness, but she did see the Sheriff scramble for his revolver. The man in the Staker hat shot the Sheriff point-blank, effectively dismantling the law of Bladestay in under three seconds. The broad-shouldered man wore a wide-brimmed white hat and a black duster coat that accentuated and disguised—respectively—the crimson of his crimes. His face was lightly splattered with blood, his knuckles slick with it. He stepped between the wicker chairs, shoving one of the leaning bodies out of his way, and smeared his hand across the window before he peered through.

Theo scrambled away from the bars and slammed her back against the brick wall between her and the man in the white hat, her chest heaving in panic. Darting her eyes up, she found Patrick staring wide-eyed at her.

The heels of the man's boots gave ominous thuds as he stepped away from the window; Patrick's eyes bounced back to the man, following the sound of footfalls.

Theo held her breath until the steps began to fade, didn't take another breath until the noise of his cadence no longer held the hollow sound of boot against wood.

Gunfire popped through the town, and soon, the beating of hooves against compact clay thundered through the street.

Patrick retreated to his cot, squinted his eyes shut, and covered his ears.

Her spine glued to the brick, Theo's eyes swept the jailhouse in a ravenous manner, seeing things in a new light, gauging what might be used as a weapon. A row of rifles lay neatly behind a metal mesh vault, but they were going to protect her about as much as the kettle was going to serve her tea.

It dawned on her that there was absolutely nothing she could do to break free and that her only option relied on the very person who put her here. Squeezing her eyes shut briefly, steadying her breath, she said, "Patrick."

Patrick didn't look at her because he didn't hear her.

"Patrick!" she said louder.

On the third try, Patrick finally looked at her.

"Give me your clothes," she said, daring a look around the corner. She saw a horse gallop by, a blur of a hunched rider as they raced through the street.

"What?" Patrick said.

"Your clothes." Her eyes flicked to the sheepskin bag at the foot of his cot. "Give me your spares."

"Why?" he said, not moving. His hands had moved off his ears, but they clutched the side of his head, rubbing his shoddily cropped cut.

"Are you dense?" she hissed. "How would you like to be a girl locked in a cage right now?"

Through the fear on his face, understanding bled through, and with it, something menacing. "Screw you, Theodora."

The barbs and brambles twisted inside her, fury a near tangible entity. Her fists balled and her tongue braced, but instead of the fighting words that begged to come forth, she said, "Patrick. There was going to be a day that would force you to decide the kind of man you are. That day came early, and that moment is now. And is this really the man you're going to choose to be?"

He wasted several more precious moments before finally reaching for his bag. He yanked out a spare outfit as he made his way to the bars nearest hers. Theo's shoulder socket was pressed between two bars, her fingers stretched out toward him by the time he had a pair of straight-leg trousers in his hands. He tossed the trousers, and she caught them and yanked them through the bars, dropping them at her feet before darting her hand back through the bars.

She began tearing clothes from her body with no regard to buttons or modesty.

"Ain't you going to ask me to not look?"

"A gentleman wouldn't need to be asked," Theo said, fastening the row of buttons that peaked at her belly button. Bare-chested and flushed with humiliation, Theo grabbed her discarded chemise from the floor and tore the thin fabric into the longest strip she could. Keeping a desperate eye on the calming chaos outside, she wrapped and bound her chest, tucking and tying the ends against her ribs. "And what's the point of wasting my breath when I already know the kind of man you are?"

"You should mind your tongue, Theodora," Patrick said in a low, unsteady voice.

"Or what, Patrick?" She yanked a long sleeve over her head. "You'll expose my ruse? Rake your eyes over my naked body? Hold me against my will and slice a knife at my head?" She donned his charcoal herringbone vest and buttoned the brass knobs down her androgynously made torso. She gathered her skirt, blouse, and remnants of the torn chemise, then paused for the first time. Leveling her gaze at him, she said, "I dare you to be more of a pig than you already are."

Patrick snarled, his face red with anger, his jaw clenching and unclenching as if working on words that he didn't know how to say. When it came to the currency of eloquence, Patrick was below the poverty line, so all he could think to say was, "You're a mean bitch, Theodora."

"That's not my name anymore. You call me Teddy if you'd like. Theodore if you're feeling fancy. Now keep your mouth shut and let me do the talking. Do you understand me, Patrick?

"Patrick," Theo repeated.

He was staring out the blood-smeared window.

"Somebody's coming," he said.

Making her way back to the street-facing wall, Theo dropped her discarded clothes and kicked them under the cot. She pressed one cheek against brick, the other against cold metal, and saw a man with a lean, wiry build heading straight for the jailhouse.

Unlike the imposing presence of the man in the white hat who was pleased to walk under the morning sun like he had nothing to hide as he coldly shot the law in the face point-blank, this man looked like he preferred to stay in the shadows, his fingers twitching in anticipation of something, anything, his tempo fluid as if he walked to a beat in his head.

When Theo first saw this man whom she would later learn called himself Brody Boone, the first thing she thought of was: music. Brody Boone was the kind of person who seemed to have found the timing to the universe, everything about him melodious, except for the literal sense.

Brody Boone was also drenched in blood. He wore a black bowler hat that was cocked to the side in an intentional way that reminded Theo of a sneer. What he lacked in sheer size, he compensated with pure swagger, a trait in his gait that was blatant even from where Theo and Patrick stood. The sun was at Brody's back, shadowing his face where the tight brim of the hat was lacking. The tendons on his neck were taut, accentuated by the slick sheen of blood, the freshness of it glistening wetly.

And he was coming for them.

Theo quickly took her place on the cot.

Brody Boone pushed the jailhouse door open with the muzzle of his six-shooter.

CHAPTER

6

B rody took off his bowler hat and set it on the sheriff's desk.

Wet splatters were slowly being absorbed by the dark felt, and although Theo knew the wetness was red, the blackness consumed it.

Brody made no attempt to tame the raven hair that bounced down his forehead once it was loose from the confines of its hat. Nor did he care to wipe the streaks of blood from his face. His black eyes assessed Theo first, gloriously brief and painfully bored, then took a longer assessment of Patrick, who was visibly trembling in the farthest corner.

When Brody's eyes landed back on Theo, a dark sort of amusement eased onto his features, one of the most haunting visions as far as Theo could recall. As he pulled the chair from behind the sheriff's desk, Theo matched his cold gaze with a grin that she hoped was mysterious and conniving, not wavering and on the brink of tears.

Her entire life, she knew, was about to be reduced to how she navigated these next moments. So, she performed a makeover of the mind and soul, determined to be a person who might be able to stand toe-to-toe with blood-soaked maniacs. Not physically—not possible—but Theo understood that prowess came in many shapes and sizes.

She had her legs hanging off the edge of the low-profile cot, her feet flat on the floor, her slumped recline propped against the wall with her shoulder blades. She had her knees spread in a vulgar flippancy, her face calm with insouciance. Her hands, which screamed to let out nervous energy, were intertwined placidly behind her head.

"You run out of paint for the town?" Theo asked, brandishing sarcasm in the hopes it camouflaged terror.

Brody tossed the chair toward Theo's cell. It clattered on four legs but didn't tip over.

Patrick let out a startled curse.

Theo grinned, knowing it was nothing but a God-given miracle that she herself didn't spook.

Brody Boone ignored Patrick, his curiosity completely on Theo as if enraptured by the possibility of a fellow maniac. He sank in the chair in a backward straddle and tapped a metal bar with the barrel of his revolver.

"What're you in for?" he asked.

She pushed off the wall to lean over her legs, propping elbows over knees, keeping her glare as direct and wolfish as possible. "Come in here and I'll show you."

Brody let out a short burst of laughter.

"What about you?" Brody asked, tilting a chin over his shoulder to look at Patrick.

"Nothin'. I didn't do *nothin'*!"

Wrong answer, Theo thought.

Brody studied Patrick for a moment, then said, "Bladestay ain't got no barber?"

Patrick's eyes darted to Theo in panic.

"Lice," Theo said.

Bringing his attention back to Theo, Brody asked, "You too?"

"Disgusting. No."

Brody watched her, letting the silence stretch. He tried her again. "What'd you do?"

"Burned down the house of God." Theo let her eyes sweep the room lazily as she sucked air through her teeth, as if bored of this line of questioning, as if she weren't battling the rising tide of bile.

Brody leaned back, so far back that he held on to the spindles of the chair, his arm fully extended, to look out the doorway he'd left wide open. "I can see the church from here."

He leaned forward again, loosely holding the wooden backing, his arms folded over each other with the revolver laid over his angled bicep.

"Look new, don't it?" Theo said with a wink. As the panic swelled up her throat, fear ballooning under her skin, her fingers and extremities demanded release, but all she could do was dig her fingernails into the scalp on the back of her head. She caught her leg, about to start bouncing, and quieted it.

"What's your name?"

"Teddy Pine," Theo said. "What's yours?"

"Brody Boone. Who's the hamster?" He cocked a thumb in Patrick's direction.

"Listen," Theo said, making a show of how inconvenient this interruption was to her day by letting out a long, slow sigh. "I don't much like that I've found myself in a conversation with you. I don't much care for the fact that you've made me miss my goddamn porridge. But most of all, Brody Boone?" Theo glanced at Patrick for the first time since the blood-soaked fiend had walked through the jailhouse door, doing her best to make it look like a look of indifference. "I don't much appreciate how you think my business is any of yours." The beat of her heart pounded so loudly in her ears that Theo was certain Brody could hear it.

Brody opened his mouth to reply, but he was just as caught off guard by the voice that wasn't his. Brody's back was to the jailhouse on trance, but Theo didn't have an excuse for not noticing the appearance of the man in the doorway.

"How old are you, kid?" The man in the doorway looked like a photograph out of magazine. He leaned his back into the doorframe, offering Theo his profile. He was holding a pipe in the corner of his mouth, but he looked too tuckered to coax it to life. The Staker hat on his head had returned to a crisp white, and Theo wondered what kind of bargain he'd made to maintain such unsoiling.

"Fifteen." As Theo told lies to the man in the doorway, she took quick note of how—in the context of subtleties—drastically Brody's body language had shifted. He tensed, his shoulders curled slightly, and the grip on his weapon became more purposeful.

"You got a bit of fire up your ass, don't you, kid?" the man in the doorway said in a deep, gravelly drawl.

"There are worse things to have up there."

The man chuckled, nodding at the floor as he fiddled with his pipe. Finally, he pulled out a box of matches. He lit the pipe, slowly working through the tobacco.

In the silence, Theo realized just *how* silent the town had become. Verily, Bladestay was a tranquil place in a peaceful valley surrounded by an amphitheater of snowcapped mountains, but to not hear the sound of a hammer on anvil, of the clatter of kitchen noises, the chatter of townsfolk, the nearly ever-present sounds of carpentry upkeep or expansion, the clopping of hooves on compacted clay—even the breeze took pause in Theo's introduction to the most terrifying man she'd ever laid eyes on.

Theo knew the inherent terror she felt in this man's presence was more than his physical daunt, that it was something deeper. Theo always thought that if the devil was going to show up on earth, it was going to be with a handsome smile and a tailored suit.

After his curated stretch of silence, the man ended it. "I have a job for you." He neither looked up nor specified whom he was speaking to, but they all knew whom he addressed.

Oddly, Theo's heart had quieted in the man's presence. Despite the horrors she already understood about this outlaw, she saw his dangerous ability to influence a room to his liking. People were scared when he wanted them to be; people were the opposite when he saw fit.

"I think you mistake me for the employable type," Theo said.

"I think you mistake that for an offer." The man tossed something over Brody Boone's head, and it landed at the base of the bars with a clang and a clatter.

Theo eyed the ring of keys not with the apprehension she felt, but with the irrelevance she wished she did. As she dragged her gaze back to the broad man in the doorway, it snagged on Brody Boone, whose finger was now on the trigger, the fluidity of his stature somehow calcified.

Appropriating all the self-control that lived within her, Theo made neither a move for the keys nor graced them with a second glance. She simply leaned back, crossed her arms over her flattened chest, and asked, "What's the job?"

CHAPTER

7

As soon as Theo was alone in the stables, she slid behind a stack of hay and vomited. She'd been forcing out images of the sheriff, a man she'd known her whole life, with half his head missing. The ferocious tightening inside had torn her raw and left her nauseous, leaving her convinced there was no possibility she could maintain this ruse. She'd given everything in the jailhouse performance, yet it had barely been enough. Men like August Gaines and Brody Boone can sense evil like a scent on a breeze—she knew this to be true.

Already, August had left her with a test. A trial of evil. An assessment of depravity.

She hadn't yet thought her way out of it. But she was working on it.

Theo hadn't dared touch the keys until August had walked out of the jail, but before he did, he'd left her with a brief but straightforward ultimatum: tend to the horses and be at the saloon in a half hour's time. Should she choose to not come back, Patrick would earn a bullet in the skull. As far as Theo was concerned, Patrick had already earned one of those, but the thing that worried her was what he might give up about her under the threat of said bullet.

Up until the ultimatum, Theo's vision of what came next had been clear: she'd foist her way out of jail time, then make a run for home and get her family the hell out of Bladestay. Central City was the obvious choice, the nearest city large enough for anonymity. But that had its own problems: if it was obvious to her it would be obvious to August Gaines, and August didn't strike her as the kind of man who let things go very easily. Digressively, the point was moot—she couldn't safely connect the dots from here to Central City, or anywhere for that matter. Theo didn't know exactly what August Gaines was after, but she did know that August reeked of revenge, as tangible as liquor on the breath.

So, Theo went back to the basics. The most important thing was to stay alive and keep as many people around her in the same fate. The trick, she knew, would be to project the opposite.

While August saw this ultimatum as a test of character, Theo saw this as a test of wits.

By the time Theo made her way to a trough, a plan began to take shape. She splashed water on her face and raked her hands through her cropped hair. Her mother had sheered shorter on the sides, above the ears, to make it as symmetrical as possible after Patrick had left her lopsided. The top of her head had loosened in volume, the subtle waves of long hair transforming nearly into curls without the weight of length pulling it straight.

She placed her hands on the metal lip of the trough and leaned over the water, waiting for it to calm. The water wavered, sending her a rippled reflection of herself. She stared at her reflection for nearly a full minute, willing herself to cry so she could get it out of her system. But as she glared at herself, she saw more and more not a girl who was sad or scared, but angry and determined.

Not a single tear came forward.

Sniffing sharply at the blond boy staring back at her in the water, she turned and headed for the row of horses who needed their tack removed and bellies filled.

By the time she was done, her stomach was aching with hunger and her mouth was sour with bile. She emulated a man's walk as she headed for the saloon, not daring even so much as a look in the direction of home. Theo forced her motions to be loose and slow as if she hadn't a care in the world, as if this was her ideal Wednesday morning. She glanced at the disarray of Main Street with an air of amusement, strolling down the road with hands shoved in her trouser pockets as if she were on her way to a picnic. She kept a slight slouch in her shoulders to hide any betrayal of curves and mimicked the crude tendencies of a man in his element—essentially, she did everything that was diametrically opposed to the ways she was taught to carry herself as a woman.

Her life now depended on her ability to control every single nuance.

"Time's up, Youngblood." August had said a sum of thirty-four words to Theo, but she knew the rumbling drawl of his voice as if she'd heard it her entire life, was as familiar to her as her own father's, an odd recognition that made her feel like a cube of ice had been drawn down her spine.

"Oh?" Theo said, squinting up at the sky as if to assess the time the sun told. She slipped her hands back into her pockets—one of her most worrisome attributes, slender and dainty and well-manicured—as her gaze settled on August. He sat upon the stairs, the batwing doors of the saloon behind framing him like angel wings. The placement of the sun above his head was an equally bizarre exposition of supernatural proportions.

"Come," he said. He pointed at the stairs with his pipe, something Theo was learning to be as much a habitual accessory as it was an addiction. "I want to talk at you for a minute."

In her panic, Theo stilled. She didn't want anyone to see her subterfuge up close. They might see how delicate her nose was. How soft the angle of her jaw was. The petiteness of her chin. Her legs carried her up the stairs, where she lowered herself as far away from him on the top step. Slouching, she let her knees recline away from each other.

"Why are you here?" Theo asked.

"Hm." It sounded like a growling purr. "Just the thing I wanted to discuss." He looked up the street one way, then down the other. "Does the name Lucas Haas or Heath Mansford mean anything to you?"

The foul scent of revenge rose around Theo like an aura.

She shrugged. "I doubt this Podunk gets a plethora of visitors."

August gave her a sideways look, the corner of his mouth tipped upward. "You ain't from here?"

"What, do I not look like I belong here?"

August's half grin deepened. "I doubt you belong much anywhere."

Theo felt a stab of something heavy and familiar. She couldn't rightly place what it was, but August was talking again, and Theo forced herself to focus.

"Where you from?"

"Taos." She remembered reading about the town in some piece of literature and figured she knew enough about it to bluff her way through, should it come to that.

August nodded as if that answered all the questions in his head. "You don't like it here."

She gave him a disgruntled snort. "What gave me away?"

Despite her sarcasm, he responded with a calm seriousness. "Indifference is illuminating."

"Indifferent?" She stood. "You don't know me. Indifference is an indulgence for the unscathed."

August chuckled. "Sit back down, Youngblood."

In her continued defiance of him, August said, "I'd prefer not to remind you of your place." His eyes flicked to the stair.

Theo sat, but with a mellow snarl on her face.

"Why were you in jail, Pine Needle?"

Theo felt this was a very heavy question. The kind that's less about information and more about aptitude. "They say I 'solve my problems with violence.'" She put air-quotes around that.

August took out a leather satchel of tobacco. "Why does that not surprise me."

She looked down Main. "So who's this man you're after?"

August packed his pipe. "You'd've been real young when this man came to town. This Lucas Haas would likely be going by another name. He has an accent. Tall. Good looking. Self-assured. Wealthy."

Her mouth went dry. *Blacksmith.* "You sure you ain't looking for yourself, Mr. Gaines?"

The sun-leathered skin around his eyes bunched in a sly smirk. "I wonder that myself from time to time, Youngblood." He lit his pipe and puffed it gently.

"What kind of accent?" Theo asked.

"He's good at sounding as he likes." He spoke around the pipe in the corner of his mouth, his teeth lightly snagging the briar wood. "But he's German."

"And you know he's here?"

"Knowing ain't the same as believing, but that don't make much of a difference when it comes to doing." August rose to his feet and smoked until the tobacco lost its light. "We have wicked business to attend to, Pine Needle." He smiled kindly down at her as he tapped spent ash from his pipe.

Theo's heart galloped at the insinuation of *we*, knowing he wasn't talking about his already established posse.

"Well, Mr. Gaines, I reckon I'd choose wicked over jail time any day."

"Yeah," came his guttural drawl. "I get the feeling we might be cut from the same cloth, you and I, Youngblood."

CHAPTER
8

Bladestay's church was a simple but attractive stucco square with a modest steeple and baby blue trim, absent of stain glass and any superfluence. The windows gleamed on a clear day, its emerald accents boasting of someone's investment and care. Where Main Street ended and sloped gently to the east was where the house of God sat, standing above all structures in the valley.

Theo could hear somebody inside suppressing sobs, but otherwise, the gathered folks of Bladestay were terrorized into silence.

Despite the mild warmth of the day, Theo felt cold all over. Her family was either inside or already dead. Her heart raced. Her mouth was filled with cotton. Her palms were slick with sweat.

August took off his hat, ran a hand through his hair, and returned it to his head as he stepped away from his gathered gang. Theo saw ten of them grouped in front of the church, but she had counted six others so far, and she wouldn't be surprised if more were on the perimeter.

Although many of the gathered ten took to sitting on boulders or leaning against the trunk of a tree, all of them were quiet and attentive.

Theo stood off to the side with as much distance as she dared without calling attention to herself, leaning against a tree with her arms crossed. Brody Boone, damn him, had followed her and was now standing too close to her.

To Theo, Brody was the epitome of a gunslinger. A six-shooter resting on each thigh, two reams of ammo slung above, and a handmade buckskin jacket that looked like he may have inherited it from the broader shoulders of his father.

Brody's eyes were expressive and inquisitive, unlike the eerie calm found in August. He'd still not cleaned the blood from him, and he now wore the dried stuff like a prize.

Theo tried not to visualize what he'd done to another human to earn such a prize. It wasn't difficult—she was consumed with the fate of her family.

With his back to the church, August's hypnotic baritone words began to ooze from his mouth. "Thanks to Hadley for securing the Bladestay census of 1860." He held a canvas ledger in his left hand that he now lifted to make it the center of attention.

Theo scanned Gaines's crew to find a man whom she presumed to be Hadley when he tipped his hat in August's direction.

"This next part is a little tough to do without it." He chuckled as if recalling a time he'd been there, done that. "Now let's get this over with." He tucked the ledger under his arm and said, "Sixer. Pine Needle. Flea. Shiner—you four with me." He pointed at them, and Theo's legs nearly buckled from under her. Theo hadn't even considered that August would take her into the church with him, and now she was about to enter a congregation where, at any time, any one of them could recognize and expose her.

The gang dispersed toward the church, assuming their flanking positions.

Trailing the gang, the appointed four followed August. Theo was lightheaded as she put one foot in front of the other. Her stomach gnarled tighter with each closing gap. A scowl hid the fear.

At first, Theo didn't understand why all those in the church had stayed put. There had been plenty of time where they had been left loosely guarded. When August swung open the front door, Theo understood. About half the town was here: all the men.

Fracture the family, cripple the fight.

"Choose your corners, kids," August muttered to the four before he strode down the center aisle. The pews were filled, not uncomfortably, so when August moved down the center, those nearest the aisle shifted and scooted away, splitting the already appointed divide. Some heads swiveled; others kept eyes forward. August neither hurried nor took his time, taking off his hat as if in reverence for the holy ground upon which he stepped, but quickly snuffed that illusion by returning it to his head after sweeping a hand through his chestnut hair.

Theo shuffled quietly to the right for a back corner, parlaying her chances of invisibility.

Brody followed, then continued past her. He walked the length of the wall and settled in the corner to the right of the pulpit.

August placed one hand on the edge of the pulpit, the Bladestay census in lieu of Scripture. He thumbed open the ledger.

Flea and Shiner settled their backs into their respective corners. Brody unholstered a revolver and held it in his hand. Fiddling with it, he scanned the congregation as if daring anyone to make eye contact with him. Looking at the back of people's heads, Theo couldn't tell if anyone did. Besides, she was too preoccupied searching for her father or any of her brothers among the throng.

"Abide carefully," August said. His voice was such that he needn't raise it for all to hear. "When you hear your family name, stand and approach." He regarded the congregation, nodded at himself, then said, "Let's begin.

"Abbot."

Tentatively, an elderly man stood to his feet, holding a weathered hat to his chest, and began to scoot down the row toward the aisle. Those in the way made more than enough room for him to pass.

Abbot was one of the town's original founders, skilled with his hands, father of four girls, grandfather of eight boys. Theo knew these things because Abbot often worked with her father at Creed Carpentry when Creed's perfectionist pace stacked his work.

Theo's stomach turned to iron, her lungs to lead.

The church was silent aside from Abbot's slow march to the pew.

"Full name," August said, looking down at the white-haired man.

Abbot gave it, and August lifted his gaze behind him. "Sons?"

"Four daughters. Are they safe? And their babies?" Abbot's voice hitched on *babies*.

August made several marks on the page, and without looking up, he said, "You're cleared."

Theo couldn't see Abbot's reaction, but August responded to it by jabbing his quill in the direction from which he came.

Abbot slowly turned, giving August several untrusting double-takes, before shuffling back down the aisle. He was about to return to his seat, but Flea called to the man, "This way, pops."

Theo darted her eyes to her left and found Flea pushing out of his corner and beckoning Abbot.

At this point, Theo had found her breath, but it only came in shallow bursts, and she did what she could to hide the jerks in her chest. She kept her spine nestled in the ninety-degree, her arms crossed firmly across her breast, her shoulders hollowed around her, and her chin dipped low, watching this unfold from under her pale eyelashes. She hated how much her body wanted to betray her in every way.

Abbot's eyes found hers, and for a horrifying moment, Theo felt her legs turn to spaghetti. Abbot frowned slightly, as one does when hitching on a recognition they can't firmly place.

By the time Abbot was back out under the cloudless day, August had the next name announced.

A terror settled deep into her bones, the dread of having to do this one-hundred and eleven more times. Not to mention, she couldn't rightly place any member of her family from her vantage.

Between A and C, Theo thought she might have developed an ulcer.

When Bram Blacksmith's name fell from August's lips, Theo held her breath.

August looked up, first at the congregation, then squinted across his left shoulder at Boone where something passed briefly between them.

"Thirteen," August said to him. Theo didn't know what that meant.

Brody shook his head and August made a mark on the ledger.

August moved on to the dreaded Cs.

Theo would discover, then, when nobody stood to claim her family's name, that it was possible to feel two opposite emotions with equal depths.

Her family was gone.

Her family was gone.

August lifted his hand to his face and gently stroked his left eyebrow. He made his marks in the ledger, then his eyes fell to Flea, who answered with a single nod before he exited. The wordless way the gang communicated made Theo feel uneasy more than anything else thus far. How does one defeat an enemy whose stitching is as tight and flawless as it is brutal and exacting?

Theo felt like she might throw up again.

August continued reading names and, when he got to another name for which nobody claimed, he looked over his shoulder at Boone again.

"Twenty-one," August said.

To that, Brody sliced two fingers across his neck.

Somebody gasped softly.

August marked on the ledger

Theo understood then: thirteen and twenty-one were birth years.

When the pews were empty, August closed the ledger, took a deep breath, and walked down the aisle.

"The wicked hour is upon us, Pine Needle," August drawled atop an exhale.

"What can I do?" Theo was surprised by three things: the airy way her voice sounded, the steadiness of her response, and the response itself. She pushed off the wall and found sturdy feet at the end of her legs.

She met him at the door, and he placed a hand on her shoulder, stopping her. "You're doin' it, Youngblood." He gave her a single pat, then walked through the threshold first, tipping his Staker a little farther down his forehead on his way under the sun.

CHAPTER

9

The corralled men of Bladestay sat in the clearing outside the church, hands bound behind their backs.

August once again stood before them, hands held casually behind his back as he studied each and every man. The gang had the town's women locked up across town in the warehouse, Theo observed, when Flea brought the census there to cross-check the attendance of the Creed women.

The span of Flea's absence was potentially the longest of Theo's life. She didn't know if she should pray for any part of her family to be here or to be gone. Theo knew August was mentally scheduling a track-and-kill order on the remaining eight members of her family, of Blacksmith, so when Flea returned with the ledger and nobody from the Creed or the Blacksmith family, August took off his hat and sat heavily on a boulder. He rested his forearms across his thighs, inching the edge of his white hat through his fingers and looked to the sky, a tic Theo was already beginning to recognize as something he did when he questioned the choices of the Universe.

August sighed deeply before he addressed the bound and sitting congregation. "Some of y'all appear to be missing."

"The Creeds are good people," Abbot said. He was in the front row, fighting the morning glare for a look at his captor's face.

August returned the hat to his head, placed his large hands over his knees, and said, "I have no quarrel with the Creed man and his family." His drawl sounded even more elongated, an indication of fatigue. "But I'm looking for a man who once went by the name of Lucas Haas and I'm starting to think your Blacksmith might be my Haas. He would have come to town about six years ago and likely would have brought a significant amount of wealth along with him." August paused to consider the craftsmanship of the church. "He's got German roots and he may or may not sound like it."

Theo's insides clenched. She stuck her hands in her pockets to fidget with loose strings and lint.

"That's him—" somebody said.

"Shut up, Nate," another said.

It looked like August's joints ached when he stood. He walked through the rows, darkness falling upon those he stepped above. It happened so fast, yet so calmly, that when the gunshot went off, Theo wasn't sure what had happened until August was reholstering his weapon in the shadows of his duster and the man who told the other to shut up was flat on his back, mouth ajar toward the pale blue sky. A clean dark red hole gaped between his eyes.

The reaction was delayed.

August was already stepping his way back through by the time horror registered among the congregation. Several closest leaned away from each other.

Two men vomited. Someone screamed. A few on the outskirts were trying to crawl away.

The posse tightened their perimeter and kicked the crawling stragglers until they wormed back in the proper direction.

August was lowering himself back onto his boulder, his face twisted in something akin to disgust.

"Nate," August said. "Please continue."

Nate, eyes huge, stared over at the dead man. "Blacksmith came here about that time. He has money. I don't know about German, but he sounds a bit like a Northerner."

"Anything else you care to share? Such as why he ain't here?"

"I don't know where he is," Nate said. "I swear. That's all I know. I swear."

"Anyone?" August said. He pulled back the hammer on his gun.

Theo felt her chest beginning to spasm.

She cleared her throat, kept her fists balled in her pockets, and took a step toward August. A hand gripped her just above the elbow. It was urgent and, if Theo didn't know better, borderline panicked. She dropped her gaze and saw fingers nearly long enough to touch at the tips around the thin girth of her bicep.

She didn't need to tilt her head farther to see a slight shake of Brody Boone's head in her peripheral.

The blood in her veins cooled and slowed. Her mind did not.

She stepped away from Brody and he released her arm as soon as he saw she wasn't going to heed his warning.

The thing about Theo Creed was that the only time she felt panicky was when she had to be patient. It's not that she *wasn't* patient or *couldn't* be, it's that her body tended to betray her most when she was still. When she had a task, the trembling in her hands ceased. The galloping in her heart slowed to a trot. The air in her lungs came and went easily. So as she approached August, her feet were steady and her gait sure.

She came to a stop in front of August, putting herself between him and the crowd. When she reached her hand toward him, it was steady.

He scowled up at her.

She leaned down slowly, putting her lips near the brim of his hat above his ear. "You're wasting precious time, Mr. Gaines." She wiggled her fingers. "Permission to try something?"

He tilted his head to the side as she leaned out, one corner of his mouth fish-hooked. "You ain't earned a gun yet, Youngblood."

Theo returned the one-sided smile. It felt dead upon her lips. "Who said anything about a gun? Let me see the census."

He leaned back a little to get a clearer look of her, and a beat later, to retrieve the census ledger. "All right." He handed her the ledger. "The floor is yours."

"I don't need that either." She flipped open to the page with the members of the Creed family listed. She didn't need the post, but she raked her eyes across it anyway. Her eyes lingered on her own name, and she felt an odd pang of loss for that girl. She snapped the ledger shut and handed it back.

"What are you going to do?" August asked.

Theo pointed to her house across the field. "I'm going to flush out the Creeds."

"They're long gone, Youngblood."

"Maybe." She shrugged. "Maybe not."

August looked across the field and studied the houses dotting the meadow, giving hers a particularly skeptical glare.

"Okay," he said in a what-have-I-got-to-lose way. He swiveled his head toward Brody and gave him his two-finger beckon.

Theo inwardly cursed. She'd hoped she could use this moment to be alone.

"Make it quick, Youngblood." Then to Brody with no attempt to conceal: "Let's see what this kid's got."

Theo didn't wait for Brody before she began walking away. When the sound of August's voice became warbled by distance, jogging foot-steps brought Brody in stride with her.

"I don't need your help," Theo said.

Brody smiled as he took an appraising look across the prairie leading to her house. He appeared entertained at the notion, as if he was deliberately imagining her without his help. "Debatable."

"But if you insist," Theo said as they neared her home. "Start there," she pointed at the house farthest from hers, "and meet me back at the Creeds.'"

"We already cleared the homesteads," Brody said. He picked at the blood caked over his cuticles.

"Clearly." She gave his blood-covered body a mock appraisal. "Just humor me, would you?" She needed a moment alone. She was about ready to beg for it if she had to. Because, truth was, Theo had no notion of what to do next. All she knew was that if she had to stand there and witness August murder her town one by one, she wouldn't be able to keep it together. She couldn't just stand there and watch. She couldn't do nothing.

"I don't even humor my friends," Brody said. "What makes you think I'd indulge you?"

This was going to take some finessing. Her mind cranked with ideas, and as it did, she found the thought of having to find a way to get rid of Brody wasn't entirely unpleasant. Because, deep inside, there was something happening to Theo.

Something she wouldn't be able to admit to herself until much later: the moment August Gaines let her out of that jail, she discovered that she was downright *delighted* at fooling a man whom she'd measured as highly intelligent. Theo didn't understand why all this felt as much of a thrill as it did a threat.

"All right, Brody," Theo said.

Theo was going up against these men because it *was* the right thing to do, no doubt, but Theo had also never had a rush like this before. She didn't yet understand why, when everything was going wrong, it was the first time in her life she felt like she was in the right place.

Theo entered her house. Brody stepped in after her and went to the kitchen, moving through it as if he owned it. He looked in the bread-basket and tossed it aside when he found it empty. He picked up a cast-iron pan and checked its underside. It clanged loudly when he dropped it.

She considered smashing something against the back of his head.

Instead, she quickly categorized the possibilities.

Theo could believe that her father, her older brothers, and the Blacksmiths had taken off the moment they saw trouble. They would have done so in the hopes of going for Clayton Creek and getting help.

Brody found an apple and bit into it.

What Theo *couldn't* believe was that her entire family would leave, fully aware that they'd left her locked in a cage to fend for herself. Her mother would never. Her sister, not a chance. Furthermore, her mother would never risk the little boys to a chase of bandits.

Something through the window caught her eye. Forcing her body to stay calm, she averted her eyes.

She knew where her family was.

She had to get rid of Brody.

Theo inhaled deeply. It smelled like leather oil and ash, tallow and smoked pork, her brothers (mildew and sweat), her sister and mother (jasmine), and her father (wood shavings and varnish). It smelled like her home always had, muted by the cold.

She stepped across the sanded wood floors.

When she stepped on a creaky plank, she dropped to a knee and gently tapped her knuckles on it. It sounded hollow, as expected—there was crawlspace below.

She looked up at Brody. He stopped chewing, cheek bulging with a bite.

"What do you reckon?" she asked him.

He unholstered a revolver, chewed his bite, and swallowed it.

"Creeds!" Theo called out.

Silence.

"Come out or we'll shoot," Theo said to the crawlspace.

More silence.

"That's your cue," Theo said.

Brody took another bite. "You know there's little kids missing, right?"

"So?" She crouched back near the crawlspace and tried to pry a floorboard loose. She knew for a fact her family wasn't down there because at the start of winter her father had laced the entire space with rodent poison.

Brody chewed. "Oh, you're a tough man, then?"

Later, if there was a later, she'd have to find a way to get Brody to take her seriously.

"Hand me a knife," Theo held her hand out.

He sent a casual look around. "Probationaries don't get weapons."

Theo stood and unhooked a lantern from the wall. "Fine." She smashed it onto the floor. "I'll flush them out myself." Oil splattered across the wood planks.

He watched her unhook another lantern. His detached expression took a turn into annoyance when she smashed the lantern in the space between them. Oil splattered across his boots.

"The hell's a'matter with you?" he said as he hopped back. He smacked at his boots as if they'd already caught fire. "You know what?" He shoved his revolver back into its holster. "Knock yourself out." He took an aggressive bite of the apple. "I reckon tough men don't need help starting a fire anyhow." He slammed the door behind him before Theo could respond.

A wave of relief made her want to laugh and cry at the same time. Theo watched him take post on the lawn through the front window, then she spun and ran out the back door.

CHAPTER
10

Theo slipped out the back and leaped down the patio stairs in a single bound. She turned left, flanked the back side of the house, and came to an abrupt halt in front of a pile of manure. This is how they did it then.

She plunged her boot into the dried pile and gently kicked some aside, revealing the cedar planks of a root cellar below. The entrance was angled severely enough to almost be considered a trap door, bolted to a retaining wall no more than two bricks high. As she swept away the layer of manure, she scanned the area for Brody or any other unwelcome gazes.

She saw no such thing, but she did spot the empty wheelbarrow, hastily propped against the side of their house. That load of manure had been sitting back here for almost a week, meant for the garden field a little farther beyond. Theo grabbed the handle of the root cellar.

She heard the terrifying, tell-tale sound of a cocking hammer.

"*Wait!*" she whisper-yelled. "*Don't shoot,*" she said. She opened the hatch and saw two pairs of eyes peering up at her. One pair was the blackness of double barrels; the other was her mother's baby blues.

They were squinting and desperately trying to find purchase in the blinding morning light.

"Mama, it's me," Theo said, sending a crazed glance at her surroundings.

"*Baby.*" She breathed out a sob, lowering the shotgun. "You're okay," she said. "*You're okay, my god you're okay.*"

Theo trotted down the stairs into the dank coolness and squeezed her mother tightly, the downwardly pointing shotgun bumping their thighs. Her mother squeezed her so hard it hurt. Theo wasn't complaining.

As her eyes adjusted, Theo saw four more silhouettes in the shadows of the cellar.

Unclenching from the embrace, Theo put her hands on her mother's narrow shoulders, held her firmly, and said, "I can't stay here."

Evangeline came up and the sisters gave each other a quick, frantic squeeze.

Theo squinted at the small, dark shapes of her brothers. "Where's Dad?"

"He went south for help," Evangeline said.

"Clayton Creek?" Theo clarified.

"Yes," Mama said. "Elliot, Zeke, and Jude went in the opposite direction with Bram as diversion." Zeke and Jude—the eldest sons of the Creeds.

"Nobody went with Dad?"

"I don't think so." Mama shook her head. "What are you doing, Theo?"

She slammed her eyes shut briefly. "Mama, you need to listen. There is no time except for you to do exactly as I say. Are you listening?"

"I'm listening, but that don't mean I'm condoning."

Her mother's voice was steady, but Theo could tell how shaken and terrified she was. Theo didn't have time to dwell—they had food, water, shelter, and for the time being, the safest place in Bladestay.

"They're going after Bram."

"Why?"

"Don't know. Once they've gone, it'll be safer to leave. Mama—" She waited a beat for her mother's full attention. "There's a chance I'll be going with whoever goes after him."

"What? *Why*?" Her mother sounded breathless.

"No time to explain. I'll cause as many delays as I can, but this man, Mama? August Gaines? He's on a warpath. He's not going to stop. He's going kill Bram and I don't know why, but we have to get out of his way."

"Honey, did you say August Gaines?"

Theo blinked. "Do you know him?"

She shook her head impatiently. "Bram mentioned that name a long time ago, but—" Her mother broke off and Theo didn't push for more information, for unraveling the past was a luxury for those whose future was secure.

"I have to go, Mama."

"Theodora, there's no way I'm letting you—"

"Let me help," Evangeline interrupted.

"No," Theo and Rose Creed said concurrently.

"You and Mom have to get the boys to safety," Theo said.

"She doesn't need my help. But you do. You've got them tricked?" Evangeline asked in a rushed way that told Theo she understood the urgency here.

"For now. Evie, these men—"

"Bring me to this man August. Make me 'confess' things. Such as where Dad's gone and what their plan is." She gave Theo a *get-it?* look. "Not only will they trust you more, but it'll take the suspicion off Mama."

Theo didn't realize she was nodding in absurd agreement until her mom grabbed her arm and said, "What's *wrong* with you two?"

"It's not worth your life, Evie," Theo agreed as she nervously peeked above ground. Every second that passed was crucial, every moment down here a greater risk. They had no time to debate this. Theo needed to make a decision and make it now, even though it never should have been hers to make.

"But it's worth *yours*?" Evangeline said. She glanced back at their little brothers. They were so small. "Please let me help you."

Theo understood her sister's insistence, how staying put could feel like the cruelest form of uselessness. "Please don't make me say yes to this." But even as Theo said the words, she heard her own lack of conviction. Because this *was* a good idea.

"You can't say no to me." She gave Theo a devious smile that did a poor job disguising her terror. "I'm older than you." Theo gave her sister a pained look, somewhere between gratitude and horror, then she looked at her mom with an apology on her face.

Their mother let out a small sob when she realized she had no say left, when she saw that even if Theo and Evangeline *could* be talked out of this, Rose Creed was also a mother of more than just her daughters. She had her young children to look after. As far as Theo was concerned, she stopped being one of those the day she sank a blade into the flesh of her peer with the desire to kill.

She wrapped her arms around her mother and said quietly into her ear, "Get the boys safe. If I don't make it back"—she felt her mother's body hitch when she said that—"they've got men in the church and the women in the warehouse."

She had no idea if that information would become useful, but Mama simply nodded.

"No matter what you hear, stay here until nightfall," Theo said. "I'll do my best to come back for you."

"I love you, baby," her mother whispered.

"I love you too." She squeezed one last time. "I'll be back tonight, and together we'll go to Clayton Creek." She said it like a prayer, a quiet, fervent plea to let this be finished come nightfall. But the other unspoken fear: Elliot, Jude, and Zeke were still out there. And sure, her brothers might be grown men, Elliot might not be much of a child anymore, but if the tables were turned, if Theo were running about the hills with someone who had a giant target painted on his back, not one of them would hesitate for a moment to chase her down and, at the very least, get the message to her what kind of danger she was traveling with.

She ached to comfort her little brothers, but all she said to them was, "Mind Mama." Then to Evangeline: "Help me get that." She pointed at an oak barrel of aging bourbon.

They carried it up the stairs, pausing before they emerged so Theo could once again make sure it was clear.

"What are we doing, Theo?" Evangeline asked warily as they rolled the bourbon onto the grass.

Theo answered her sister with a *you don't want to know* look, then turned to close the cellar doors behind them.

The last thing she told her mom before she covered her back in darkness was, "Don't move, don't *breathe*, until night."

One of her little brothers began crying at that, hurting Theo's heart in way she'd never felt before. She was officially responsible for the lives of her family with these decisions. She and Evangeline spread the manure back over to hide the doors.

Together, the Creed sisters carried the barrel up the stairs and rolled it into the house.

"Get the matches and anything flammable," Theo said.

"Theo . . ." Evangeline said, understanding.

"This is how we survive," Theo said.

Evangeline looked around sadly, then started to tear through their house. While she did, Theo changed out of Patrick's oversized outfit and slipped into her little brother's clothes and boots. She heard Evangeline let out a soft sob from the next room. Theo clenched her teeth together and forced herself to remember the helplessness she'd felt in the jailhouse as innocent people were murdered right in front of her face, and just like that, rage eclipsed fear and she didn't feel like crying anymore.

As Theo buttoned her brother's shirt down her torso, she went to the front window and peeked out to check on Brody. She paused on a button, unease rippling through her.

He was gone.

She continued buttoning, coldness kissing her cheek when she leaned close to the glass. Still, Brody wasn't in sight.

Fastening the final button, she ran to the other side of the house, looked out the back window for him there.

Nothing.

The thundering hoofbeats of Gaines's scouts returning made her return to the front window.

For any of this to work, Theo had to assume the information the scouts brought back was based on tracks in the dirt, not any actual sightings. If the Blacksmiths and her brothers could just manage to keep the gang occupied long enough for her father to get to Clayton Creek for help, then the only thing Theo had to do was survive.

Evangeline touched Theo's shoulder. "Here." She held up a handful of matchboxes.

Theo took a box, struck a match, and flicked it into a broken mess of glass and lantern oil. It caught fire with a whoosh.

As Theo shoved the remaining matchboxes into her pocket, her sister held something else out to her.

"Remember when Bram gave this to dad?" Evangeline asked.

Theo picked up the straight razor from her sister's hand. Theo nodded as she smoothed her thumb against the scales of the polished bone where it was inlaid with a gold cross. She flipped open the jaws and touched the razor, which was wickedly sharp all the way to its uncommonly acute toe. "Three Christmases ago."

"Four," Evangeline corrected over the quiet crackle of things catching fire.

"Yeah," Theo said as she went over to the barrel in the center of their living room. "I think you're right." She knelt next to the bourbon and ran a fingernail along a seam.

She stabbed the razor there, then shimmied it out. A sieve of bourbon sprouted.

"Come on," Evangeline said, tugging her sister by the arm.

The curtains had caught fire and the smoke churned and curled toward the rafters.

As they hurried out the back door, Theo affixed the razor against her ribs midaxillary, under the edge of her bound breast. She slid it under the tightened chemise upside down so she could remove it by yanking downward, toward her hips.

Outside, the sisters paused to watch their home catch fire. They exchanged something unspeakable.

"We're out of time," Theo said as they clung to the backside of their house. Theo peeked around the corner and saw August holding council with his scouts. She looked at her sister. "It's not too late to go back to Mom."

"You know," Evangeline touched her sister's shorn hair, "I've seen the way you spot bluffs at the poker table. And I've always thought, if they'd just give you a chance, if they'd just let you play *one* hand, you'd bleed them dry."

"What a chance, huh?"

"I'm not going back, Theo. Just like you aren't. Whatever happens next, it's on me. I chose this. Remember that, okay? Now please," she said. "Let me help you."

Theo hugged Evangeline, nodding against her. "Thank you."

"What do we do?"

"If Bram and Jude and Zeke went up the mountain," Theo said, "they're probably going for the inn at the pass." They both instinctively turned to look at the mountain range due north. "Tell them that. Tell them Dad went too."

Evangeline nodded.

"But Dad'll get help," Theo whispered. "We're going to be okay." Her throat was tight and painful. Their house started to crackle with loud pops, exhaling smoke. "Run, Evie."

Evangeline pulled away from Theo, her eyebrows pinched together.

"*Run.*" Theo darted her eyes across the prairie. "I'll catch you."

Evangeline pointed her finger in Theo's face. "Don't pull your punches when you do."

"You're crazy," Theo said with a sad, breathless laugh.

Evangeline pecked her sister on the cheek and then took off running.

Only then did Theo indulge in tears. She dismissed them as swiftly as they came and then she took off after her sister.

Behind her, the explosion was more aggressive than she expected. But by then, her sister was far across the meadow and Theo had her at the end of her fingertips. Theo clawed her to the ground and Evangeline fought hard but ultimately Theo did what she was supposed to. She disguised her sister's face with blood and mud, severing whatever resemblance from the Creed line might tie them together. Then Theo took a handful of her sister's thick brown hair and used it to drag Evangeline to August's feet.

August hardly acknowledged Theo.

"You a Creed?" August drawled at Evangeline.

Evangeline sobbed at the grass, her hair a curtain around her. She nodded.

August opened the ledger. "Which one are you?"

Evangeline was shaking all over, unable to answer at first.

When Theo would later look back on this, she wouldn't be able to understand how she got through this moment. It wasn't the first time she experienced this phenomenon: the sensation of not being inside her own body, like she was instead sitting off to the side, watching herself. She could recall with great clarity that her hands were steady inside the front pockets of her (brother's) trousers. Her face was scowled. Her posture was sure. Both feet planted heavy on the ground, assuredly.

"Evangeline," her sister said.

"Tell him what you told me," Theo said.

That was when August acknowledged Theo, really looked at her, and when he did, she saw a hopeful fire burning in his eyes. She nodded a curt assurance at him.

"My dad—" Evangeline broke down for a moment and Theo knew that if she had to use her own voice in that moment, it wouldn't have shown up.

She took her eyes off her big sister and took in the surroundings. Brody Boone was standing in the outskirts of the gathered gang, arms folded over his chest, leaning under the shade of a spruce. Theo never saw him approach, he was just suddenly there, watching the scene with apathy.

Theo counted six of August's men, not including the man himself. She'd spotted six guarding the women on the backside of town. She could see straight down Main Street and clocked eight more. She guessed there might be more, considering how swiftly they took over a town of over three hundred souls, but she didn't have an idea of what that number might be.

"My dad and Mr. Blacksmith," Evangeline tried again. "They went that way." She pointed north to the pass saddled between two peaks.

"And the rest of your family?"

Evangeline began to cry in a manner in which no words were possible. But she only pointed to the house that was on its way to embers.

August looked at Theo.

"She's the only one who ran out when I started the fire," she replied.

August looked over his shoulder, asked a silent question to Brody. Brody nodded his answer.

August sniffed. "I'm sorry for your loss, Miss Creed."

Evangeline hugged herself across her stomach, bent her head, and cried.

"I'll make you a promise, Evangeline Creed," August said in a kind, almost tender drawl.

Evangeline looked up at him, tears tracking through blood and dirt.

"If your father conducts himself with honor up on that mountain," August continued, "no harm will come to you."

Evangeline glanced up at Theo, but Theo didn't dare meet her eyes.

August beckoned Flea over and told him, "Put her with the others. Give them what they need to clean her up."

Theo's legs felt like they were filled with nothing. She steadied her stance to make sure her knees didn't fail her.

"Sir," Flea said. He pulled Evangeline to her feet and walked her back to town.

August stood and looked down at Theo. "Not bad, Youngblood." Then to the rest of his gang in earshot: "Secure the men back in the church. Pathfinder, Jester, Rook, Shiner, Sixer, John, Spartan—you're comin' up the mountain with me. Prepare the freshest horses. Pathfinder and Spartan, assign the remaining men their posts. If I called your name and you ain't yet eaten, do it now. I leave in twenty minutes and y'all better be ready by then, hear?"

"Hear," came the collective response.

"What about me?" Theo asked.

"Kid, you?" He clicked his tongue and sent a glance to Brody before he looked back to her. He patted her on the shoulder. "I ain't decided on you yet."

CHAPTER
11

B rody and Theo sat shoulder to shoulder at the bar, annihilating a bowl of sticky oats and a tray of cold bacon congealed in its own fat. The only sound in the saloon was the clatter of their spoons scraping porcelain and the crunch of bacon between their teeth. Rays of light highlighted floating dust, a reminder that there is no such thing as settling.

Brody kept giving her sideways glances, ones that lingered too long, ones she knew were trying to work something out.

She dropped her spoon with a theatrical clatter and angled herself to face him, her elbow on the bar.

"Why does August call you Sixer?" she asked.

He shrugged. "Suppose you could say I got a way of readin' a person." He slid another room-temperature bite of oatmeal. He chewed as Theo glared at him. Streaks of dried blood were starting to flake and peel off. Black hair fell across his forehead no matter how many times he pushed it away, invisibly matted by the gore of whatever he'd done to bathe himself in blood. Theo found herself noticing the angle of his jawline, how it most certainly was forged from steel, sharp and hard. "He calls it my sixth sense."

"Bet you're a hell of a poker player."

"Bet," he said. He set his spoon down and pushed his bowl away. When he looked at her, Theo held his harsh gaze unapologetically with her chin shoved in her palm.

When he said nothing else, she only nodded, as if they'd come to some silent understanding, even though Theo felt increasingly off-balance every time he directed his attention on her. She didn't like the way the blood seemed to drain from her head when his eyes traced the outlines of her face. The way she felt exposed no matter how hard she made her shell.

"And what's your read on me?" Theo asked challengingly.

Brody sneered a smile, like a reaction to an inside joke. Instead of answering her question, he said, "Boss man ain't gonna include you up the mountain."

Theo kept her relief from spilling over the edges and into her mannerisms, even though she knew it was possible there was no truth to the statement, that Brody was just pushing buttons and seeing which ones lit up.

"Okay. I don't want to go."

Brody made quick movement of shifting on the barstool, his face close enough to hers that she could feel his breath on her cheek. It was a move that was meant to unnerve Theo, which it did, but she was once again able to keep things from spilling over the edge.

"Then what *do* you want, Teddy Pine?" Brody said, the fake name intentionally coated with a different tone, a taunting one, Theo decided.

Theo held her ground, not without difficulty. "Do you have a problem, Brody Boone?" She mimicked the taunting tone around his name.

"No." He stood and picked up his bowler hat. "I don't believe I do." His eyes wandered up to her fresh haircut, and as he pressed his hat atop his thick waves of raven locks, he said, "You've got something in your hair, partner."

When he bumped through the batwings, it took Theo a moment to realize her rigidity. Her fists were clenched. Her spine was erect. Her leg was bouncing lightly. Not even August Gaines, with all his powerful command, set Theo on edge the way this boy did. Theo didn't understand it. She wasn't afraid of him, not any more than anybody else who'd come into town in the last twenty-four hours, but there was something unknown there.

Once Brody was out of sight, she raked her hands through her hair. To her horror, she found a little brown hairpin that had survived the scuffle and the cut. She stuffed it into a pocket, eyes racing around the room, hoping she would never have to spend another moment under the observant gaze of Brody Boone.

That boy was dangerous.

Theo grabbed the last two pieces of bacon, scraped the scabbed remains of oatmeal from the bottom of the cauldron, stuck the bacon in the sticky mess, and headed down the street. Up and down Main, Gaines's men were posted with such efficiency that it made Theo's stomach curl and flip.

They were going to keep her town captive until August came back down off the mountain and Theo just couldn't figure out *why*. Why wouldn't the force of his entire gang stay at his side? Maybe this wasn't just about revenge.

Maybe they were after something else.

But that was a concern for another day. Right now, she had to prepare herself for the immediate contingencies.

If August was going to leave her behind, she just needed to wait out the day. In the cover of night, she could help Evangeline, her mother, her baby brothers. Together they would make their way to Clayton

Creek, meet up with her father, and wait for the law to administer justice. Simple.

If not? If August meant for Teddy Pine to accompany him? She didn't have a plan for that. She simply reminded herself over and over that she could do it.

Gaines's gang treated her with a respectful ambivalence, rarely acknowledging her as she passed by any of their given posts.

She entered the jailhouse with no raised brows and no qualms.

Patrick scrambled to his feet, making frantic glances about. He opened his mouth, almost blurting something, then he pressed his lips shut before chewing on the bottom one.

He finally settled for, "Hey."

"Have you been fed?" Theo asked.

Patrick shook his head.

"Here," she handed the bowl through the bars, having to tilt it to fit.

"Thank you," he said. Patrick stepped back and sat on his cot, taking a greedy bite, then another. With an apprehensive look on his face, he asked, "How'd you do that?" he asked around a mouthful.

"Do what?"

"That. *This*. When that Brody fella—" he swallowed as he studied her. "I didn't even *recognize* you."

"Well, that was the point."

He took another bite, mumbled, "Suppose so." He glanced outside. "You have any water?"

"No, but I'll get you some."

"Why you being so nice to me? It's my—" He swallowed what was in his mouth and put his eyes on the floor so he wouldn't have to look Theo in the face when he added, "It's my . . . this is my fault."

"I'm overjoyed we've come to that understanding," she deadpanned. "But listen. Locked up here, locked up there . . ." Theo nodded in the general vicinity of the church, then lifted her shoulders. "Collateral either way."

Patrick's eyes went shifty before asking, "Do you know what they want?"

Theo blew off the question. "I'll be back for you tonight," she lied. Whichever way this went, she definitely would not be coming back for Patrick Holmes. "I'll get you out, and we'll go get help." But she did have a reputation to uphold, and she didn't need Patrick saying anything that contradicted Teddy Pine. "Lie low, can you do that for me?"

"I thought you hated me. Why would you bother?"

"I *do* hate you, Patrick. But you kept your mouth shut when you didn't have to. You keep my secret, and I'll use it to help you. Deal?"

Patrick blinked. "Have you always been so cold, Theo?"

"I don't rightly know, Patrick. I reckon it don't rightly matter either though, do it?"

"You're telling me you'd rather be fair than kind?"

She hated the way he always tried to bait her. "Lie low, Patrick," Theo said again, doing her best not to slam the door on her way out.

"Theo," he called lightly after her. "Wait! I need to tell you something."

Moron, she thought, hoping nobody else heard him call her that name. She stepped down the stairs and headed back down Main, the sound of clopping hooves jogging her way. She stopped at the intersecting alley, stuck her hands in her pockets, and looked up at the thinning smoke from the embers of her home. She made a silent prayer for all the things they'd lost, followed up by one for all the things they hadn't.

Brody had his hat pulled low and a horse in tow. He trotted over, sat deeply, and *whoa'd* his gelding. Looking down at her, he dropped the lead line of the ponied horse at her feet.

Numbly, Theo took hold of her horse.

"Reckon we get to see just how tough you really are," Brody said. Then he reigned his horse into Main Street and trotted away.

Dread slammed into her.

August Gaines means for me to accompany him.

She put her foot in the stirrup.

You can do this, she told herself.

She reached for the reins with a handful of mane and hauled herself up.

You can do this. She pushed down fear and drew the rage. Already, the exchange was getting easier.

She was going to survive this day. Then she was going to survive the next day, and then the one after that.

She put her other foot in the stirrup, adjusted the reins to be congruent and flat, checked the security of her pack and the capacity of the waterskins. She was going to survive as many days as it took to dig a grave for August Gaines, with bare hands and broken fingernails if she had to, because she refused to let her family be the collateral in someone else's revenge plot.

Over and over, she told herself she could do this.

She could camp out for an undetermined about of time with a gang of bandits without revealing herself.

She could track down her own flesh and blood, knowing what the end entailed.

She could keep her cool.

She could make it through a menstrual cycle without supplies.

She could cut a throat with the straight razor harbored against her ribs.

She could outthink a seasoned brigade.

She could find a way to derail a plan that has been years in the making.

And then Theo remembered she was supposed to have testicles, so she made the proper adjustments. Down the street, a bandit wearing fingerless gloves was watching her.

Theo dipped her chin away from him and dug her heel into the horse's ribs, making the horse pivot easterly. As soon as the horse's nose pointed toward the church, she squeezed the horse forward.

"Ey, kid," a voice called. She found the bandit with the fingerless gloves walking toward her. She slowed her horse to a standstill, resisting the urge to take off. In that moment, she thought this was the end. She'd been made. She'd been caught. And now he was going to tear her off this horse and say, *Look everyone, look what I found. This little boy ain't a boy but—*

The bandit took off his faded black hat, smoothed his matted hair, and extended it to her.

Theo looked down at the hat, at the man, then slowly reached for it, still unconvinced this wasn't the end of everything.

"You'll get ruddy as a radish out there, young'un."

She took the hat tentatively, and before she could find her voice that was buried somewhere beneath the panic in her chest, the bandit spat the brown of chew, gave her a smile as he wiped his chin, and stepped back.

She pressed the man's hat atop her head, tipped it at him, then loped the horse down the street. Theo felt the panic start to melt. She needed to keep moving forward. Nights, she knew, would be the hardest. She tried to focus on the things she could control, which narrowed things considerably. She would focus on the art of machismo. She would seek and find the soft spots of August Gaines's soul. She would outsmart her own fear.

She didn't focus on the fact that she had just burned down her own house in the name of control. She didn't think about how striking the match didn't make her any more in control of events because, if she did, she would be reminded that cutting off the rest of her hair didn't mean that she had wanted it gone.

II

SYCOPHANT

THE PROBLEM WITH THE DEVIL ISN'T THAT HE'S EVIL,
THE PROBLEM IS THAT HE'S CHARMING.

CHAPTER

12

August was in a foul mood when he announced their place for camp. The ten men who comprised their search party kept a wide berth, including Theo and Brody. Brody took August's horse as soon as the man dismounted.

"You stay with me," Brody Boone instructed Theo.

The outfit carried out their tasks with sharp precision. Theo imagined their fluidity and cohesion akin to an orchestra, each with their own place with their own talent, playing in time with the other.

As Theo played groom's assistant with Brody, she observed the group. Flea, Jester, and Pathfinder handed their horses to Brody and walked straight out of camp in different directions.

Shiner, a white man with a purple birthmark below his left eye, tied his horse to a tree and immediately began to gather firewood.

Rook, a man with a massive beard and closely cropped head, had the job of unpacking the saddle bags as Brody and Theo untacked. He brought the blankets, canvases, furs, and cans of food to where August stood, apparently designating the center of camp. August had chosen a flat area lush with ferns but clear of trees.

Spartan, a heavily muscled man with long dreadlocks, was in charge of weapons.

John, a man who'd earned no nickname, hadn't uttered a single word since Theo knew him. Theo didn't know if he couldn't, or if it was just that he didn't. John helped Rook set up camp as Shiner brought back armfuls of stones, then armfuls of kindling. Shiner had a pit dug, established a rock perimeter, and was working on ignition by the time Spartan had a pot of beans ready to be heated.

Even with the new members of the gang, camp sprang together flawlessly. The horses were grazing on dinner. Everyone had a bed laid. The fire was roaring.

When Flea, Jester, and Pathfinder returned, Spartan was ready to spoon hot beans back in cans for them.

"I'll take first shift," Flea said, nodding his thanks to Spartan when he handed him an open can filled with hot pintos. "I spotted a perfect little lookout thataway," he added. Then he walked out into the direction in which he'd pointed, off to his task.

"I'll take second," Shiner said, mouth full.

They went around the oval shape of their camp, each taking responsibility without complaint or argument. When it got to August, he said, "I'll take last post. Pine Needle—you'll accompany me."

Her stomach lurched; she nodded calmly.

"Where's the river?" August asked, pulling out his pipe. The moving water gurgled in the distance, but the acoustics of the small valley it ran through made it difficult to pinpoint where it was.

"Right down there," Pathfinder said as Flea pointed north.

"Clean yourself up, Sixer," August said grumpily as if he was tired of looking at the kid in his current state.

"Sir," Brody Boone said.

As they began to scrape the bottom of their cans, August pulled out a bottle of whiskey. He uncorked it, and everyone stilled, wiping their mouths and finishing the food that was in their mouth.

When August held the bottle out in front of him, toward the fire in a gesture meant to be all-inclusive, Theo knew she was witnessing tradition.

"We honor the past so it does not dictate us. We remember the fallen so they do not haunt us. We never underestimate the enemy so they do not surprise us." August got to his feet and walked over to Theo. Her body wanted to curl up and cower, but she simply looked up at him. "We welcome new friends . . ." August looked over at Brody, whose designated spot wasn't six feet from Theo's.

Brody finished the sentence: "For they become family."

August smiled. It was genuine and kind and it made Theo's insides uncoil and relax. He stretched his arm somewhat behind him, toward the fire, and tipped the mouth of the bottle until he'd emptied the approximate amount of a shot glass. "For the past." Then he extended the bottle down to Theo. "And to the future."

Theo reached for the bottle, and August released it to her grip.

She placed the bottle on her lips and took a deep swig. It burned and raged down her throat, but it turned her stomach into a furnace, spreading outward through her limbs and leaving her head feeling like it was filled with something effervescent.

August smiled again, nodded toward Brody, then went back to his spot.

Theo took the cue as Brody being next in line, so she handed it to him.

It was the first time she saw Brody Boone show his teeth in a kind or peaceful way, and yet, it was somehow more menacing through the dark maroon of his crimes.

He took a drink, coughed once, took another drink, then got up and passed it along on his way out of camp.

As the bottle made its rounds, the men settled into conversation with the kind of ease forged by shared struggles, successes, goals, battles, losses, gains, and the countless confides and mini alliances that encompass a family. August was grinning, enraptured by a private dialogue with Spartan, who was telling an animated story as he leaned on an elbow toward August. Packing his pipe, August laughed at something Spartan, who was mildly loose with liquor and laughter himself, said.

It was an unnerving scene for Theo to take in, but she also supposed that when you sleep with the enemy, you're bound to discover something redeemable about them. She scooted to the edge of her bed, stretching toward the flames and a blanket loose on her shoulders. She watched and listened to conversation, but she didn't know how to speak in the nostalgic grooves that the group's intimacy had slowly engraved in all the years prior. Often, she found herself grinning at stories she could follow, enraptured by others, flat-out horrified by few.

When Brody walked back into camp, Theo did a double take.

He was wearing nothing but his drawers and boots, his shirt and trousers slung over an otherwise bare shoulder. His presence felt invasive, obtrusive, and utterly disrupting. Theo wanted to know why nobody else felt completely rocked by his return. It set her on edge as momentously as if a wolf wandered into their camp, but the men hardly gave him a glance as he crouched next to the fire to lay out his wet clothes. She tried not to watch the way the muscles on his back moved under his brown skin. She definitely would not watch the rivulets that hurried down his neck and shimmied the slope of his shoulders. And when he swept a hand through his wet hair, Theo absolutely didn't notice how graceful even his most mundane movements were.

She scooted back, suddenly no longer needing the heat of the fire. Theo lay down in her bed, cocooned herself in her blankets, and flipped over to put her back to Brody.

That boy was dangerous.

CHAPTER

13

"**D**o you know why I brought you with me, Pine Needle?" August asked. He sat propped against a tree, one knee drawn up, hat tipped back off his forehead, loading his pipe with tobacco.

"Presently," Theo leaned against a nearby trunk of her own, "or previously?" Her chest ached deeply, the razor digging into her ribs. She peered back at camp, slices of orange glowing through the thick forest. August had posted their first night watch about fifty yards from the sleeping men.

"Sure," he said.

She crossed her arms over her chest and squinted at the glow through the darkness. Theo had to be insidiously careful here.

"Because you think you know me," she said. She resisted the urge to spill her constructed story, one she'd crafted in her head on the trail, but she knew she had to make August work for it, to make him feel like he'd pried something from her, but she was struggling to concentrate.

Every inhale deepened the bruising ache on her side. Her breathing turned shallow. It did little to relieve the pressure.

August folded the tobacco back into its leather satchel. He tucked it into a pocket at his breast, exchanging it for matches. "Let me make something very clear to you, Youngblood." He struck flame. The breeze threatened it, so he cupped his hand.

He sighed as he flicked the spent match into the shadows and got another.

She pushed her fingers against the razor, trying to slide it out of its bruised indent.

His eyes dropped to her chest, noticing her discomfort. "I'm rather particular about new blood I bring into the fold."

She inched the razor back. The relief was great.

When he struck the fresh match, Theo saw the way his eyes narrowed at her. "Catch me, Youngblood?"

She nodded, but she was starting to wonder if she actually did.

He stood, and somehow he seemed bigger than the last time she saw him on his feet.

Theo regulated her flight response. On her next inhale, sharper and deeper than she could control, she felt a gentle pop, followed by a horrible loosening. The razor slipped out and tumbled down her torso. Completely reactionary, Theo's hand darted to catch it, but it tumbled past her fingers.

She felt it land next to her foot.

He stepped close to her. "You got bugs in your britches, Youngblood?" He dragged his eyes up and down her.

Run, run, run—but he was too close and she couldn't even breathe.

"I'm just—" Her voice was small. "Cold." It had an audible tremble.

"Hm." He placed the pipe in his mouth. He leaned down so their faces were level, examining her closely.

He held out his box of matches.

She took it cautiously, sliding her foot over the razor.

"You think I don't know you." He kept his eyes steady on hers when he cupped his hands around the end of his pipe.

She swallowed.

"I *do* know you."

The world slanted, tilted off-kilter. *There's no way he knows.* Theo felt like she might be sick.

"I know who you are. I know *what* you are."

This isn't happening. She considered going for the razor. Wondered if she could be fast enough.

She doubted it. Unable to think of what to do or what to say, she simply did what was expected of her.

Her hands shook when she struck the match.

"What do you have to say about that?" He drawled, coaxing the embers with gentle puffs as she stoked the pipe with the flame.

She held his gaze, refusing to cry. If she wasn't leaning against the tree for support, her legs would surely have given out by now.

"Mr. Gaines . . ." Sweat prickled the back of her neck. Her nervous system was revolting.

"It's not a bad thing, kid. To be seen." Smoke swirled around his words. "Because I can see that you're missing something."

The sweet spice stung her eyes.

"And maybe," he said, "I could give it to you."

Theo's forehead creased into a frown.

He didn't step out of her space. "Maybe," August stuck the pipe between his teeth and took off his coat, "I could show you a thing or two about the world you could have."

He held it out for her.

She looked at it, stifling disbelief. She looked up at him. *Pull yourself together.* She took the coat. *He doesn't know.*

"Why do grown-ups do that?" She was lightheaded with adrenaline and her voice was still weak with panic. "Always pretending you understand me. *Get* me."

He gave her a small, knowing smile and turned.

Theo doubled over, clutching his coat to her stomach as she took a silent, devouring breath behind his back, her mouth stretched open in a silent scream.

She clamped her mouth shut.

She snatched the razor and sneaked it up her sleeve.

By the time August had returned to his spot, Theo was upright, pulling the coat across the evidence of hyperventilation.

As he sat back down, he answered her. "People think 'cause they lived an age before that they lived your life before."

She slowly gathered her confidence back. "But not you."

"Imagine that." A hint of a smile crossed his lips as he puffed.

"Yeah." She felt her insides relax. "Imagine." Just a little sarcasm. Her hands started to go steady. She unfastened a button under the protection of his coat and slipped a hand into her shirt.

"So, Youngblood. If I can sum you up, I'd like something from you in return."

You can do this. "What's that?" she asked with as much conviction as she could muster.

"I want you to rid your shoulder of that chip."

She lifted her chin slightly, bluffing contemplation. She found the wayward end of the chemise and pulled tight. The ache in her torso resumed.

"Whatever you say, Mr. Gaines," she said, a little flippantly.

"None of that."

"Fine." She tucked the end of the binding back in place.

"No."

She sighed. "Okay." She softened the edges of her tone.

"Say it."

She took a purposeful pause. "I promise."

August nodded.

Puffed.

Looked her up and down as if just now sizing her up, as if he hadn't already come to all these conclusions prior to this moment.

She denied a shiver when the cool air hit the sweat on her skin, when his eyes assessed her.

"You lost your parents when you were little. Probably never knew them."

Theo tightened her lips and steeled her stance to be slightly defensive even though she felt overwhelming relief.

"You get into trouble all the time, thinking the world owes you something for the things it's already taken. You're reckless because you feel like you've got nothing to lose. You think that, by doing this, you're challenging the world to give you something worth losing. Nobody you've ever lived with knows what to do with you. You're a ruffian, borderline dangerous, dancing closer to that border the older you get, but nobody takes you *too* seriously because you're small. Which compounds this complex.

"You're an orphan in a small town which is somehow worse than being an orphan in a big city, but you couldn't handle the anonymity anyhow, no matter how much you crave it, and you've lived just long enough to find that people do one of two things with people like you, sometimes both things, but never neither thing: they pity you or they can't stand to be around you. You've spent a brief lifetime bouncing from town to town, constantly runnin' away from your hurt, looking for a home in any house that'll have you, but it's not like you'd accept it even if they gave it to you because, kid? You don't trust it no more because the first family you were given was stricken. And now, well, you've got yourself a problem. You seek the very thing you won't take and to make matters worse? You're smarter than everyone. You're too smart for your own good and because of that, you're constantly bored. When you lost your family, a violence was planted within you that you have no idea how to handle. You have this *rage*. Yeah, I see it—it's *boiling*. And not just any kind of anger, no, it's a singular kind with a fuse lit by powerlessness."

Her breathing turned shallow again but had nothing to do with the pressure of the bindings.

"People tell you to be good, but they don't know the definition of it. Adults tell you they understand, yet they couldn't tell you why you feel the urge to scream during every waking second; why it feels like you're filled to the brim with something inside of you that, while it's a part of you, it *ain't* you; why you feel an unholy urge to take a blade and run it across your own skin; why those thoughts inside your head feel like yours but they ain't yours because no matter how much you will them, they just won't be *quiet*, not for a moment. Nobody gets this loneliness you carry, how it's both empty and heavy." He held his palm open in front of him as if to weigh something there. "Men—they stand on podiums of power and privilege and when you squirm under the pressure of their thumb, they chide your disobedience.

"Adults, we can't tell you why a good man dies while the evil one thrives, so they just say, well, kid, that's simply God's will and you just have to trust that, but you don't, you *can't*, and Christ, Youngblood, how could you? You don't even understand your own damn self."

Tears broke free and skipped down Theo's face.

She felt simultaneously filled and hollowed.

She'd expected he'd likely peg her as an orphan, she just didn't think he'd go on and on the way he did, hitting several true marks along the way. He might have been wrong about the source of the pain, but still, he *saw* things.

The tears were planned; the ease in which they came, was not.

She pulled his coat tighter, feeling shielded by it.

"Life don't have to be so hard, Youngblood." August puffed.

"So you have all the answers then, is that it?" Theo asked, but the challenge in her tone was lacking.

"Not even close. But I'll promise you something: I won't ever pretend I do. But more important?" He paused for effect. "I'll teach you something ain't nobody bothered to show you before."

She swallowed, disturbingly eager for what he was going to say next.

"I'll show you how to live without them. I'll prove to you they ain't necessary."

She was nodding before she knew she was. "How did . . ." She didn't want to finish the question. It was too vulnerable. Even cloaked in lies, it felt too real.

"How do I know how that thing in there operates?" He tapped his temple with the mouth of his pipe, his brows lifted.

Theo wiped her cheeks, her mouth tight.

"Haunted recognizes haunted, Youngblood."

That was the first time she felt it. Something quietly antithetical.

She sniffed an inhale. She nodded. "Same cloth?"

August smiled broadly and somehow, sadly, as if he pitied the mind that worked like his as much as he delighted in it. "You got it."

Theo was thinking, *This turned out to be too easy*, but the mirrored thought to that was: *August's probably thinking the exact same thing.*

CHAPTER
14

What Theo didn't know until three days later, was that the night shifts were solidified on that first night. Flea had claimed first shift that first night, and so it would be for the duration of their mission. It was the same routine every day and every night.

Theo learned her place in rotation, which was always attached to someone's already established one, usually either Brody or August, but sometimes Flea too. On the trail, somebody always scouted ahead; that was Pathfinder's job, but often interchanged with Jester, whom Theo was beginning to think earned his name ironically.

Theo was pleased with how easily she slipped into their routine, how quickly she found herself slipping into the established grooves of intimacy.

On the morning of their third night, before the sun began to dilute the horizon, a large hand shook her out of sleep.

A rumbling drawl coaxed her awake. "We're up, Pine Needle."

She sat up and he handed her a cup of black sludge. It was acrid, gritty stuff, but it was hot, and it sent lightning bolts throughout her nervous system. That morning, Theo was surprised by how well she had slept. Her sleep had been black and dreamless, a void where time doesn't make sense—she had just laid her head down five minutes ago but now it was seven hours later.

Theo rolled up her site efficiently and quietly but left the neat pile where it was for the crew to finish packing up when the sunlight roused them. As they stepped out of camp, Theo saw that August's site was already tidied, an indication that he'd been up before the previous shift could awaken him. She looked over her shoulder, checking Brody's site. His bed site was empty, making Theo deduce August intended to supersede the shift early. Arguably, the shift Brody Boone had landed was the one attached to a short stick, but it never seemed to bother him.

When August and Theo made it to the relative high ground of the post, Brody was pacing quietly. His footsteps were quiet and precise, his alertness at the end of his shift a testament to how seriously he considered the task.

"Morning," he said to August, but gave Theo a polite dip of his chin.

Theo gave a small nod over her cup.

Stretching, August asked, "When did that happen?"

At first, Theo wasn't sure what he was referring to, but then she saw it. Or rather, didn't see it. The fire they were getting closer to every night, was gone.

Brody scanned the inky forest, the dark shapes of night yet to show lines of definition. "Twenty-four minutes ago."

"If only everyone were as precise as you, Sixer." August dragged his eyes along the undefined horizon. "Ninety minutes or so till sunup." August turned his profile toward Theo. "Want to go down to the river and wash up, Pine Needle?"

Theo thought her heart might stop right then and there.

"What about them?" she asked about the extinguished fire. "If they're moving, shouldn't we?"

August smiled. "Nah, Youngblood." He pulled out his pipe. "That right there? That's an invitation for an ambush. We don't travel at night. Not unless we're the ones being chased."

"Brilliant," Theo said. "Meanwhile, they tire themselves out and we can push the string harder today."

August packed his pipe. "You got it, kid."

She smiled.

Theo knew it could happen. Perhaps even understood that it *would* happen. She just didn't expect it to happen so quickly. This act melding to actions, persona becoming personality, façade becoming easier than the factual.

It was the one thing she tried very hard not to think about. She'd been gifted with the powers of a chameleon, and she was focusing on counting the blessings that came with such a gift. But she also couldn't shake the memory of Faust, that when he entered a bargain with Mephistopheles, he did not miss his soul, for that came later, when he realized his corruption was irrevocable.

"Sixer ain't going to fall back asleep," August said.

Brody crossed his arms and kept appraising the hillside.

"He can help me keep watch if you want to go on 'n' wash up."

Theo cleared her throat, relief so intense that it made her head light. She nodded, untrusting of the way her voice might tremble should she try to use it. Taking a large swallow of bitter black, she muttered softly, "Appreciate it."

August waved her off as he lowered himself to the ground. Brody's eye found her, then lingered longer than she would have liked.

She left them to it, and as soon as she was out of sight, she began running toward the sound of water.

The bank was a gentle slope on this side of the river, but steep and rocky on the other side. She needed to be quick, preferably back in her clothes before pink started to dust the sky. The cold sank its teeth into her naked flesh, and when she began to unbind her chest, a deep, permeating ache was released. Her skin was an angry rose color underneath, indents etched into her skin around her upper torso. Her breasts hurt from the constant pressure, and as much as she had been dreading the icy water, it felt glorious on the aching parts of her chest, sides, and back. She ran a tallow bar across her skin and over her head, truly appreciating her botched hair for the first time since she lost it. It took no time to wash it, and even less time to rinse.

Theo was painfully rejuvenated, her breath visible in the emerging grays of presunrise. She was smiling through clattering teeth, filling her lungs as deeply as she could, and letting it out felt like a purge. The river was thick at this junction, the land fairly flat, and the current relatively gentle. Theo dared to swim against the current, leaving the wading calm of the shore, trying to get her blood to pump some warmth through her body. She fought the current as hard as she could, pushing against it with kicks and strokes until her body screamed for relief and the cold didn't feel like punctures, then let the current carry her body back to the bank where she'd left her clothes.

She was breathless with exhilaration when she reached her toes down to find the sand, her hands floating to the surface, outstretching her fingers.

"Get out," a voice called lightly from the shore.

Theo jerked her arms back to her body, found the bottom of the river with the bottom of her feet as she found the shadow on the bank. Her arms wrapped protectively around her bosom beneath the star-speckled surface, the water eager to reflect any pieces of light.

She recognized the silhouette of the bowler hat before she did the voice.

"Breakfast's up. Wrap it up, Pine."

"Okay," Theo said. Sobs pushed against her throat, a hot buildup screamed in her eyes—this was the moment she'd been dreading, when these men would discover her and punish her for being what she was and no one would be there to judge their actions except for the mountains, so when she saw the agile form of Brody Boone turn and lope back up the gentle hillside without seeing an inch of her skin, she took in as much air as her lungs could hold, slipped her head back under the water, and screamed until there wasn't a bubble of air left in her chest.

CHAPTER

15

It took two days to travel no more than thirty miles, the terrain increasingly treacherous, but Pathfinder estimated they had closed the gap between them and the Creeds and Blacksmiths by about half. That night, August was in a pleasant mood, telling stories and commanding the conversation. With the fresh scare of almost being discovered two mornings ago, Theo's guard was back in place. A newly uncorked bottle made its rounds as August regaled the camp with a particular war story that only two of the men present now were present then: Pathfinder and Spartan. They held the bottle longer during their turns, during the story. Their faces slacked at hard memories; their eyes traveled away from the now.

August was an indulgent storyteller, never an embellishing one; his defense for fact as strict as his disregard for truth left his listeners both mystified and enticed, like a sleight of tongue, telling you one thing but disproving it in the same breath. He did this the most, Theo noticed, while on the subject of authority. He could lay out all the virtues of leadership while telling a time he'd dismantled it. He would explain how a lawless nation will crumble like a sandcastle while equating himself to a tidal wave during the details of a heist. He'd tell you the methods of castration while speaking about the importance of loyalty, then go on to tell you an instance of duplicity that was for the greater good. There's no such thing as a great con artist who hasn't mastered the art of duality.

And while these stories helped guide Theo into the grooves of the familiarity, none of them helped her understand this seething feud that had driven Gaines to give up his life for the path he was on now. What could Blacksmith—if he truly was this Lucas Haas—have done to have derailed Gaines's life so thoroughly?

Theo craved the answer, needed it, *required* it.

She'd given up so much to join this quest, and it unsettled her how nobody seemed to need a prerequisite when it came to August Gaines.

Unsettled her, yes; confused her, no.

In order to poke that beast, however, there was something she needed to do. Because a conversation like that is one that had to be earned.

The next morning, she got up before Gaines.

She put on a spare sheepskin coat, stepped into her (brother's) boots, filled a cup with the black mud water that remained suspended above embers all night, every night, and crept quietly out of camp. Jester was snoring a riot, but nobody stirred as Theo chose her steps carefully. She climbed to the lookout, a rare location of three-sixty proportions. Boone tipped his nose over his shoulder, an acknowledgement of her approach.

Automatically, Theo handed the hot tin to him as she sat. Just as seamlessly, Brody took a drink before handing it back.

"Gaines?" he asked softly, glancing back at camp.

"Sleeping."

"He'd want you to wake him."

Theo reached over and took Brody's right wrist in her thin fingers and rotated his arm to check the time. She had never seen anybody wear a timepiece on their arm before, so she took a moment admiring the getup. The pads of her fingertips lingered on his skin next to the thick leather strap that was fastened around his wrist as she turned the glass face of the timepiece to catch the glow of the fire. Her touch was brief and intentionally benign, but when it happened, Theo became very aware of their proximity. She could smell the way sagebrush interacted with his skin. Brody, she noticed, became very still. Theo was quite certain he wasn't breathing.

The moment lasted just that, and Theo withdrew her hand.

"He still has some time," she replied.

Brody was watching the mountainside with an intensity.

"Did you see their fire tonight?" Theo asked.

He nodded. "It appears they packed up about half an hour ago."

"Do you really think they're waiting to ambush every morning?"

He shrugged. "It doesn't really matter. They ain't gonna outrun us."

"What makes you so sure?"

"See that pass?" He pointed to the silhouetted mountain range, intimidating heights with sharp angles. "They gotta go through that to keep running. It ain't thawed enough to take that risk. Their horses will be ragged by then and to risk a foot pursuit in what looks like knee-high snow—" Brody shook his head. "Madness. They're gonna make their stand at the inn. It's their best play."

He was right.

August may be gaining on the Blacksmiths and the Creeds, but maybe Blacksmith had a clever plan. Maybe he was letting Gaines think he had the upper hand. Maybe he was coaxing Gaines into a false sense of confidence. Maybe they *would* keep running. Knowing what she knew about Gaines and his crew, running through the pass probably *was* the safer bet. *Please have a plan. Please keep running. Please—*

Brody glanced at Theo. "You good?"

Theo looked up at Brody. She got lost in her thoughts too easily. She hadn't even noticed that he'd stood. He was unbuckling his gun belt. She was staring at him. She should say something.

"Did you hear me?" he asked, slinging his gun belt over his shoulder.

She cleared her throat as if she was going to respond, but she only shook her head.

"Are you okay?" He adjusted the watch on his wrist under the cuff of his sleeve.

She'd never seen him look like that. Concerned. Kind. Brody may be one of the deadliest people she'd ever met, but it was hard to see that when his guard was down. It was also hard to ignore that he was unreasonably handsome. Her mind, without her permission, reminded her of what he looked like without a shirt. She felt her cheeks redden.

"I'm fine," she said. "Are you going somewhere?"

"I'm gonna go water a tree. I'll be back in a minute."

"Don't leave me alone without a gun," she said.

Brody looked at the wilderness as if gauging the dangers. Then he nodded, drew a pistol, and spun it to offer her the grip. She took it. It was cold and heavy, and she ignored how fervently aware she was when their fingers brushed against each other, hotly contrasted.

"Don't hurt yourself," he said. There was a lightness to the way he said it, not quite teasing, but not far off either.

"You don't hurt *yourself*," she snapped, which was, admittedly, not her best retort.

He smiled, holding the unbalanced weight of his gun belt over his shoulder.

She narrowed her eyes at his back when he turned. When the dark foliage swallowed his silhouette, she popped the cylinder and emptied the bullets. Flicking the cylinder back into place, she pocketed the bullets.

She checked August's bed site. No change.

It was time to escalate things. They were closing in on the Black-smiths and her brothers too quickly. A confrontation was imminent. She needed to disrupt August and his men. She also needed to wedge herself deeper into the trusted fold.

She was confident she could kill two birds with one stone here.

First, she was going to carve some more trust for herself. The thing about men is they think trust is earned through threats and humiliation. She was fluent in that language too.

Brody returned, buckling his gun belt across his hips.

She slowly took out her straight razor, keeping it hidden under her arm.

"Are you trying to get me killed?" Theo snarled the question when he sat back down next to her. "Or do you just not trust me?"

"What?" he replied.

"You give me a pistol without any bullets?" She shoved the gun flat against his chest. "Why."

He took it, confused. Checked the chambers with a creased forehead. "I don't . . ."

Theo dumped the hot coffee into Brody's lap, flipped open the straight razor, and pressed the edge against his jugular. Brody fell back but grabbed her arm. The hat tumbled from his head, and she took control of his scalp with a handful of hair. The bulletless gun fell from his lap. Theo pressed her knee deeply into his groin and pressed the blade until his skin broke.

"Jesus!" He breathed hard, wincing. He kept his fingers wrapped around her wrist, but put his other hand up, signaling submission.

"Easy!" he growled through clenched teeth.

"Hassle me and I'll carve your throat like a goddamn jack-o'-lantern," she hissed.

"*Listen*—" He tightened his fingers and counteracted the pressure of the blade on his throat, but he wasn't fighting back like she thought he would. "I—"

"What's the fuss, Youngblood?"

Theo darted her eyes around, but his voice came from somewhere out of reach.

Theo dropped her eyes to the boy at her mercy, and when she did, his eyes held no malice. *Fight me!* she wanted to yell.

"Get off me," he said. He sounded stern and steady, but not angry.

Theo pulled the blade from his neck and removed her knee from between his legs.

He winced and pressed his hand to the thin laceration left by the razor, checked it for blood, then sniffed, shoving hair from his forehead as he retrieved his hat and his gun.

Theo clicked the razor shut as she slowly turned to face her fate.

Gaines leaned against a tree, a foot propped against it, his hat tipped down his forehead to block the subtle breeze as he stoked his pipe.

"Why'd you do what you did, Pine Needle?" He exhaled smoke and lit another match, sounding disappointed.

"He took my coffee, Mr. Gaines."

"A sacred thing." Theo was certain the comment was facetious, but she heard no such notes. "Sixer?" Gaines prompted.

"It's as Pine said," Brody seconded, then let out a soft laugh. "Don't come between this kid and his morning coffee."

Theo shot him a look. Maybe Brody was going along with the lie to cover his own mistake of allowing her a weapon. Then again, he could have easily pushed the knife from his throat and overpowered her. What was he up to?

August chuckled gravelly as he pushed off the tree and approached Theo. Nodding, he said, "All the same." Then he swung his fist against her temple and she saw stars, then nothing briefly, then her face was in the cold, damp pines that carpeted the ground, the entire left side of her face lit with pain, her jawbone the epicenter.

August was kneeling in her line of sight and his massive hand was pressing down, clutching almost her entire skull in a grip so powerful it felt mechanical. Theo blinked hard against the daze, her fingers digging in the earth, searching for grip in a spinning world that was blurred at the edges.

He thumbed open the straight razor and gently ran the spine of the blade down the slant of her nose. "The next time you turn a weapon on this family, you better be starting with me. Catch me, Youngblood?"

Theo nodded.

August leaned down close to her ear so whoever may be close enough to hear, wouldn't hear this: "You've got nothing to prove. Hear me? If you did, you wouldn't be at my side today. Catch me, Youngblood?"

Theo nodded again.

He leaned back out but kept the same pressure on her skull. "You pack camp today. You saddle every horse today. You set up camp tonight. You don't eat until supper. Reparation is the price of forward motion, and your penance is over at sundown. Catch me, Youngblood?"

Theo nodded for a third time, still unable to find her voice, let alone use it.

The penance August described would turn out to be much more shameful in reality than it was on paper. While the gang ate a breakfast of dried venison and hard biscuits, they would do so with their backs turned to Theo while she rolled blankets, loaded packs, saddled the horses, filled the waterskins and canteens. By the time Theo would get on her horse at first light, she would already be exhausted and hungry.

August clicked the razor shut and dropped it in front of her face as he stood.

As he walked away, she heard him chuckling, repeating in disbelief, "*Because he took my coffee.* Goddammit, Sixer." His chuckle turned warm. "Goddammit."

With tears still dripping across her face, Theo smiled.

CHAPTER
16

August roused Theo earlier than usual, not to get an early start on the day, Theo knew, but because it was the morning after her day of penance and there existed a period of time following such a beating where subservience could go one of two ways: harden to resentment or soften to the alpha. Fear was hollow without esteem.

He handed her coffee, and she followed him to the lookout.

The sky was filled with a million stars, and August looked at the sky with an undying reverence. He lowered himself down onto a fallen log, drinking from his steaming tin. He let out a contented noise and said, "Sit down, Youngblood."

Theo did as she was told, holding the mug in both hands between her knees. The side of her face throbbed and it hurt when she chewed.

"Mr. Gaines," Theo began softly.

"What did you do to land yourself in the Bladestay jailhouse, Pine Needle?"

Theo frowned into a drink of her coffee, jolted by the question even though she'd rehearsed the answer in her head countless times. When going up against a man like August Gaines, there's one thing to grasp, and one thing only, and that was learning how to play his game.

Theo watched Gaines. Every night and every day, she observed him, and she noticed one consistent thing above all: his dedication to headspace was stringent. It would be accurate to call Gaines introspective, but more precise to call him a strategist. He was quiet because his mind was loud. His opponents were chess pieces, the world was sixty-four squares, and he never stopped playing out every move in his head.

Theo learned she had the acuity for such mind tricks, and that all it took was practice. She spent as much time, if not more, as August, trying to outplot and outplay whatever he might be strategizing.

"I'd rather not say," Theo said.

"I'd rather not make you." August said things like this, malice in the intent, kindness in the delivery.

Theo felt along the short places of her hair, a calculated hesitation, before she said, "Tried to steal a horse."

August nodded and began to work on his pipe. "And you're ashamed of this?"

Theo shrugged. "No."

August was quiet, waiting.

"I just . . ." She took a sip. "I don't know, thought it was rather ordinary."

"You didn't want to say because it wasn't a colorful enough crime, is that what I'm to understand?" Theo couldn't help the warmness that settled across her, held her like a blanket, when she heard the amusement in August's voice.

"I reckon that's part of it," Theo admitted reluctantly. "I suppose I'm mostly just ashamed I got caught."

August laughed, and a smile inched across Theo's face.

"You know, I've not known any man to get the jump on Sixer," August said.

"People tend to underestimate me."

"I ain't one of 'em."

Normally, during their morning talks, they spoke in hushed voices, rarely elevating past a whisper, but now August spoke in his normal rumble, and Theo couldn't help but wonder if there was something he knew that she didn't.

"Mr. Gaines," Theo said softly.

He looked at her sideways, lighting his pipe.

"I've never . . ." She took a slow inhale. "You were right, what you said earlier."

August flicked the match into the dew and shadows and lowered the pipe from his mouth, letting his hand rest upon his knee. He waited with rapt attention for her to continue.

"I've never belonged anywhere before." She hung her head, swiping a hand down her face.

Theo almost screamed when she felt the weight of August's arm settle over her shoulders, but then his hand squeezed her arm—briefly, fatherly—before the weight fell away, and Theo was so overwhelmed with dissonant emotions that she barely registered what August had just said to her.

"I know it, Youngblood," he said.

"Why haven't you yet told me what Lucas Haas did to you?"

He puffed. "You ain't asked."

She drank. "I'm asking."

August stared into the fading night with a silence that Theo didn't dare touch. "All right, Youngblood. It ain't a pretty story."

"Ones worth telling rarely are."

With the corner of his mouth slanted slightly upward, he looked at her sideways again, the way he did that made her feel seen, heard, *understood*.

"Lucas and I were very close once. It's rare to find a soul that sees yours in a profound way, to see the world the same way so you don't feel so crazy—catch me, Youngblood?"

She nodded, swallowing down an angst that was building in her throat. She couldn't tell exactly what made the emotion cinch around her the way that it did, just that August had a way of dictating sorrow in a way that nobody else seemed to grasp.

She sensed he lived with the same twisting barbs in his insides, how it tweaked and yanked and made a person feel like peace wasn't an attainable thing.

"That's what Lucas was to me. Brothers, bonded by something that transcends blood. I ain't gotta ask if you catch my meaning on that, because I already know you do. We met when we weren't much older'n you are now. We met at the academy, served in the same infantry, and when it came down to it, loved the same woman." He scowled when he amended: "Women." He packed his pipe. "We disagreed over politics. That was first. Then it was over my first wife, Elana. Lucas loved her, but she loved me. I didn't really love Elana—not *in* love, I mean—but I married her anyway."

"That's cold, Mr. Gaines."

"Nah, we're still in the tropics, Youngblood." He lit his pipe. "Elana couldn't get pregnant. I lost interest. About a year later, Lucas marries a woman named Maureen. All be damned, I fell in love with Maureen. I fell hard, and it was for real this time. We had an affair. I know; I *know*," he said even though Theo kept her reactions contained. "Then that terrible farce of a recon mission happened. We got our asses handed to us. I made it home; Lucas did not. I thought he died and that's what I told everyone. When I went home, Elana had returned to hers in England. Maureen and I got married. I looked after Lucas's boy like he was my own. Soon after, Maureen bore my child. Several months later, Lucas surprised us all by coming home. As you can imagine, things did not go well. Lucas raged. He killed Maureen and my infant daughter."

Theo put her hand over her mouth, closing her eyes.

"He burned my home to the ground and then he took every last cent my family had to their name."

Silence hung between them, in which Theo calculated her response. "In all these years . . ." she trailed off, pausing. "Did you ever, I don't know . . . consider letting it go? Moving on."

August smiled as he stoked his pipe back to life. "Are you asking for life advice or my personal take?"

Theo shook her head slowly. "I suppose I just want to hear you say what I reckon I already know."

"Hmm," came his growling purr. He blew rings of smoke as he procured his answer. "We chase after peace and happiness, catch me? We chase after these things as if that's the pinnacle of the human experience, yet we sabotage our chances every step of the chase as if we, deep down, know peace is a fable, a fairytale that not even the perspective of adulthood changes, yet if you lose your belief in peace, you find . . ." He didn't finish the sentence.

Theo sensed it wasn't because he struggled to find the words, but because saying things out loud tends to make sentiments more tangible, more real.

She finished it for him. "You find that the only thing left to live for is pain."

August tapped the ash from his pipe, and Theo would swear that the man looked hauntingly close to tears. His face was a stone, etched with a deep disquiet.

Theo thought he looked like a man in need of bailing, so she did him the courtesy of breaking the turbulent silence.

"It's a burden, isn't it?" Theo prompted.

August looked at her, his features just quizzical enough to urge her to continue.

"To see the world for what she truly is."

He let out a soft, slightly amused, somewhat awestruck exhale.

His chin dipped, a half nod. "More so when it's recognized at such a young age."

"It's like you said, Mr. Gaines." Theo held his gaze meticulously. "Same cloth, you and I."

CHAPTER

17

The next night, after the stories had quieted and the flames had been reduced to embers, Theo lay awake, rolling the bullets from Brody's gun between her fingers. She watched the glowing, pulsating orange in the center of the slumbering men. Shiner was on duty. Pathfinder was twitching and whimpering quietly in his sleep. Brody was sprawled on top of his blanket, using his arm as a pillow. August was curled on his hip, holding a large, sheathed blade against his chest like a comfort. Rook was so still he looked dead. Flea's mouth was hanging open, his predominantly gold teeth glimmering. John and Jester were both breathing steadily, but Theo couldn't see their faces.

Theo fingered the ammo. She watched the men. She considered the fire.

She saw the window to the Bladestay jailhouse, in her mind's eye, at the moment it got covered in the sheriff's brains. It was a scene on repeat in her head, and no matter how tightly she closed her eyes or how wide she kept them, she'd see the window, clear one moment and bloodily obscured the next, and that window would just pop into her head—clear one moment, splattered the next.

Without sitting up, Theo took out a bullet.

Clear one moment, splattered the next.

She swept her eyes across the camp once more before she tossed the bullet toward the fire. The embers swallowed it with a modest display of sparks.

Clear one moment, splattered the next.

She pulled out another one. She chucked that one too.

Clear one moment—

The first bullet detonated.

The window disappeared.

Theo was amazed by the swift reply. Everyone responded in a moment, their eyes wild and wide as they readied their guns in their hands and went for cover. Some, like August, merely crouched where he was, his knife replaced by a revolver, as he scanned the surroundings. When his eyes landed on Theo, he put a hand out, lowered it to the ground, then put a finger to his lips. She nodded and checked on Brody.

Brody was on his feet, standing behind a tree as he kept ducking his head around its bend. He darted his head to her and beckoned her to cover.

The other bullet detonated.

Brody leaped over to Theo and yanked her to her feet. Shoving her behind a tree, he swept his gun at the darkness.

Pathfinder yelled something indiscernible as he took off into the night.

"Pathfinder!" August called after him as he got to his feet to go after him.

"What the hell?" Brody muttered under his breath as he watched the two disappear into the woods.

Theo squinted at the figures as they vanished.

"Stay here," Brody said, and then he too was after them.

In moments, the camp was cleared.

Theo ran through camp, searching for a pistol left behind. "Suckers," she whispered to herself as she dislodged a revolver from one of the men's holsters. She sprinted to the lookout and found Shiner desperately surveying the midnight chaos.

"Pine," he said, dropping his aim from her when he recognized her. "Did you see Haas? You know what's happening?"

"Pathfinder took off and everyone went after him."

Shiner cursed. "I tell August all the time, tell him to leave that broken man behind. Not the first time Pathfinder done something like this."

"Why?"

Shiner shrugged. "The war haunts him."

"Fascinating." Theo raised the revolver and shot Shiner in the chest. When he fell, she put one more in his head. Then she emptied the cylinder and threw the bullets into the bushes. On her way back through camp, she returned the gun to its rightful holster, then proceeded to go after the shouts and commotion in the distance.

Running down the slope, she and Flea almost collided in the dark. He had a pistol out, sweeping surroundings. Theo mentally berated herself, that Flea had seen her coming before she'd seen him. She almost shrieked when he caught her arm, hand tight around her bicep as he kept alert to the shadows.

"Heard more shots," Flea said in a low voice. "You see anything, kid?"

She shook her head. "Ran when I heard the first one." She stepped back and out of his grip.

"You got matches?" he asked quickly, almost panicked.

Theo patted a pocket, nodding.

"Get on down to the riverbank, quick-like," he muttered as he continued past her, his frame bent low as he jogged up the gradient with his pistol held in a proficient, two-hand position.

Theo burst through the tree line to find several of the men in a scuffle while the rest were splashing in the shallow shore of the river wading back and forth, shouting August's name.

Brody had an arm hooked around Pathfinder's neck, trying to restrain him from behind as two others tried to help. Pathfinder wasn't a huge man, but he was a skilled fighter and strong as an ox. He got free of Brody and swung at him. Brody ducked, dodged the blow, and Pathfinder's own momentum threw him off-balance—Brody dove for his midsection and the two tumbled to the ground.

"August!" the men shouted through cupped hands at the inky, midnight water.

August must have gone under water and not come back up.

"Handkerchief!" Theo yelled as she sprinted to the shore, snatching a fallen branch from the ground on her way. "Somebody give me a something dry to catch fire!"

Rook splashed over to her as he plucked a handkerchief from where he kept it tucked at his breast.

"Flea's gone to fetch matches," he said as his eyes darted toward camp.

"I've got some." She snatched the handkerchief from his hand and wrapped it around the stick, scanning the surface of the water for any signs of August's body, but found it just as impossible as the men had.

"Ready little runt, ain't ya?" Rook said.

"How long has he been under?" Theo asked as she struck a match.

"Less than a minute."

"Good." The handkerchief caught fire and Theo waded deeper, sweeping the temporary light across the surface. The yellow light caught the break in the surface, a hand or a foot or an elbow gently bobbing away from them in the slow current.

"There!" she called, pointing.

Rook and John dove after August, and moments later, they were dragging the lifeless body of August onto the shore. They laid him in the sand and knelt around him. Pathfinder had finally come back to himself, his understanding of the reality he was in finally registering. He'd been stuck in the past, trapped in a trauma. He curled his body into a crouch, his head in his hands as he muttered something to himself.

"Move," Theo said as she shoved Spartan, who had his head bent low over August's face, his ear nearly touching August's lips in an attempt to find a breath, out of the way.

Spartan said, "He's not breathing."

She wrapped her fingers around August's wrist and felt a strong pulse.

"Come on, August," she muttered as she snaked her hand under his neck.

When she'd thrown the bullets into the fire, she hadn't expected it to lead to August edging death, for if he died right now, fingers might point at her, but worse, they were liable to pack up and return to Bladestay. This was too soon. She couldn't afford his death right now, not yet.

She lifted to tilt his head back as she stuck her fingers into his mouth to pry it open. The moments of silence that passed were chilling. She could feel the building anger of the men, their silent glances among themselves a vow to avenge.

Come on, August, comeoncomeoncomeon.

He gasped and coughed roughly, his body constricting and tightening as he rolled onto his side. Everyone stepped back a pace, aside from Theo, who put a reassuring hand on his shoulder. It was a mindless response, a biological impulse to comfort a person who was dragging themselves back from the grave.

Propped on an elbow, August coughed and hacked the water from his lungs.

As understanding of his situation began to dawn, August pushed himself to his feet, holding his chest as he continued to regain his breath. He spun slowly in a stumbling circle, placing his hand on Theo's shoulder momentarily to steady himself, then his eyes landed on Pathfinder and his hand slipped away.

When he reached Pathfinder, August knelt in front of him. He coughed again, clearing his chest of the river.

Theo tensed, wondering what retribution August might have for Pathfinder. She stole a glance at Brody, who was watching August with a similar apprehension.

What August did next didn't surprise the established gang, but what Theo witnessed was the single most thing that would continue to haunt her long after this was over. August placed his hands on either side of Pathfinder's head, over Pathfinder's own hands, and moved his head to force Pathfinder to look him in the face.

"I'm sorry," Pathfinder said with so much torment that it tugged on Theo's heart.

"It's over, brother. It's over." Then August leaned his forehead against Pathfinder's—it was brief, but Theo had the urge to look away, that this was too intimate for a crowd. "It's over," August said once more before laying a hand on his knee to shove himself to his feet. When he got there, he reached his hand down to Pathfinder; Pathfinder gripped August's forearm and August hauled him to his feet.

"Shiner's dead," Flea said. He stood there almost aimlessly, his arms dangling at his side, one of his hands in a fist where Theo presumed he held the too-little-too-late matchbox.

They all turned.

"*No*," Rook said.

August hung his head, rubbed his eyebrow, and began to walk up the bank back toward camp. He stopped when he went by Theo, at her side, close enough that the edges of their arms were touching. Raking his hand through sopping hair, he looked down at her.

Their eyes locked as if he were talking to her, but when he spoke it was loudly for all to hear: "Who's responsible for me being upright?"

"Pine," came the collective response.

August nodded, curled his hand over her narrow shoulder, gave a gentle squeeze, then continued back to camp.

"Haas ain't working alone," August announced as he walked up the hill. He took a deep inhale and said, "I smell a cahoots," as if he could literally sniff it out.

August paused, then said, "Ain't no Creed getting off this mountain alive."

Theo felt like she'd been punched in the gut.

"Hear?" August said.

"Hear," came the collective response as the men started to follow August back to camp.

But Theo couldn't move. When she lifted her gaze into the dense shadows, she found the silhouette of Brody Boone, and although she couldn't see his black eyes, she knew they were watching her.

CHAPTER
18

rody emerged from the black shadows after the gang disappeared over the hill. He stopped when he was directly in front of her, the tips of his boots almost touching hers. For the life of her, she couldn't lift her chin to look him in the eye.

"We're overdue for a conversation, you 'n' me. Come my turn on post, you're gonna tell me the things you've been hiding—"

"Such as?" Theo said, which was, admittedly, an unnecessary taunt.

"Such as why you picked a fight with me for no damn reason. My pistol was loaded when I handed it to you."

"That so?" Theo said.

"That's so."

"Then why'd you cover for me?"

"You know, Pine, August's too arrogant to think you'd cross him." He leaned down a little closer, his cheek close to hers as he added into her ear: "But I ain't." Then he breezed by her, angling his body to flow around hers as if he couldn't be bothered with the extra steps it would take to go around, like an apparition he moved by her without touching her at all, and like a ghost, it made Theo feel cold all over.

As she listened to his dreadfully quiet feet move past the sandy bank and into the underbrush, Theo slammed her eyes shut, balled her hands at her sides, and forced a steadiness to her breathing. She stood like that for about a minute until the tension fled, her thoughts leveled, her heartbeat slowed.

If August himself would have muttered such a threat, it wouldn't have left her half as unbalanced. Brody Boone was the most turbulent calm she had ever encountered.

A rustle in the brush made her send a scowl over her shoulder. Brody was already lost to the shadows.

She stepped down to the water's edge and crouched there, sinking her fingers into the cold sand below the shallow. Pressing the cold over her face, she submerged her hands and did it again. Again and again, anything to keep her from going back to that den of monsters.

Something—some*one*—grabbed a handful of hair at the top of her head, and before she could think to draw breath, plunged her face into the shallow. She screamed into the water and kicked blindly behind her. Her heel hit something, and for a moment, the man who had her by the hair faltered and loosened his grip. Theo squirmed and flipped her body, coughing out pieces of the river. About the same time she caught her breath, the man had the edge of a hunting blade pressed against her jugular.

"Quiet," her attacker warned in a low, deep voice. "Or I kill you."

She blinked.

She knew that voice. "*Zeke?*"

Immediately, the weight of his knee was lifted from her chest and the sharp edge taken from her throat.

"*Theo?*" he whispered.

There was a violent bloom of relief in Theo's chest.

Zeke scooped her up and hugged her, both of them on their knees, his knife still in hand against her back.

"I don't believe it. I can't believe you're here. Where's Mom?" His whisper was desperate. "Eve and the boys?"

"Safe," she whispered back, even though she had no way to be certain if that was the case.

He let go of her and pulled her up with him as he stood. They moved down the riverbank before they spoke again. He kept the hunting knife gripped at his side.

"What are you *doing* out here?" he asked. "You their hostage?"

"Something like that," she whispered back. "Where's Jude?" She sent nervous appraisals at the night. "Did Dad get a clean break for Clayton Creek?" They had to keep moving.

Zeke jutted his chin to the northeast, vaguely in the direction of where August and crew were headed. "Jude's with me. Dad's gone ahead with Elliot."

Her brother started to move down the riverbank, tugging Theo with him.

"Wait—what?" she whispered after him as she followed. "Elliot and Dad's gone ahead *where*?"

"Come on—quickly," Zeke said, not slowing.

Theo glanced around then trotted after her big brother.

After winding down the curves in the river, Zeke stopped around a sharp bend where the trees went all the way to the waterline. Once under relative cover, he returned the hunting blade to the sheath strapped to his calf.

"You armed?" he asked.

"Just a knife. Where's Jude? And Bram?" She took a scrupulous look through the trees. "And why did you all separate?" There were too many contradictions, and she couldn't sort a single thing out in her head.

"You're safe now, Theo," Zeke soothed. "Relax. We got a plan. Okay?"

"Who's we, Z? What *plan*?"

"You don't need to worry anymore. Come on, this way," he said as he started back down the waterline, but this time he started to weave into the trees.

"What *happened*, Zeke?"

Zeke kept walking, and Theo thought he might actually continue to blow her off. "Dad was supposed to take Elliot to the pass." Zeke again jutted his chin to the northeast.

"You seriously telling me that he didn't go to Clayton Creek?"

Zeke shook his head.

"Then who did?" After all that—Evangeline had been dragged out of safety only to tell August the truth. Theo wanted to scream.

Zeke shrugged as if that didn't concern him. Then, to her utter shock, he just kept walking. As if this wasn't one of the most important conversations she'd ever had in her life. As if that piece of information wasn't the difference between life and death for their mother. Their sister. Their brothers. For every Bladestay townsperson.

"*Damn* it, Zeke!" She stopped following and fought the urge to stomp her foot at him. "What the hell's a matter with you?"

Zeke stopped but didn't turn around for a moment, only tilted his head back with a small groan as if dealing with this, with *her*, was a typical, day-to-day little-sister inconvenience that interrupted whatever his plans were.

Finally, he turned to face her. "We was trying to divert Gaines's lot. Get his attention off the town."

Old news. "And how's that working out? There's still at least a dozen men holding our town hostage." It bothered Theo that the name of August Gaines was in her brother's mouth. She had an uneasy idea who put it there. Quickly, she added, "What good is any of this if nobody's actually gone for help?"

"Listen, Theo. We've got it covered. Okay?"

"You don't know what you're up against, Zeke," Theo said. "They're after Bram. Do you know that?"

"Come on," he said, pulling her forward. "This way."

She tore her arm away. "Why does none of this concern you? Nobody's gone for help and Mama and Evie and the boys are just sitting at home, *waiting* for it."

Zeke went still. "August don't know who *he's* dealing with."

Theo fumed. "What's that supposed to mean?"

"Would you just—" Zeke rubbed the spot between his eyes in a way that made Theo feel like a little child.

"Where's Jude, Zeke?" Theo snapped. "Is he okay?"

Zeke softened. "He's okay. Would you just let me show you?"

"Fine." She gestured angrily. "Show me."

Zeke kept walking and Theo kept following. South, south, due south.

Theo peered into the trees. She'd snag a glance of the stars every time there was a break in the gangly limbs of the forest above.

Still: *backtracking*. Not at all on the way to the pass.

Finally, they rounded a sharp corner against a steep hillside and on the other side was—

Theo stopped abruptly.

Blacksmith had his profile to Theo. Next to him was Jude. They were laughing at something.

But that's not what made her breath catch.

"No, son!" Blacksmith laughed, elbowing Jude playfully. "Like this—"

Blacksmith blinked at her.

Jude glimpsed his brother and sister, did a double take on the latter, his smile frozen in place. He dropped the rope he had in his hand and crossed camp to her, encasing her in a hug so warm and familiar that Theo almost broke down.

"You're alive," he said, squeezing her a little tighter.

She stepped out of Jude's embrace with a strained smile and looked past him to the other side of the fire. She recognized wild black hair and ever-ready posture. Brody was glaring at him with accusation so intense that it made her stomach flip. Next to him was John, staring at her with just as much accusation but not quite as much hurt. She felt an overwhelming need to explain herself to Brody. But he was tied to a tree like the enemy he was and before she knew it, Theo was encased in Blacksmith's arms and now she *was* crying, quietly clutching him. Her body jerked in silenced sobs and Blacksmith held her tight, held her in such a way as if he understood the exact weight of all the dread she'd been carrying up this mountain.

"It's okay," he said softly, his words too quiet for the prisoners. "You're safe now."

And she felt the truth in it, the absolute clarity that relief brought when you were able to defer to somebody older and wiser.

"Come on." Blacksmith stepped back and led her forward. "Over here." He walked her toward the tree to which Brody and John were secured but kept her in a safe distance. When her eyes met John's, he spat on the ground, at her. He didn't need to say the word *traitor* for her to hear it in her own head. Brody's glare followed her. The meager fire reflected a dancing gold in his ferocious eyes. When his face fully came into view, she saw the remnants of a bloody nose across his lips.

That's when she felt it again. That unrestful thing.

That antithetical thing.

CHAPTER
19

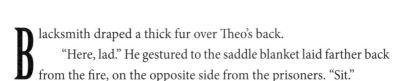

Blacksmith draped a thick fur over Theo's back.

"Here, lad." He gestured to the saddle blanket laid farther back from the fire, on the opposite side from the prisoners. "Sit."

Theo tugged the fur over her shoulders, mind racing. *Blacksmith was playing along.* She held back a frown. Feeling numb, she lowered herself onto the blanket. Jude sat down next to her. Zeke brought her a canteen. She drank from it, closing her eyes in relief, drinking deeply when she discovered the depths of her thirst.

John averted his eyes downward. Brody pressed his lips together.

Blacksmith watched the brief interaction. Studied the way his prisoners reacted to Theo.

"Are you hungry?" Blacksmith asked Theo.

She was, a little, but not enough to eat in front of Brody and John. Already, quenching her thirst while these men had their hands tied behind their back felt wrong somehow. She shook her head no.

He jutted his chin at Zeke, and regardless of her answer, he fetched her a satchel of wild berries.

She didn't touch them. Zeke backed several paces from her, from Blacksmith, when Blacksmith unsheathed a large hunting knife. The blade glinted, winking the orange of their small fire.

"Were you their prisoner?" Blacksmith asked Theo. John stiffened when Blacksmith approached them. Brody gave Blacksmith a passing glance before returning his accusations on Theo.

"It wasn't like that," Theo said, unsure why she said it defensively.

Brody dug a heel into the dirt and pushed himself a little more upright when Blacksmith lowered to a crouch. As he did, almost imperceptibly, he moved his head side to side. *Keep your mouth shut*, it said.

"No?" Blacksmith said. He had a calmness to his voice that put Theo on edge. "Then what *was* it like?" Blacksmith pressed the blade against John's cheek then glanced over his shoulder at Theo.

Theo shrugged. "I tricked them."

Blacksmith's forehead creased as he smiled. "Did you now." He focused back on John. "What's your name?" Blacksmith asked, keeping the blade pressed gently to John's cheek.

"He can't speak," Theo said.

Brody was trying to tell her something with the way he was looking at her, trying to convey something to her, like he knew something she didn't. She didn't know what that was, but she was certain he wanted her to shut up and keep shutting up.

"Can't?" Blacksmith flicked his eyes between Theo and Brody. "Or won't?" He withdrew the blade from John's face and draped his arm over his knee. "And what about the Mexican? Can he speak English?"

"Quite right, old chap," Brody deadpanned.

Blacksmith laughed, genuinely amused. Then, quick as a viper, Blacksmith struck John across the face. It was a hard backhand, the gold ring splitting skin on his cheekbone.

Theo flinched.

Her brothers shifted uneasily.

Brody glared at her. Motionless. Reactionless. Glaring at her as if he could will her to do the same.

"Speak," Blacksmith said. He touched John's lips again with the edge of his hunting knife.

"Bram," Theo said. "I know as much as he does."

Jude put a hand on her arm, a silent plea matching the one on Brody's face: *stop talking.*

"We can't be sure of that, though, can we?" Blacksmith said. He struck John again. The blow dazed him, and he tried to shake it, but he didn't make a noise.

Theo's breaths started to come a little quicker. Brody too, his chest expanding a little larger with every breath.

"I'll tell you everything you need to know," Theo tried again, but she was beginning to see the futility. Beginning to understand why everyone was telling her to back off. And that's when she started to notice things. Zeke had bruising around his right eye. Jude's hand that was gently clasped around her arm in caution had two fingers bandaged together.

"I know, lad." Blacksmith struck John again, this time with a closed fist. "I know you will."

John whimpered as blood strung from his mouth.

Blacksmith clutched the underside of John's jaw and smiled kindly. "That's a start." He touched the tip of his knife onto the open laceration on his cheek. John tried to yank his head away, his face twisted in agony.

Theo categorized everything as quickly as she could.

At what point did Blacksmith and her brothers circle back to put them as the ones in pursuit? At what point was her own family hiding in the trees, watching her and Gaines and his crew go by as they took up the rear?

Her mind revolted against the truth of what was happening.

Her father and Elliot, the carrot stick they'd been following, only two of them sitting at the campfire they closed in on every night as Blacksmith and her brothers stalked them from behind. Blacksmith and her brothers must have simply been waiting for Gaines's crew to catch up to Elliot and her father, to pin Gaines between their two parties and ambush. She was annoyed at the brilliance of it; confused by the protraction of it.

Blacksmith pressed the tip of the knife harder and John cried out louder.

"Good," Blacksmith encouraged. "Now words."

This wasn't strategy. This wasn't about extracting information. This wasn't Blacksmith. This was—

"Lucas Haas," Theo said.

A hush washed over them. Blacksmith went still. A moment passed. Another.

Blacksmith slipped his knife back into the holster in his boot and let his hand fall away from John's face. Then, slowly, he pivoted on his heels and glowered at Theo, the short fingers of the fire flickering between them.

"Who?" Jude asked.

Zeke mirrored the question on his face.

Brody's nostrils flared, strands of hair splitting through his savage glare. He darted his eyes to Blacksmith, then back to Theo.

Theo grinned even though she felt foolish.

"Oh, he hates you so much." Foolish to believe that she could shake the person she'd become once she'd gotten to this point, as if she could return to pretending she was still a child, as if seeing the needless cruelty of men was something you could unsee, as if engaging in the games of adulthood was something that could be retracted, as if you could undiscover who you are there, as if she'd ever wanted any of that anyhow.

Blacksmith was showing her who he really was; it was only fair to return the courtesy.

Blacksmith stood to his feet. "Well, the feeling's mutual."

Not that she needed the confirmation, but it was nice to have it

Jude's hand slipped from her arm.

"You need a plan, Mr. Blacksmith," Theo said.

"A *plan*?" Blacksmith said it as if it was the most absurd word in the dictionary. He came to a stop in front of her.

She nodded slowly as he crouched in front of her. Her grin deepened as he knelt in front of her. She folded her legs to cross them, unflinching as she lowered her gaze to hold his.

"Do you remember Harry?" She could see Brody in her periphery, could feel the angry heat of it. She didn't dare look at him as she continued. She understood what this was now.

She knew what she had to be.

Nobody went for help, was all she could think.

"Harry loved to chase squirrels. Rabbits and coyotes too. Harry never caught any squirrels. They're too fast and can go too many places dogs can't."

Blacksmith narrowed his eyes at Theo with a hint of curiosity and a tinge of disbelief.

"But rabbits?" she continued. "Harry'd spent a lifetime chasing them, never catching one. But one day . . . Harry finally caught one. Do you remember what happened?"

What happened was Harry was so shocked that he actually caught a rabbit, and in his surprise and naivete, let go of the rabbit, just for a moment, but a moment is all it takes when it comes down to the difference between life and death.

Blacksmith swapped reality with: "Harry shook that fuzzy fucker until his neck snapped."

Theo smiled. "You don't have a plan, Mr. Blacksmith." She held the same tone—a taunting one—around Blacksmith's name, the same way that Brody had done with hers over a bowl of oats. "The only reason you've got two of them now is because of the mayhem *I* caused. Did you hear those gunshots? They were *all* me and not a single one of them knew it."

She heard the pride in her voice. She was beginning to think there was something very wrong with her.

Blacksmith smiled widely when he saw the fury on the prisoners' faces, a confirmation of her story.

"I can deliver you August," Theo said.

Blacksmith nodded with a mock agreement and a dishonest smile. "Surely." He got up, walked back over to John, then swung his arm back and plunged the blade into John's temple.

The suddenness of it caused an upheaval inside Theo. The extreme change from the Blacksmith she knew gave her the sensation that she was falling, backward, with nobody to catch her. But somehow, just like in the jailhouse, she was able to keep all her reactions beneath the surface.

Blacksmith watched Theo watch him. He was very obviously gauging her reaction.

She watched with a patient calm—bored almost.

John's face went blank, then slack, then he fell over, the handle of the blade sticking out the side of his head.

Brody went stiff. His chest compressed, breathless.

"Mr. Blacksmith . . ." Jude said. He sounded like he might be sick.

Blacksmith gave her the slightest nod. Approval, Theo thought.

Zeke looked back and forth between the disturbing calmness of his sister and the eerie ambivalence of Blacksmith. Her brother looked terrified, completely unprepared for Blacksmith to take it that far.

Maybe Theo showed Blacksmith who she really was (*what* she really was) because she knew her brothers were out of their league. She told herself it was to protect them. Her father. Elliot. And she might even be able to admit that a small part was for Brody too. But she hoped someday she'd be able to understand why it felt like it was her turn to draw a card and as much as it was about drawing weapons.

"Jude," Blacksmith said as he put John's cheek under his boot. "Send the body to the wolves, would you?"

Brody turned his face away as if he could get away from the sound of blade pulled from bone.

Jude swallowed apprehensively. Looked at his sister. Then, after another moment's hesitation, got to his feet and did what Blacksmith said.

"Z, watch the Mexican." Blacksmith returned to Theo and offered her his hand. She took it and he pulled her to her feet.

"If he tries a single thing," Blacksmith continued, "put him out of our misery."

"Yes, sir," Zeke mumbled as he pulled out a revolver.

"No—" It sounded like Blacksmith was on the verge of losing his patience.

"No guns, Z," Theo said.

"Let's not draw any more attention to ourselves," Blacksmith agreed.

Jude began to drag John's corpse into the trees and down a slope, swallowed by shadows.

"Right," Zeke said, exchanging the revolver for his knife. A slight tremble to his hands almost made him drop the weapon as he exchanged them.

Blacksmith placed his hands on her shoulders. He smiled. It was now the Blacksmith smile, the kind one, the one she'd grown to trust. Then he wrapped his arms back around her.

She hugged him back.

"Now just where in the world has *this* girl been hiding?" Blacksmith said quietly so only she heard it.

Theo knew how he felt. If she'd been able to glimpse the truth of Blacksmith, maybe she wouldn't have felt so alone most her life. Maybe she would have found she belonged somewhere after all. Maybe she could have known somebody who truly understood her.

"Reckon in the same place Haas was," she said.

Blacksmith leaned out to look at her, grinning sideways.

She returned the sly smile. "I have an idea."

"Let's hear it."

He nodded in delight as she laid things out.

August Gaines didn't stand a chance.

PROXY

THE TRUTH SHALL SET YOU FREE. BUT THE FACTS?
THOSE BASTARDS NEVER LET YOU BE.

CHAPTER

20

lacksmith left Jude and Theo on watch around the time of night
when everything went silent, when few things stirred. Jude's eyes
were going bleary, and not long after Blacksmith's soft snores began, Jude's eyelids dragged, getting heavy.

Theo scooted next to him and hooked her arm through his, leaning against him. He patted her mindlessly, yawning. She watched Brody, who was now blindfolded. His chin kept dipping toward his chest,
dancing along on the edge of sleep, tortuously never able to reach it
with his hands tight behind his back.

"I'm wide awake, Jude," she whispered. "Go on 'n' close your eyes."

"No way," he muttered back. He yawned again.

"Those bastards trusted me on watch." She nodded nebulously toward Brody. "You can too."

"Y'sure?" Jude asked.

"I promise to kick you awake at the first sign of trouble."

Jude wrapped an arm around her shoulders for a quick squeeze, then said, "Just a few minutes, 'kay?"

She nodded and he reclined, stretching his legs out toward the embers and cradling his hands behind his head. He was out cold in under a minute.

She paused on her way out of camp. She made her footfalls as silent as possible, but when she neared Brody—where she paused—Brody angled his face in her direction, chin still tilted downward.

He said, "They'll kill me."

This jolted her even though she knew it to be true. She flipped open the jaws of her straight razor, stepped carefully behind Brody, knelt there with her blade ready.

He tilted his blindfolded face over his shoulder. He might have been about to say something, but Theo placed the sharp edge of her blade against the soft place in his neck.

In his ear, she whispered, "Give me one good reason I shouldn't do it for them."

She could feel the thump of his heart reverberating through the blade and into her fingertips. Theo wasn't sure she'd ever felt a greater feeling than the one of holding somebody's life in her hands.

"Because I know what you are," he said.

It felt like time came to a violent stop.

Brody moved his face forward. "But if you really believe I'm your enemy, go ahead and do what you're gonna do."

She wasn't falling for this again. "What do you think you know about me?"

"You ain't no fifteen-year-old boy."

She jerked the blade from his throat. Her brother grumbled sleepily and rolled over.

Theo had a lot of questions on her mind, but whether she was leaving Brody to die wasn't one of them. "Can you run?" she whispered.

He nodded.

As she started to saw him free, she put her mouth next to his ear. "You don't hurt them. We do this my way."

He hesitated, then said, "Ain't that what we've *been* doing?"

His bindings were loose and he was on his feet, yanking down the blindfold before he was upright.

He grabbed her arm, expertly twisting her hand behind her back, and pushed her into the dark woods. He held her hand perfectly on the brink of pain as he shoved her into the forest, away from camp. He had the straight razor stripped from her grip before she even had her feet underneath her. She stumbled loudly, her toes repeatedly catching roots and clumsily rolling on pine cones so Brody switched tactics. He let go of her fingers and wrapped his hand around her small wrist, gripping hard.

Sweeping to be in front of her, his pace was fast and his steps unbelievably sure over roots and fallen branches and ruts and sodden soil, all without an inkling of morning light. She stumbled and he kept constricting his hold to keep her from falling.

"Brody—"

"Keep your mouth *shut.*"

They walked in silence for a long time. Once safely distanced from Blacksmith's camp, he stopped and pressed his knuckles against her shoulder and pushed her until her back was against a tree. His grip on her wrist hadn't loosened. The straight razor was in his fist pressed against her collarbone.

At some point, he'd unsheathed the blade. No part of the razor was touching any part of her, but it was angled toward her neck and it wouldn't take much effort on his part to slice an artery wide open. She wasn't fighting him—she'd already accepted this was a necessary, immutable confrontation.

He had his head cocked to the side, taking in every part of the night.

"Explain yourself," he said.

"Which part would you like me to explain? The part where we were both stupid enough to let them get the jump on us? Or the part where I singlehandedly got us out of it?"

He darted his head toward a soft noise. "The part where you tell me who you are."

But he didn't wait for her to answer; his hand went over her mouth.

After he determined that whatever he'd heard wasn't of consequence, he whispered, "Why are you doing this? You've been playing an angle since August let you out of that jailhouse. You tell it to me now or you take it to your grave."

She gently placed her hand over his. Instantly, his grip loosened. His fingers brushed her lips when he lowered his hand.

"You know what August told me?" Theo asked.

"What's that."

"No man's ever got the jump on you."

He looked her hard in the eye.

"That true?" she asked.

"If that were, Pine, I wouldn't've been at the mercy of your razor two times over, would I'uv?"

"Exempt me."

"If you're askin' me something," he said, "do it outright."

"You didn't get jumped back there. Not like I did. You got caught coming after me."

"That don't sound like a question."

"Okay," she said. Suddenly Brody's closeness didn't feel threatening. It felt— "Why'd you do it?"

"Do what?"

"You could've gone back and alerted Gaines. You risked your life to do something stupid."

"Is that what you are?" Brody asked.

She scowled at him. She felt chilled and hot at the same time. "When did you figure it out?"

His eyes danced along her face and he leaned even closer still, just a fraction more, giving Theo the absurd notion to pull him closer still, to stand on the tips of her toes and snake her hand around the back of his neck and—

"Straight away," Brody said. It sounded like a confession and somehow, also like a boast.

"How?" She was desperate to know where she'd slipped.

"Found pretty blond hair in a wastebasket, a dress under the cot."

Theo closed her eyes briefly. She had a flash of Patrick at the jailhouse: *Wait, I need to tell you something!* He'd known the whole time. "Why would you do that? Why would you keep my secret?"

"I ain't ever seen one bad thing from holding cards close to my chest."

She shook her head, annoyed at the deflection.

"Now the question is: why did you choose to sacrifice that Creed girl instead of hiding with her?"

Theo's eyes widened. "You *saw* that?"

"Did you really think I'd leave you unsupervised?"

She wanted to fight that notion, but she didn't know to what end, so instead all that came out of her mouth was: "I owe you my life."

He stepped back from her, releasing his hold on her. He looked something akin to offended. "You owe me *nothing*. Do you understand me?"

The electricity in the air changed. They looked around as if just now remembering their dire placement.

"We have to keep moving," Theo said.

"Yep," Brody said.

They continued their trek through the woods. Brody sent constant looks over his shoulder at Theo. Untrusting. Wary.

By the time the early morning sun had turned the eastern mountains into silhouettes, Brody slowed, then stopped.

Theo halted, and Brody turned around to face her.

She took a step back from that look in his eye, the same accusatory one that he'd had at Blacksmith's camp when he saw her embrace his enemy.

Her family.

She took another step back.

"Brody—"

He shook his head and held a hand to his forehead as if he felt stupid for not putting it together earlier. "You're the other Creed sister, ain't you?"

She shook her head, but not in denial.

"Those boys with Haas were your brothers?" The next look on his face was something Theo couldn't identify. Like he was disgusted. "You brought your own sister out of hiding?" The lines in his forehead deepened as he looked her up and down. "Why?"

"It . . . she . . ." But Theo's throat was too thick with anguish to say anything else. She only shook her head.

Then Brody's face softened. "The rest of your family."

Theo watched him angrily.

"You did it to save them."

She said nothing.

"Didn't you?" he asked.

"Yes."

He took a step toward her and although Theo had the urge to take another back to keep the distance, she didn't. Brody scrubbed his fingers along his jaw. Neither of them said anything for a stretch.

Above them in the trees, the birds rejoiced at the start of a new day. The pines smelled wet with dew. Theo's chest ached in its restraint. Theo registered these things, but they were distant. All she could think was how what happened next hinged on what happened now.

"When I first met August . . ." Brody said quietly, so quietly that Theo could hardly make out the words.

Theo held her breath, an anticipation so sharp it was excruciating.

A *crack*.

Brody's hand went to his hip reflexively. He pivoted toward the sound. He flexed his hand when he found nothing to grip, holding out the other in caution to Theo as he searched the woods. He took a careful step backward, toward her, as he pulled out her straight razor, flipped it open, and held it in front of him. He took another step back to her, quietly rolling on the balls of his feet. He was close enough now to touch her, but his hand out to her was still one of caution to keep still and silent.

A melodic, two-whistle chirp almost blended in with the cheerful birdsong, and Theo may not have picked it out of the noises of the morning had it not been for Brody's reaction.

His shoulders relaxed. He dropped his hand and folded the razor shut. He stood straighter.

Before anyone came into view, Brody handed her the straight razor. She took it, her fingers touching his. He held on to it for a moment, letting their fingers press together. He said in a voice just loud enough for the two of them, "I've got your back."

Why? She wanted to ask again. What did he possibly have to gain from keeping her secret? From taking her side? But the comfort and heat she felt throughout her whole body when their fingers were simply touching was—

"I—" She was about to make a similar promise when Brody quickly withdrew his hand and two of Gaines's men came into view.

CHAPTER
21

"He's *lying*," Jester hissed.

In their new camp farther up the mountain, August studied Theo carefully. He twitched a scowl. He took off his hat and looked briefly at the sky, a dark blue of midmorning. He went back to studying Theo. Theo only took her eyes off August once, and that was to check on Brody, who was cleaning a pistol with an intensity as if his life depended on it.

"Why would I do that?" Theo asked. She stood in the center, the gang loosely gathered around her.

"Yeah, why *would* you?" Spartan said, insinuating.

When Theo told them the lie she'd crafted, she figured it might be difficult for them to wrap their heads around this. Ten years of chasing come down to this? She could understand how that might be disappointing. She could understand how their egos might take a minute to warm up to this.

"Tell us again how you did it," Flea said, shoving his hat back on.

"How many times you gonna make him tell it?" Brody snapped. He shoved his overly polished revolver back against his hip and pushed off the tree.

"You saw him?" Pathfinder asked Brody. "You saw Haas's body?"

"Like I said, I was blindfolded," Brody said. "And by the time Pine cut me loose, it was full dark."

"So Haas coulda been sleeping?" Flea asked.

"And not dead?" Spartan added.

"I cut myself loose, I cut the bastard's throat, I got Sixer free, we took off." Theo snarled the fear away. "What is so damn unbelievable about that?"

"Haas woulda checked you for weapons," Pathfinder said.

"He *did*," Theo said. "He missed it."

"Bullshit!" Spartan yelled.

"No way you pulled this off, you little runt!" Flea said.

"We should turn back, August," Spartan said, "turn back and check for this supposed body and catch this little bastard in his lies and then show 'im what we do to liars—"

August held up a hand.

They fell silent.

Theo had to try very hard not to smile. Instead, she marched up to August, ripped something out of her pocket, and slapped it against August's huge chest.

He frowned down at her and slowly placed his hand over hers and the gift that was held there.

"I thought I was your family." She held his eyes for a moment. Just a moment. But it was long enough to see just how much that stung him.

Then she ripped her hand away, shoved her forearm across her face as if she might be on the verge of tears, and bumped into Flea on her way past him and away from them all.

"Youngblood." August's voice rumbled after her. She knew better than to keep walking. This moment was everything. She stopped but didn't turn around yet.

"I believe you," August said.

Theo slowly turned back around. She desperately wanted to take Brody out of her peripheral, but she had to stay focused.

August was looking down at the gold in his hand. Then he closed his hand into a fist around it and closed the distance between them. "I believed you before you showed me this. I don't think I wanted to, but I did. And I know that ain't meanin' a whole lot now that you've handed this over, but . . ." He looked around at his men before back to her. "Well. This all just feels a little . . ."

"Innocuous," Pathfinder said.

"Innocuous," August agreed.

"Haas was going to kill us," Brody said. Everyone looked at Brody, but Brody was only looking at one person. "For sport," he said as if directly to Theo and only Theo. "I was inches away when he drove a knife into John's temple." Brody rammed a finger against the side of his head. "That was after he beat him. I was up next." He swept a hand through his hair. "If it weren't for Pine, I'd be dead."

"You know as well as us that this just ain't about *innocuous*," Flea said. "Haas was the *only* person who knew—"

"Watch your mouth," August said. His tone chilled Theo, made her feel brittle.

Theo pretended to be entirely uninterested, but all she could think was: *The only person. The only person. The only person who knew* what?

August stepped over to her and Theo looked up at him.

"Forgive us," he asked.

When she saw the pain etched all over him, there wasn't a single part of her that felt like she was playing a role, not in that moment, not when she had the overwhelming urge to hug him and confess everything, that whatever Haas knew, August still had a chance to find out, that Haas hadn't taken it to his grave, hadn't taken anything to his grave, not yet, that August still had a chance at Haas, a chance at *peace*—

"Always," she said, softening her face.

He smiled kindly.

August held his fist up to put it between the two of them and let the gold drop. Blacksmith's chain swayed from his fist, two gold wedding bands dangling just below her chin. There was blood smeared across the rings and the chain, now dried.

At the time that Blacksmith had handed this over to her, Theo had thought that was a nice touch, but now, looking up at August's sorrowful, grateful face—

"I can't take that," Theo said.

August spread the chain and put it over her head and let it rest around her neck. "You've earned it." The two bloodied bands landed just below her breast. He gave her a pained half grin. Then he placed his hand on her shoulder, gave it a single squeeze, and walked back through his men. Theo expected him to shout or do something provocative, but August once again surprised her. He simply nodded at them, said, "It's over." He retrieved a bottle from his saddle pack and uncorked it.

"We camp here tonight," August said.

"Yes, sir," Flea muttered.

Funny how none of them could really look her in the eye right now.

"We drink here tonight," August said, a little livelier.

"Yes, *sir*," Flea and Spartan said.

"It's over," August said again, nodding. He spun slowly. "We *celebrate* here tonight," he said, louder.

"Hear, hear," everyone replied. Everyone except Brody.

August came over and handed Theo the bottle. She smiled, took a drink, and handed it back. He held it up at her then took a drink of his own. It was a deep, long pull, and when he took it off his lips, there was no more sorrow in his smile.

When August passed it to Spartan, Spartan hesitated, but then lifted the bottle in her direction, tipped his hat, and took a swig. Spartan passed it to Flea, who did the same thing, who passed it to Pathfinder, who took the longest hesitation before he, too, finally gave in and held the bottle up to her. He passed it to Rook who gave it to Jester, until finally it ended up with Brody. He came up to stand alongside her. The men proceeded to set up camp as Brody took his time holding the bottle.

"You owe me an explanation," Theo said.

Brody looked confused. "On what?" He put the bottle to his lips and tipped it back but Theo doubted that he drank.

"Your loyalty."

Brody scoffed, slight surprise.

"Why are you going along with this?" she asked.

"You're the most obtuse genius I've ever met," he muttered. Before she could ask what he meant by that, he said, "You really think this is about *loyalty*? And here I was, thinking we wanted the same thing."

"What's that?" Theo asked.

"Things that were taken from us."

Theo scowled up at him.

Haas was the only person. He was the only person who knew.

"What was it?" Theo asked softly. "Whatever Haas took I can help you get it back." It felt like a riddle: What was a thing that could make loyalty obsolete and a man betray a brotherhood?

But Brody just shook his head. He scoffed again, this time as if she was no longer worth his time. "Jesus, Pine."

She flinched at the way he said her fake name. "Just *tell* me, Brody. You owe me. You owe me the truth. What was Flea going to say?"

"You're right. I do owe you that." Brody returned the bottle to his lips and, from the looks of the way he bared his teeth after, drank. "So here it is: Haas will act with no prejudice when he comes for August."

"Just because Blacksmith's Haas, that doesn't mean—" Theo paused abruptly, frustrated. "He would never hurt me. My brothers too."

"You want the truth? The one that we're really dealing with? We're talking about blood, lots of it, not a drop of it good. And then there's the other thing. The thing you think will give you answers? Truth is—" he sent a wary glance at the men. "The truth is," he repeated, quieter, "you find out what that is and it's liable turn you into a monster, same as the rest of us." He gave her a look of warning. "There's no such thing as loyalty out here."

CHAPTER

22

August knelt at the edge of the riverbank, his bare back to Theo as she approached. The cuffs of his trousers were rolled up and his shirt was folded neatly on a nearby rock.

The water gurgled pleasantly, but August clocked her approach first with a mild annoyance at being bothered, then modified to a warm smile when he realized who it was doing the bothering.

"Do you mind?" Theo asked. She approached, her arms full of canteens and waterskins. If Brody wasn't going to give her the answers she wanted, she was going to get them another way.

Haas was the only one who knew.

Brody's warning should have extinguished her curiosity, inciting self-preservation, but it begged the opposite.

"Not at all, Youngblood." His neck was lathered with soap and his hair slicked back from a recent wash. He pointed with the tip of his knife to the river's access point next to him, upstream.

She set the canteens down, unscrewed the first one, and dipped it into the cold, heavy current.

August lifted his chin, leaning over the water, and scraped the edge of his blade against the hair on his neck. He winced as he did.

Theo screwed the canteen shut and started on the next.

"I'm sorry, August."

He sent her a sideways glance. "What for?"

"I took something away from you. For what Haas did to you . . . it should have been you. You should've been the one to bleed him dry. I didn't realize that until just then."

August rinsed the sudsy blade. "I have one rule, Youngblood. It's a simple one." He made another pass at his soaped neckline, inhaled sharply in pain. "Goddammit." He touched his neck and checked it for blood.

Theo pulled out the straight razor and held it out to him. "This thing has a wicked edge."

August considered the razor, then got up off the bank to sit atop his neatly folded shirt. He lifted his chin in her direction and put his palms on his knees.

Theo froze. Was he inviting her to put a blade to his throat?

"Would you?" he asked.

She kept her hand outstretched for a moment, Bram Blacksmith's straight razor offered there, unable to process the two thoughts that entered her mind:

It can't be this easy.

He trusts me.

She felt resistant to the first thought, humbly softened by the second.

Theo got to her feet and unhinged the razor. She put August's chin in her thumb and forefinger and tilted his head back farther. He watched her carefully as she placed the edge of the straight razor against his neck. She ran it upward, leaving smooth skin in its wake.

She bent down, rinsed it, and placed the blade back against his throat.

One swift slice was all it would take.

She couldn't think of a single reason she shouldn't do it. She could hide after she opened his neck, wait for her backup to arrive come sundown.

She smoothed another portion of his throat.

"Can I ask you something?" Theo asked.

"Always," August said.

Theo paused on that response.

"Why haven't you told me what Lucas Haas took from you?"

August gave her his half grin. "We've had this conversation."

She slowly scraped up to his jawline. "Have we?" She rinsed the blade again. "You told me a story, but that was before you trusted me to run a blade against your throat," she said as she did just that. "I would think we're beyond pretenses now, Mr. Gaines."

He leaned back slightly. "You think I was lyin'?"

"Not all pretenses are false." She tilted his head to the side and made another pass. "This ain't only about revenge, is it?"

"Not much escapes you, do it, kid?"

Theo changed her approach.

She touched the side of his head, at his temple where sprouts of gray had emerged. "Do you ever think, Mr. Gaines . . ."

He narrowed his eyes at her.

"Do you ever think what it would be like, to have a single moment of quiet up here?"

He swallowed. "All the time."

She dropped her hand back to his chin and nodded sadly. She scraped the last strip of scruff on his neck. Then she kept it pressed there, in the crook of his jawline, slightly more pressure than necessary to raze hair.

He calmly held her gaze.

"Does is it ever get easier?" She made her whisper sound like a plea, the knife against his throat as if this were the information she was extracting from him.

"In a manner." He made no move to withdraw her hand, no effort to take the blade from vulnerability. "You learn to find purpose in it."

She withdrew the blade.

He made no reaction, as if she had never pressed the blade there to begin with.

"Those demons that plague you?" he said. "You learn how to harness them. You learn how to use them as a weapon." August sighed wearily. "I'm not sure that makes it easier. But I believe it makes it worthwhile."

Theo stepped out of his personal space and swiped at her face. She shook her head. "What's the rule?"

August frowned. "What rule?"

"You said you had one rule."

"Ah." He slid off the rock and knelt back at the water's edge. "You don't apologize." He splashed the remainder of the soap from his neck and chin. Then he looked up at her and said, "Not when it comes to the choices made in order to survive."

As August redressed, Theo finished replenishing the waters.

"Thank you, Mr. Gaines," she said.

He pressed the white hat onto his clean hair. "Nah, it's me who owes that to you, Youngblood." August held his hand out and Theo handed him the filled waters. "But what're you thankin' me for?"

"For giving me a place to belong."

He smiled. He slung the straps of the canteens over his arm. He looked at the river. Frowned at the treetops. "A diamond."

Theo followed his gaze to the sun-frosted tips of the trees, thinking, at first, that he meant the way the glittering dew drops caught the sun looked like diamonds, for it did.

"He took a diamond from me." He held up his clenched hand between them. "As big as your fist. Valuable beyond belief." He looked back down at her. "It doesn't matter anymore. None of it does." He gave her a sad, sad smile and Theo felt the barbs inside her clench, a sick, dawning epiphany that all this bloodshed might be more about the loss of a rock and less about the loss of life, more about the betrayal of wealth than the loyalty of blood.

"And now," August heaved a sigh as he turned to leave, "it's gone forever."

CHAPTER

23

The first half of the night passed in harrowing peace.

They ate freshly cooked venison that flooded Theo's mouth with tender flavor, and Theo finally learned how Jester had earned his name. The man told stories with such a deadpan stoicism that nobody had any idea they were jokes until he got to the punchline, never once smiling or indulging in laughter himself.

The longer they sat fireside, the more saturated they became in liquor, and the group let loose in a way that Theo hadn't experienced. This dark shadow that had hovered over them for so long was finally gone.

Theo sat opposite of August in their circle around the fire. Jester and Brody were on either side of her. Pathfinder and Spartan on either side of August. Flea to Brody's right. Theo would catch Brody's eye, a cautious smile on his face that, in opposition to the loosening of the gang, grew more cautious as the night progressed.

On edge. Anticipating. Waiting for Lucas Haas and Jude and Zeke Creed to ambush their laughter and bleed out their illusion.

Somewhere in the trees, an owl asked its incessant question. The smoke spread upward, hazing the stars and the waxing slice of the moon, shadows dancing in tandem with the fire.

Beyond August, a shadow moved incongruently to the fire. It defied the shapes of the woods, moving smoothly, drawing closer. In the center of the silhouette, a quick wink of fire against metal reflected yellow. Theo had the urge to scream a warning, but she caught the yell at the peak of an inhale, keeping it in place by holding her breath. The shadow edged the tree line, reaching the clearing. She darted her eyes to Brody. She saw that he saw it too.

The silhouette almost halved its size, crouching, half crawling as it headed directly for August's back.

Brody's fingers curled over the gun against his thigh.

The silhouette was halfway through the clearing now.

She dropped her eyes back to August.

She caught Jester staring at her in her periphery. She looked at him.

Theo saw the gears in Jester's mind click into place in the span of a second . . . two. He witnessed Brody. He noticed their tension. He followed Brody's line of sight.

Theo's wide eyes went back to August as her hand darted toward Brody to—

Jester whistled a loud, sharp chirp. She hadn't ever heard any of them make that noise, but she didn't have to be acquainted with it to know its intent: ALERT, ALARM, DANGER.

She saw one thing very clearly before bodies blurred into action in front of her and chaos descended around her. August, in a maneuver that was so fast and calm that it seemed expectant, ducked and rolled, yanking out a knife as he did. He was on his feet in an instant, slicing at the shadow that could have been her brother, her father, Elliot, Blacksmith.

Then the camp was chaos and the next thing she knew, Jester had her knocked on her back and an elbow jammed in her neck. His nose was almost touching hers. His eyes were angry and searching, and then, knowing.

She couldn't breathe.

She kicked her legs and tried to scream.

She was clawing at him when he pressed the cold, round end of his revolver into her cheek, under an eye.

The altercation in camp was unnervingly quiet. No yells or shouts, just shuffling feet and heavy breaths and pained grunts, so she heard Jester's hammer click back into place just as much as she saw it down the length of the barrel.

The weight of Jester's body was tackled from hers.

She gasped air into her lungs as she scrambled backward.

Brody and Jester were in a tangled brawl. Theo desperately searched the ground for Jester's revolver, but it was nowhere. In a brief upper hand, Brody yelled at her: "*Run!*"

She stumbled to her feet and spent another moment searching for a weapon, and in that moment, Jester landed a heavy blow to the side of Brody's head. It dazed him but didn't knock him unconscious.

Jester was on his hands and knees. He looked up at Theo.

She took a step back, toggling her eyes between him and Brody, who was moving slowly, trying to get control of his daze.

Theo watched Jester's eyes land on metal glinting in the light of the fire. It was just out of his reach.

It was way out of hers. She turned and sprinted for the trees.

A gunshot chased her. She ducked midstride but didn't slow. When she hit a cluster of trees, she wove through them, branches slapping her and roots tripping her. Another shot. Bark sprayed her in the face. The heavy steps of pursuit crashed behind her. They grew louder with each moment. Theo was out of her element. She couldn't outrun Jester. She certainly didn't have a chance in combat.

She pushed one final sprint, running as fast as she could, then turned sharply behind the biggest tree she could find, and pressed her back flat against it.

Already, the pursuing footsteps had slowed to a walk. At first, she couldn't hear them over the pounding of her ears and her own ragged breaths.

As she waited for Jester to find her, she pulled out her straight razor. She readied its blade. She held it close to her heaving chest.

The shape of Jester rounded the tree, preceded by the outline of his revolver. Theo sliced down. The blade fell heavily across his wrist and he cried out, dropping the gun. Theo spun to run, but his hand clapped over her skull and slammed it into the trunk. The jagged bark of the tree bit into the side of her face. She reached out for something to catch her fall. For a moment, nothing about the world made sense. The sky became the ground. The trees were upside down. It felt like she was floating, spinning. Then her face hit a bed of fallen needles, prickling her cheeks and eyelids.

She knew she had to move. She had to get up. She had to run. But the world wasn't behaving. She was in a depthless ocean, desperately swimming toward the surface, but she was going the wrong way, swimming deeper the whole time. She dug her fingers into the earth, smelled mud and tasted blood. Her stomach burned hot and her arms stung cold.

Distantly, she was aware that Jester wasn't killing her. Every moment that passed, she expected it. Fingers around her throat or a blade into her heart or a bullet into her skull. But Jester brought nothing and at first, all she heard was ringing. When that started to fade, she heard something else. It sounded like the noise of a serpent dragging its belly across mud, like a large animal writhing slowly in wet leaves—then she heard an attempted breath.

Theo woozily pushed herself up. She managed to drag a knee underneath her. Then she saw. Brody was wrapped around Jester from behind, his legs coiled around Jester's midsection, his arms caged around Jester's head and neck

Theo didn't understand why Brody hadn't just shot him, but she did understand why he couldn't now. The dominance that he was precariously holding would be lost in the moment he shifted it. Jester himself made a move for one of the guns, but he had the same problem. Any time either relinquished a fraction, the other gained dangerously.

Then Jester made a smart move. He feinted for the gun, drew Brody's attention there, and in the narrow window, Jester rammed his knuckles, hard, into Brody's knee.

Theo pulled herself to her feet, swaying into the tree.

Brody grunted and tried to regain what he'd lost, but Jester managed to loosen Brody enough to earn better body shots. Brody clenched his teeth and strained as Jester landed another blow to his knee.

Theo dropped to her knees and searched for the gun or the knife. She found neither, but her fingers did find the smooth, cold surface of a stone about the size of a grapefruit. She half crawled, half stumbled to them. Brody watched her as he struggled to keep his hold. Theo swung the rock at Jester's skull, but the blow was thwarted when Jester drew his knee back and kicked her. His attempt on her was partially thwarted by Brody, but the blow still knocked her away and onto her back. The stone grazed his head and then tumbled into the underbrush.

Scrambling back, Theo reached for Brody's revolver.

She yanked it out but Jester struck, hard and fast, sending the gun flying from her hand before she could get a good grip on it. It too was swallowed by the dark, spindly limbs of the brush.

In her distraction of looking for where the gun landed, he managed to grab her hard by the hair. It was a short-lived maneuver, a tactic to get Brody to counteract. It worked, costing him more leverage. Jester twisted hard and jerked them to the side, loosening Brody's control of the headlock. Quickly, Theo clutched Jester's shoulder and tweaked, hitting him in the face as hard as she could. Jester hit Brody's knee again.

Theo didn't think her next move through. She clambered onto both of them and hit Jester in the face with her fist again, this time with better leverage.

"Get back!" Brody spit out.

She hit him again, feeling the crunch of his nose that time. She pinched her lips together and drew her fist back again.

Jester elbowed at Brody then swung at her. She ducked and only managed to dodge him because of Brody's continued efforts. Then she went flat against him, straddling and hugging her arms around them. As expected, Jester hooked his arm tight around her and squeezed so hard she thought for sure he was going to snap ribs.

Brody relinquished one arm of the headlock and grabbed onto Jester's sleeve, straining to keep him from crushing her.

Jester wrapped his other arm around Theo. Brody's weight was leaning onto the hip and pinning the other revolver out of reach. Jester squeezed harder and harder, ounces away from crushing things inside her body, but by then, Theo had unsnapped the holster that intersected Brody's spine.

Theo sank the knife into Jester's spleen.

His hold on her jolted and slackened. He cried out and reached for the knife.

Theo sat up, raised the knife with both hands, and stabbed him in the heart.

The last breath to pass through Jester's lungs was a faint, surprised gasp. His eyes glazed, then closed. His limbs went limp.

Theo rolled off him, first onto her hands and knees, then she sat back onto her feet, panting.

Brody uncoiled from Jester and moved from under the body with a shove of his boots.

He crawled over to her and wrapped his hand around her fist, the one holding his knife. "Are you—" He breathed hard, swallowing harder. "Are you okay?" His voice was low and uneasy.

Theo nodded. But then she felt a sharp pain on her waist. It was unique and wrong. The blade tumbled from her hand so she could hold on to the hot pain.

When she removed her hand, it was coated in blood.

CHAPTER

24

Theo didn't remember lying down, but there she was, flat on her back. The moon smiled at the tips of the trees. She could hear the shootout waning, scattered gunshots popping nearby.

She didn't realize she was squirming until Brody's voice found its way to her ears through the chaos telling her to *Stay still. Be still.*

His hands were under her shirt. His touch was traveling up her torso. His fingers found the chemise binding. They fumbled to get the binding loose.

He was shirtless.

Through the haze of shock, she swung at him and tried to kick at him. Words in her head refused to connect to each other.

Brody gently deflected her weak attempts, his face all screwed and tense, a sheen of sweat covering his skin.

"I know it hurts, but I got you." He said this over and over and then the pain got really bad where the bullet had chewed through her flesh.

She let out a whimper and grabbed at his arm. But the pain didn't go away, only seemed to grow and grow and build and spread until Theo thought she would die or lose consciousness. Neither mercy arrived.

She felt the loosened binding of the chemise being slid down her abdomen, then the pain exploded to new heights as Brody began tightening the chemise in a new spot in a place that intersected her belly button.

"You're gonna be fine," he said as he lowered her shirt back down over her stomach. "You're gonna be okay," he said as he slung his buckskin coat with the copper rivets over his bare shoulders, slipping arms back into the sleeves. "But we can't stay here."

She nodded, and he didn't wait another moment for her to contemplate what came next. He shoved his hand between her shoulder blades and the cold flesh of the ground, slinging her arm over his shoulders, then hauled them to their feet.

The pain shattered and went deeper still, touching places inside that she didn't know *could* feel pain, such a violent agony that it briefly dropped a black curtain over her eyes. She dipped and buckled, making Brody's hands go strong and steady over the places where he held her body. For the first few steps, the pain was so unpredictable and enormous that she couldn't possibly do this. But Brody didn't allow her to slow, her feet practically dragging as he took large steps away from the dying gunfight and deeper into the forest.

Her head settled in the hollow of his shoulder, one set of her fingers clutching his side, the other set clutching hers. There was a mass of something balled against her torn flesh, and she realized it was the shirt off Brody's back.

He grunted each stride, their breaths a disconcertingly thick fog.

Theo felt the rhythm of his limp, then fell into it. The pain didn't dull, but it evened, making movement manageable. She forced her feet to take steps, to hold their weight.

"Brody," she said breathlessly.

"Shh," he said, looking around at increasingly hopeless wilderness. Already, the forest had swallowed them in a directionless void.

"Your leg," she managed.

"I'm okay."

"Gaines?" she asked.

"I don't know."

Theo didn't know it was possible to be so weak that your tongue no longer had the strength to form words, but her body was starting to funnel all resources to her ability to put one foot in front of the other, so that's all she did. Clinging to a man who was an enemy just days before, she walked and walked and walked until her body refused to do that.

Theo's legs buckled. Brody held her steady the first few times it happened, but then he nearly went down with her. Instead, he planted his feet, and helped lower her to the ground, leaning her spine against the trunk of a thick evergreen. The shift in movement made the pain go sharp and deep and unpredictable again, and Theo let out a pitiful cry.

Brody knelt next to her. He pointed directly in front of them without taking his eyes from her face. "See that, Miss Creed?"

Panting, she followed his finger to the black mouth of a cave.

"We just gotta make it there. Okay?" He panted. "That's it. We're so close."

She nodded, squeezing her eyes shut, chest rising and falling rapidly.

"Brody," she said.

"Don't talk."

She nodded again, squeezing her fingers against his, realizing that he'd never let go of her hand.

Then, before she could protest, he lifted her to her feet, and they fell back into limping rhythm.

The cave was shallow, but it was angled from the icy breath of the elevation's steady breeze. Brody found the flattest, softest place in the hollow, and settled Theo there. She refused to let go of his hand because she knew what he had to do, that he had to leave her alone while he gathered wood for a fire.

"I won't be long." He took a revolver from his thigh and replaced his grip on hers with the gun's. "It's loaded. I checked." He gave her a grim grin.

She tried to return the smile, but she only made a noise of pain.

"I'll be right back." He pushed himself off the ground, moving like he had geriatric joints, and disappeared around the corner of the cave.

The next thing Theo knew, Brody was shaking her back to consciousness.

She jerked, swinging the gun. Reflexively, his hand caught the barrel.

"Hey, hey, hey. Where are you right now?"

"I don't know."

"Fair." He helped her settle the gun in her hand to rest in her lap. "What's my name?"

"Brody Boone."

"Good. You think it's about time you tell me yours?"

She grimaced a smile. "Theodora Creed. I prefer Theo."

"Suits you better than Teddy," he said as he scooted a few feet away. "How old are you really?"

"Eighteen come December."

He nodded as if he expected that.

"You?" she asked.

"Eighteen last week."

"Happy birthday," she said.

He let out a soft laugh. "Yeah, ain't it?"

She smiled painfully as he shifted away from her, toward the mouth of the cave.

"Keep talking to me," he said. "Do you feel dizzy?"

Theo shifted painfully to see what he was doing. "No."

"Can you tell me where we are?"

"In a cave."

"Spot on." He pulled out a matchbox. "What's your favorite color?"

"Pink." She settled her head back down.

"Mine too," Brody said.

Theo laughed, then whimpered. "Don't make me laugh."

"I wasn't foolin'." He leaned down, his palms flat on the dirt underneath him, blowing gently on the small flame. "But that does sound like a challenge." His cheek hovering close to the ground, he glanced at her, hoping to glimpse her smile.

Theo obliged, but with a grimace. "You're nothing what I thought."

"You're just about everything I thought," he replied.

He blew on the flames, coaxing them hotter and larger. He watched her face for a moment, and when he realized he'd rendered her speechless, he said, "Why were you in jail that morning? I'd say you don't strike me as the troublemaker type, but I wouldn't be able to do so with a straight face."

Theo managed a smile without a grimace. "All right, Brody." With great difficulty, she tried to adjust again. "Truth for truth."

Brody came to her side and helped prop her up against the rough stone of the cave wall. "You'll tell me yours if I tell you mine?"

She nodded.

He held his hand out to her, and it took her a moment to realize he meant to shake her hand, as if they were entering some sacred pact.

She put her hand in his. He wrapped her hand in his and moved his thumb across her knuckles, back, and then across again, never once taking his eyes from hers; it was quite possibly the most electric handshake Theo had ever experienced. The pain against her waist was vanquished for a moment, a glorious, brief enchantment.

"Deal," he said.

By the time Theo was finished telling him her tale of what had landed her in a cell alongside Patrick, the fire was raging and Brody was scowling lightly at the orange. "What a prick."

Theo let out a thin laugh. "Well. Small towns. What can you do?"

"Right," Brody said, "*That's* the problem with the likes of Patrick, Small towns."

Theo laughed again. "I was trying to be nice."

"Why?" he asked.

"Well, up until then, being nice had kept me out of jail."

"Yeah, but it weren't gonna keep you alive."

Theo nodded slowly. "So what's your excuse?"

"My excuse?"

"For being nice to me."

Brody fell into a state of contemplation, mesmerized by the fire. "It ain't about nice, Miss Creed. It ain't even about loyalty. This is about trust."

Theo no longer heard a taunt in the way he said her name, but there was something else in his voice and it gave her a boldness to take her time looking at his face, really look at it—the elegant curve of his lips and the stunning color of his eyes and the perfect shape of his brows and the cutting angle of his jawline.

"Brody," she said softly.

He took his eyes off the fire to look at her.

"Are you just going to stare at it, or are we going to do this damn thing?" She lifted the hem of her shirt, carefully guiding it over the bloodied binding across her belly.

He took a deep breath and pulled out the bandana. Leaning toward the fire, he picked up the scales of the razor. He inspected the orange-tinted blade, then set it back down in the fire.

"I can do it if you can't," Theo said.

Brody went to her side and knelt there.

"I can't do it," he said. "But I will anyway."

She closed her eyes, nodding.

She understood that catechism. "Strange how easy and necessary don't like to go together, isn't it?"

He took the gun from her hands and set it aside. "I've never known anybody like you, Miss Creed." He began loosening the binding.

"Please stop calling me Miss Creed." She winced when she arched her back for Brody to make an unwinding pass behind her back.

"You got it, Mr. Creed."

She barked a painful laugh as he made another round.

He smiled back, but it dissolved quickly into his task. When he got the binding free, he slowly pared his shirt from her wound. Her flesh was ripped at the zenith of her waist. The bullet had torn off the skin and muscle, like an animal had taken a bite out of her side—the luckiest location of a bullet wound to the gut. It was clean in the sense that the bullet was a short-term tenant, leaving no fragments behind on its way out.

"You're fortunate it wasn't an inch to the left."

"Fortunate would have been an inch to the right."

"Fair enough. Let's get you on your side." He held his hand out to her, the tips of his fingers already printed in blood. She gripped it, and together they got her body propped on her opposite hip.

Brody stripped a branch and broke it into a short piece before placing it between her teeth. Her flesh sizzled and popped when he cauterized the wound, but what Theo would remember more than the pain, long after the wound had healed, would be the smell of her own skin burning.

She spit the wood from her mouth, dug her claws into the earth, took three long breaths, and on the exhale of the third, she screamed. She did so into the crook of her elbow to muffle it because she didn't know what lurked in the woods, didn't want to attract more trouble than she already had. Brody wrapped his body around her, and she curled and melded against him, where she could dilute her screams into his chest. He held her tight, and through the haywire effects that pain often brought about, she valued how his embrace didn't imply she was fragile.

When her screams were demoted to staccato breaths and finally eased until something akin to steady, she said, "You owe me. You owe me a story, Brody Boone."

"I suppose I do," he said, quietly, so Theo heard it more from the ear pressed to his chest. He said nothing for a little while after that, but when he started his story, it began with this: "It happened six years ago."

CHAPTER

25

B rody took a step closer, finger now on the trigger. "Don't you want to know my name?"

August poked a finger on the underside of the brim and lifted the hat from his face. He gave the young man a slow appraisal as if considering a piece of livestock, then said, "I haven't decided yet if that's pertinent."

"What's your business on my land, mister?"

"*Yours*," August echoed.

Brody stole a glance around. Somehow, the trees felt closer. The horse seemed larger. The fire, hotter. Swallowing past the feeling of cotton in his throat, Brody regripped his weapon.

Before Brody could respond, August spoke again. "Sit down, boy."

Brody was itching to do the opposite, felt the mistake of his choices before the vaporous reasons turned solid. From the corner of his eye, he thought he saw movement. He swept the rifle in that direction, took a step back to angle himself better between a possible threat in the woods and the potential one on the ground

"Good lord, boy. You're making me nervous." August sat up and leaned his back against a propped saddle. He pulled out a pipe. "Sit down a beat, would you? I gather I'm not going back to sleep anytime soon, so I'd like to talk at you for a minute." He reached into the saddle pack, paused to make purposeful eye contact with the boy as to convey his nonnefarious intents, and once he received a single nod from Brody, he pulled out a moccasin water bag. Without taking so much as a sip for himself, August lifted the water in the boy's direction.

Brody glanced at it but made no move for it.

August tossed it at Brody's feet.

Brody was very thirsty, and the way he saw it, he was the one with the gun, so why not drink the man's water? He picked up the moccasin sack, tried to unscrew the cap, but couldn't do so and keep a finger on the trigger at the same time.

"Stop, stop," August said. He unbuckled his holster and tossed it at Brody's feet. "I don't mean you no harm, partner." He struck a match, lit his pipe, and invited Brody to join him fireside with a universal take-a-seat gesture.

Brody eyed August as he kick-scooted the man's holstered weapon farther away. He moved his aim off August, and on further consideration, set it against the trunk of a tree. The fire popped between them as Brody took several greedy pulls from August's supply.

"Thank you, sir," Brody said as he screwed the lid back in place.

August shrugged as he puffed. "It's your water."

It took Brody a moment to understand August meant he'd replenished from the nearby creek.

"How much land to your family out here?" August asked.

It didn't feel right to answer the man's questions while standing at his fire, drinking of his water, even if it was on Boone land and from rivers that ran through it, so Brody sat. "About five hundred acres."

August let out a low, impressed whistle. "I would've liked to settle in a place like this. You been here long?"

"I was born here. So was my father. And his before him. Why didn't you?"

"Settle?"

Brody nodded.

"I'm more of a travelin' man." He lit another match. "Not my first choice, mind you. But still mine, nonetheless. Catch me, kid?"

"No, sir. If you coulda chosen the first one, why wouldn't you?"

August held on to his pipe with his molars as he reached into his saddle pack. "It's like this, kid."

Brody wrapped his hand around his rifle, but August only pulled out a bottle of brown liquor filled about halfway.

"Choices are illusion. There's a current in the Universe, young man, and it plays our emotions like the strings of a banjo. And mankind, see, we dance. Every choice we make is because of a feeling. I don't care what no man's ever told you. Only one ingredient to decision-making and that ingredient is how a thing makes a person feel. That current controls anything that holds the power of self-awareness. That current's called Destiny."

Brody considered this, a frown slowly lining his forehead. "That ain't destiny, sir. I believe that's called pretext."

"Excuse me?"

"Smoke and mirror. Guise. That's just an *excuse*, Mr. Gaines."

August sputtered a surprised chuckle. "Prove me wrong."

"You say you do things because of the way a thing makes you feel, so you ride the strongest current."

"Couldn't'a put it better myself."

"You say there's no honor in swimming up current."

"Incorrect. Gotta do that sometimes. You're still manipulated by the current, whether you're swimming against it or riding with it."

"Manipulated and swept away are two different things."

"You still haven't proved me wrong. Give me a tangible. Give me a scenario, and I'll tell you the emotion that drove it."

So the banter went, on and on and deep into the night. Brody began to see what August meant by the time he was drunk, saw his point when most every answer Gaines said was *greed* or *love* or *hate* or *jealousy*. Brody saw that the man wasn't entirely wrong, but he also saw how convenient it was that his worldview supported an ideology that said you should do whatever it is you feel because that was just how the current of the Universe flowed. If Brody were to have a proper retort with a mind clear of a buzz, he would have turned Gaines's own argument against him and told him the fact of the matter, that Gaines's core current was cowardice. It's not poetic or glamorous to believe in Fate, it's an amorphous pillar to hide behind, a justification to ride the current even when it was red with hate and greed. Mighty effortless to believe in the futility of choice, easy to buy into the idea that tells mankind are free of liability.

"Well," August Gaines said. "It doesn't exactly matter what you believe now, do it, kid?"

Brody didn't realize he'd drifted into the haze of drink until Gaines's voice was rumbling much closer. His blinked his bleary eyes. He stiffened when he was staring down the barrel of his own gun.

"You ain't pliable enough to my liking." Then August pulled the trigger. The gunshot echoed against the cavernous jaws of the valley, and Brody Boone was dead on the ground before the last echo came back to them.

Around the bend of dicelegs, Billy Boone startled awake.

He'd followed his brother by the ashy light of the moon, crawled to the outcropping after his brother had slid off it, where he watched the beginnings of his brother and the stranger's interactions. Billy felt the unease that his brother exuded, but was comforted when Brody shed his coat, set down the shotgun, and joined the man in discussion that was a little too far above Billy's head for him to follow. The slow grind of the stranger's voice was fatherly and kind, and Billy was lulled to sleep about the same time Brody was.

Tears were spilling out of his unblinking eyes in rapid succession.

Last thing Billy remembered was his brother smiling and laughing. Now he had a huge hole in his chest and his eyes were open but they weren't looking at anything.

It happened so fast yet took all night. Billy didn't comprehend what he was looking at. As a boy on the cusp of teenage hood, Death was still as abstract a concept as what lay beyond it.

Billy watched August Gaines stand over Brody. Watched him drop the dead boy's shotgun in the grass so he could relight his pipe. Watched him go back to his reclining place. Watched him not have a single shred of remorse for the life he just stole.

August was just riding a current, he would have said.

Billy thought he couldn't possibly be any more terrified than how he felt in that moment, but when he saw seven shadows emerge from the forest and step into the orange glow of the fire, Billy couldn't move. He couldn't breathe. Urine spread across his crotch. He held his mouth closed with both his hands.

Inaction is the best example of riding a current, August would have told Billy; that current would be Fear. In fact, he *did* tell Billy that, years later, when the memory of shooting Brody Boone was hardly a thing that touched August's mind. Fear was August's least favorite current, he would tell Billy, without any idea that he'd given Billy's older brother the same spiel. Fear, August droned one night, carried you places you shouldn't go. That was a current you should swim against, August would have said, did say, and would forever continue to say.

And if you're really good at feeling the current of the Universe, you'd find another layered beneath Fear—that one was Rage. And if you went deep enough, it would take you in another direction altogether.

IV

ALLEGIANCE

MORE DANGEROUS THAN THE MAN WHO HAS NOTHING LEFT TO LOSE,
IS THE MAN WHO BELIEVES HE HAS NOTHING LEFT TO LEARN.

CHAPTER

Theo was very still in Billy Boone's arms. The fire crackled in the following silence. She wanted to shift, to get out of his arms to look him in the eye, but he was holding her so tight, and she realized she was wrong before—it had nothing to do with her fragility.

"Billy," she said softly, trying the name in her mouth, testing the way it landed between them.

He flinched as if she'd pinched his skin.

"Why did you take your brother's name?" She knew the answer, but she thought he needed to finish this purge. To say the truth, the facts, the reality out loud to remind himself the lie he was shrouded in was nothing more than what it was.

The tension in his muscles melted as he gave his answer. "He never even learned Brody's name. And the best part?" he said with a bitter laugh. "Boone ain't even our family name to begin with. It's Barba."

"Your whole family changed their name?" Theo asked.

Billy nodded, loosening his hold on her slightly when he ran a hand through his hair.

"Why?"

"Because—" He halted, maybe considering how to put it. "Because twelve years ago, our land—my family's land—became America's land. Because twelve years ago when a con man won his war, we learned that when the United States reassigns your nationality, you play the part or you pay the price." He picked up a piece of debris off the cave floor and tossed it into the fire, muttering, "As if pretending to be a gringo has ever made a goddamn difference to one."

"What happened?" Theo asked gently.

"I promised him. I promised my dead brother that I would kill August Gaines in Brody's name. I took his bullets and his revolvers. I took his coat. I *became* Brody because—" The rest of the explanation became ensnared in Billy's throat.

Theo shook her head. That's not what she was asking about. She was asking about the price they'd paid; how much it had cost them to become something else.

She took a steadying breath. "Because ghosts aren't real. Because ghosts can't avenge themselves. Because Brody deserves a second chance at August Gaines."

He nodded at the fire. "Yes," he said. Theo could hear the tears in his eyes by the tension of his voice. "Yes."

"What did you do next?" Theo asked.

"I didn't move. For so long. It was night the next day when I finally had the courage to crawl out of my hiding place. The black pit from the fire was cold, but Brody—his body was colder. They left him there. Left him for the coyotes to tear his body apart. I didn't even think about that until later. Until it was too late to go back."

Theo didn't say anything in the long, composing pause Billy took. "Gaines and his crew packed up and made their way to the next town over before I even had the nerve to move. I went home, but my parents were gone. For the longest time, I blamed it on Gaines. Told myself he'd come and killed them too. It took me a long time to let the truth in: my parents were out looking for me and Brody. But I didn't allow myself to believe that, because I had already made up my mind, so I just believed what I needed in order to do what I wanted. I took what I thought I needed. I took all their money. I took the best horse and let loose the rest. I hurt my family so much deeper than I needed to. I did it because I was guilty. I was ashamed. It was my fault my brother was dead, and I was going to go fix it." Billy took another long pause, his inhale shaky. "I didn't fix shit. I've ruined everything. And now I can never go home."

Theo wormed her way out of his embrace, and Billy's hands sort of hovered around her. She sat back heavily, holding her seared side, grimacing around labored breathing.

Billy watched her warily. "Maybe this is where I belong. I can't face my parents after all the things I've done." He shrugged defeatedly. "Lord knows I've earned my place next to Gaines."

Theo sat still for a while. Quiet. She gathered her thoughts, then settled on: "You say you're ashamed." She waited for Billy to grow the courage to look her in the eye before she sent the real sting. "Is that because Gaines killed your brother on your watch, or is it because he's manipulated you into loving him despite that?"

The sharp angles of Billy's jaw flared and tightened as his chest decompressed, as if all the air was vacuumed from his lungs. "That's—" He cleared his throat. "That's a cruel thing to ask."

"I know."

His eyes traveled along the walls of the cave as if searching for his answer. There was a hatred burning through the tension of his body.

She decided to bail him from his hatred. He deserved that.

"One time," she said, "Elliot and I and a few other kids were out playing. Patrick was with us, and he was in a really bad mood. We were all playing tag or hide-and-seek, but Patrick was throwing rocks at anything that moved. He was having no luck, and he got angrier every time he missed a target. Well, there were these crows circling." She twirled a finger upward. "They weren't even doing ordinary crow antics, just . . ." She put her hand out dreamily. "Riding the wind."

Billy rubbed his knee, watching her.

"Patrick throws a stone straight into the flock and—just . . . *nails* one of them. You could hear the thud of that rock hitting its little body. Patrick shouts, points, laughs, and starts dancing around like you'd imagine an idiot might. That bird falls through the air in a flutter of feathers, lands in the grass. Patrick goes running over to it, and pretty soon we're all standing around the thing. It was so . . . *sad*. That helpless little crow, trying to walk, trying to fly, trying like hell to just get away, but all it can do is spin in circles. And Patrick, he's just laughing. He picks up a stick and is going to mess with it more. I remember so clearly this look on Elliot's face. He was looking at me, and I didn't realize how angry I was about it until I saw it mirrored on his face." Theo touched her cheek absently. "Elliot snatches that stick out of Patrick's hand so fast that Patrick yanks his hand back to find he'd drawn blood. Elliot yells, 'What is *wrong* with you?' I mean, Elliot yelled so loud that it even made me take a step back from him. Elliot's younger than me. By a few years, and Patrick? He was always a bit big for his age, but at that time, the age gap made their size difference laughable. But Elliot's never been afraid of this boy three years older and twice his size. They've gotten into it before and Patrick knows that's a losing battle, and soon it's just me and Elliot with this poor crow. There's no way it'll make it on its own. Elliot takes my hand, squeezes it, and says, 'We have to help him.' So we take it to my dad and he makes us this enclosure for it—he's good at that."

Billy smiled softly. "Creed Carpentry?"

"One and only."

"Did he survive? The crow?"

Theo nodded. "Three weeks it took. Nursed him back to health. By the end of those weeks, that crow was eating out of our hand. We named him Aardvark. I can't remember who came up with it or why. It just fit him."

Billy added a light frown to his smile.

"At the end of three weeks, we go out to the field where Aardvark fell from the sky. Bring him out in the box my dad made. We let him go. That bird hopped out of the box, and I swear he looks at us like he knows what we did. Elliot and I look at each other in disbelief, wondering if the other saw what we'd each seen. Aardvark hops a few more times, spreading his wings, then . . ." Theo paused for a second. "Liftoff."

"That must've felt good."

"It did." Theo nodded. "Until that pack of crows comes out of the trees like a wild gang and attacks Aardvark back to the ground. Elliot and I sprint over, waving our arms like madmen, chasing the crows off. But we were too late." Theo shrugged again. "They'd killed him. Pecked him to death."

"Goddamn," Billy said, alarmed.

"Elliot was crushed. He was on his knees. Scooped Aardvark into his arms and just looked up at me so helplessly. That was the first time I saw him cry. We buried that poor bird in the same box we healed him in."

"I'm sure there's something poetic there."

"Yeah, I reckon," Theo said. "But you know what I think? I think there are two different kinds of men. The kind that breaks things, and the kind that fix things. I think the most special kind of person is the man who doesn't want to break things, but I think the most noble is the one who *wants* to break things but chooses to fix them instead. Elliot was the special kind." She paused, gathered all her courage, and said to Billy, "I think you're the noble kind."

Billy went very still when she said that, chose to study the inside of the cave, and Theo could tell from the way he made his face turn into a stone that he didn't believe what she said, didn't accept it, and was trying very hard to not let her see the way that comment made him feel. He shook his head, his lips pressed together. Finally, he turned his eyes back to her.

"You don't know the things I've done, Theo."

"Maybe it's not too late to stop doing them. At least, I hope so, for my sake too."

"That's not the same. You got caught up in a fight that ain't yours and you've only done what you had to do to survive."

She smiled kindly at him, gave him a soft look that suggested that's exactly what she'd been trying to say all along.

He nodded. "That's—" He shook his head. "It's not the same thing."

"If you say so."

Billy was looking at her with such a beautiful intensity that Theo had to look away. Like he just couldn't believe that anyone could possibly see anything in him that wasn't reprehensible.

"So what I can't figure out," Theo said, shifting the conversation a little, "is how does a boy like Elliot come from a man like Haas? August said Lucas murdered an infant. I can't wrap my mind around that, Billy. I mean, I saw how Blacksmith was the other night. What he did to John. What he—" Her breath caught a little when she looked into his eyes. "What he was about to do to you. I can't stop thinking about it. And I'm not even talking about *what* he did—" She broke off.

"But how he did it," Billy said.

"Like he'd been waiting a long time to do something like that," she agreed. "I'm fairly confident there's something wrong with me, Billy. But Blacksmith?" She shook her head. "I think there might be something broken with him."

"Theo," Billy said. "There's nothing wrong with you."

Theo looked at the small fire sitting at the mouth of the cave, then looked upward at the glow it cast on the smooth stone, refusing to let a single tear escape. "I have to tell you something."

Billy waited a moment, then said, "Okay."

But she still didn't say anything.

And when she kept saying nothing, Billy reached over and placed his hand on hers.

She looked down at his hand, tightening her fingers over his. "You're not the only one," she said quietly, keeping her eyes down, watching his thumb follow the grooves of her knuckles.

"The only one what?"

"I had my razor to August's throat."

Billy's hand went still.

"And I couldn't do it." She finally looked up at him. "I asked you how you could love August after he killed your brother. I wouldn't ask you something so cruel if I weren't asking myself the same question."

Billy's nostrils flared. "How?" he said. Then a little softer: "Tell me how you had a blade to August's throat and lived to tell the tale."

"I gave him a shave."

Billy snorted something like a laugh. "You're foolin'?"

She shook her head. "He also told me about the diamond."

"*What*?"

She nodded.

"Theo," Billy said. But then he stopped, stayed in a surprised state of contemplation as if still trying to wrap his mind around what Theo had just told him. "You need to understand something . . ." He stopped again. Finally, he continued. "August, he don't *love*. When he lost his daughter, something inside him broke and since, I don't think he's ever been . . . capable."

Theo gave him a puzzled look, recalling warm nights of sitting fireside with August, remembering especially the moment when August placed his hands on Pathfinder's face and leaned his forehead against his. If that wasn't a gesture of love, of deep connection, Theo couldn't be sure what was. "But you?" she asked. "His crew?"

"No." Billy stared at a place in the cave for a long time, taking his time with that truth as if having to face it for the first time. "He don't care about us."

Theo didn't try to fill the silent pain this time.

"It feels like he does." He nodded. "And he's real good at making us believe that. And you know what? *He* might even believe he does. But he don't. Because it wasn't just the loss of his daughter, it was the way she was taken." There was another pause, like the words themselves were heavy, and to hold them in his mouth made him weary. "Lucas didn't just break the part of August that loves, but the part that *trusts*. I once saw August sacrifice a man he called a brother in hopes of gettin' the upper hand with Lucas. August had a family once. He hasn't had one since, no matter what he says. August is broken, Theo. August would *never* trust a person to hold a knife to his throat. Never."

"What are you saying, Billy?"

"I'm saying—" He broke off, but instead of saying the obvious, that Theo had somehow found a way past the ice surrounding August's heart, Billy slid closer to her and held her hand in his lap with both of his and said, "I'm saying that there's something wrong with August, not you."

She looked him in the eyes for as long as she dared, then she closed the inches of space that remained between them and leaned her head on his shoulder. He responded by gently placing his chin on the top of her head, pressing his lips into her hair for just a moment.

"You know what this means, right?" she said.

"What's that?" he said.

"That if there's nothing wrong with me, then there's nothing wrong with you."

He exhaled a soft, warm breath of laughter into her hair. "Your logic is undeniable."

Theo smiled, then winced at the searing pain. She held on to it once more, made a small adjustment, but didn't let go of Billy's hand.

"How are we going to get out of this?" Theo wondered aloud, not expecting an answer or a solution.

But Billy just held her hand a little tighter and said, "Together."

CHAPTER

27

A gunshot in the distance yanked Theo and Billy from a state that wasn't quite sleep, not quite wakefulness. Billy quickly but gently untangled his limbs from Theo's and scrambled to his feet.

He let out a surprised cry of pain and buckled under his swollen knee, grabbing at it. He cursed his way through it, yanked his revolver free with an air of frustration, and caught the edge of the cave with his shoulder, keeping the gun close to his chest as he peered into the forest.

"Are you ready?" Billy asked as he scanned the downward slope of the woods, pale in the morning light.

Theo took a moment after he asked that. In it, she discovered how much she admired Billy for knowing her enough to understand that she wasn't going to stop.

Theo stood and pressed her hand against the cave, doubling over the curve of her waist. It still felt like it was on fire. "I don't know if I can . . ." Theo winced and refused to finish that sentence. *Can* was a matter that was neither here nor there when *can't* meant death.

"Yes," she said. While there was still a threat to her town—yes. While her family was still in danger—yes. While she was still breathing. Yes.

Billy grabbed Theo's straight razor and slipped it into the pocket at her hip. He returned his weapons to his body. Their height difference was too disparate for him to duck under her arm, so she snaked her hand up his back and clutched his shoulder.

The sound of the river grew louder as they followed their path back down the hillside. At an approachable intersection, they sank down next to the roiling water. They cupped mouthfuls of bitingly cold water until their thirst was quenched. Theo unwrapped the chemise from her stomach.

"How's it look?" she asked.

Billy took the rust-stained binding from her. "Like it hurts like hell. But clean." He balled it up and plunged it into the river that tried to yank it from his hands, then brought it back to Theo to let the icy water wash over the angry flesh of the cauterized wound.

"Oh," she said in surprised relief.

He soaked more water and washed her wound again.

"Good?" he said.

"One more time."

He plunged for more water and wrung it out over her bruised, burned, and puckered skin. "Better?"

She nodded.

Billy redressed the wound, winding the chemise back around her waist as she held her torn and bloodied shirt out of the way. He hopped to his feet and offered his hand to her. She took it and he hauled her up. The cold had felt good, but already the relief was fading.

"Hold up," Billy said. He climbed up a steep hillside to a blanket of snow under a large patch of perpetual shadow and cupped a handful, packing the ice between his hands as he stepped and slid carefully back down to her. Briefly making eye contact with her when he lifted her shirt for her to again hold it up out of his way, he pulled back the chemise and slipped the packed layer of compacted snow against the cauterization. Then he laid his hand over the layer of ice and chemise and gently molded it to the curve of her waist.

"Thank you," Theo said.

He nodded. "I got you."

They continued to follow their own path back down the hillside until they came to the spot where they'd left Jester's body. It was gone.

Billy checked his guns before they continued on through their final stretch back to the last place they held camp.

"What's our play?" Billy asked.

"Stay hidden. Figure out what happened, who survived, who won. Then we come back into the woods and make a plan."

He holstered his guns. "Agreed."

Billy's limp eased the more he moved it and Theo felt more clearheaded than she thought possible. The mechanisms in her mind were cranking again, and she began to shroud her mind in character, trying to pull the wool back up between her and the world, starting to anticipate what she was about to discover. There were so many options, her head was swimming in them.

If he survived, August would have learned that she lied to him about cutting Lucas's throat.

She knew he no longer had a reasonable incentive to keep her alive.

She also knew she had to confront the reality that her father, her brothers, Elliot—any one of them may not have survived. She tried to tell herself she'd find a way to move on, to keep fighting for her mother and her sister and the boys. She really did. But the thing was, it didn't really matter if Theo had an hour or a week or a year, nothing could rightly prepare her for what she saw when they came into view of the clearing.

CHAPTER

28

Theo was sprinting with no regard to the pain in her side.

Her father's legs were still kicking.

In a single moment, she forgot it all. When she saw her father hanging by his neck from a tree, she forgot everything about who she was and who she was supposed to be.

Theo was screaming something.

August was scowling.

Pathfinder and Flea looked to August, their weapons drawn but low, unsure.

Billy caught Theo around her ribs, high up her waist to avoid her injury, and wrangled her in a tangle of aggressively thrashing limbs.

August, slowly, turned and looked up at the face of the man strangling at the end of a rope, then back to Theo, once more to Harrison Creed—his face twisted into something that nobody, not even those who knew August best, could read or understand.

Bewilderment. Shock. Malice. Devastation. Glee. Frustration.

August gave a loud, two-whistle chirp, running his hand perpendicular across his throat in the elimination gesture.

Without hesitation, Flea raised his revolver and aimed it the tangle of knots tied to a branch, and pulled the trigger. The boom of the gunshot jolted and froze Theo, who was still in a subdued cage of Billy's arms.

The rope frayed and snapped, and Harrison Creed landed on the ground below.

Theo fell to her knees, the pain in her side screaming.

A great shadow fell upon Theo, and a moment later, August was kneeling in her line of sight. The cold metal of the end of a revolver touched the underside of her chin and forced her to upturn her face.

August's eyes bounced across her features, desperately searching for something.

"Goddamn it, Youngblood," he growled. He dropped his head, a temporary mourning. "Go ensure that man don't die just yet, Sixer."

As Billy stepped past them to his task, August dropped the gun from her chin and instead pressed it into the grass, his other arm draped across a knee. Theo held his gaze angrily, her lips pressed together so they wouldn't tremble, her eyes glaringly motionless to keep the tears from escaping.

August's eyes trickled down her body. He reached out and took the unbuttoned hem of her open vest between his fingers and peeled it from her torso.

"God*damn* it, Youngblood," August said again, and this time Theo didn't know if he was referring to the unbound swell of her chest or the massacre a little farther down.

He pulled the mouth of the vest back over her torso and stroked his eyebrow. He put his hand on the side of her head, leaned over her, and kissed the top of her head.

Theo began to tremble.

"I wish you hadn't deceived me." He stood. "But I need you to know that what comes next is about the blood in your veins, not what you claimed was between your legs." He patted the side of her head, his large palm briefly gentle as if in apology for when his fingers turned hostile, clutching a fistful of hair from the top of her head. Stepping behind her, he yanked her head back, exposing her jugular as he reached down and slipped the straight razor from her front pocket.

She struggled as she realized his intent, clawing for her weapon.

He tweaked his stronghold again, rocking her backward, forcing her to sit hard on her ankles; the edge of the blade touched her throat and Theo's fingernails broke August's skin on the inside of his wrist. It didn't faze or hinder him, and she froze like that, her life held wholly in the movements of August's fingers.

"August," she said in a squeaking whisper.

And nobody saw it. Nobody noticed the soft spot that Theo found when she said his name, pleading mercy, that his grip softened, even if just for a moment, the edge of the blade releasing less than an ounce of pressure. It was small, so small perhaps, that Theo thought she might have imagined it.

"I didn't understand why you'd lied to me about Lucas," August said as Billy dragged her father over.

She gritted her teeth against the pain in her side, the dread of bleeding out, the horror of seeing her father swaying from a tree.

"I reckon I do now." He tightened his fingers, pulling harder on her hair, tilting her head back more.

Billy shoved Harrison Creed, who had landed in a jumble of elbows and knees, several yards in front of his daughter.

His lips were blue, his eyes were red and bloodshot, and the noose was still around his neck. He gasped his every breath, the air through his swollen throat making a rasped, strangled noise. With his hands still bound behind his back, the side of his face landed in the cold earth. Harrison's hazy eyes rolled in their sockets, his mouth swallowing air in panicky gulps. His legs squirmed beneath him, heels digging into the grass, trying to find any semblance of control of his own body.

"That's it, Creed. Come back to us."

Theo tore her eyes from her father to glance at Billy, whose face was all stoic, no emotion. She wished she hadn't looked. It only made the pit of despair less manageable.

Harrison coughed and shuddered, his legs fading into slower movements as his brain drank the oxygen and settled his nervous system. He let out a groaning, growling noise that sounded like he was trying to say something.

"How long've you known, Sixer?" August asked as Harrison blinked back to awareness.

"Last night, tending to her wounds," Billy said.

August made a noncommittal growl of a "Hm." Then he said, "She killed Jester?"

Billy nodded without looking at her.

"Jesus," August said in a way that straddled disbelief, respect, and grief all at once.

When her father finally had the awareness and clarity to recognize what was happening around him, his entire body went tranquil. He blinked at Theo. The muscles on his uncharacteristically unshaven jaw popped. When he glanced up and behind Theo, at August, a fire blazed in Harrison's eyes in a way that Theo had never seen and Harrison had plenty of clarity to understand the means in which August Gaines planned to destroy him.

When he made a similar groaning, crying sound, this time he wasn't trying to say anything at all. It was simply a noise of pure anguish.

Theo choked on a sob.

"You have been granted a second chance," August said.

"*No*," Harrison cried.

August ran flat side of the blade up Theo's cheek, promising violence with a caress.

"Confess," August said.

"I don't know!" Harrison tried to yell, but it was only a hoarse whine. He directed his attention to Theo, his words quick and damaged.

"Theodora, I love you. You hear me, honey? I love you."

"I love you too, Daddy."

He nodded at her, his cheek dragging against the dirt.

"Confess," August said, returning the blade to her neck.

"I'll tell you everything I know," Harrison said. "Please just let her go."

"Where is Blacksmith?"

Blacksmith was still alive. That meant Elliot and her brothers could be too.

"I'll tell you after you get your hands off my daughter."

"This daughter?" August said. "The same one you left defenseless in a jail cell when I came into town?" He dragged the blade down through Theo's forehead, across her eyebrow, leaving a track of hot pain. He kept the blade there, hovering above her eye socket, intersecting her pupil. She looked again at Billy and noticed the white-knuckled way he was holding his gun, one hand holding his own wrist as if to restrain himself from getting involved.

If her daddy didn't come up with some kind of answer, Billy was going to spark something that Theo didn't believe anyone would walk away from.

"Okay, August Gaines," Theo's father said. "I'll confess something to you." His lips brushed the ground. "I don't know where your godforsaken rock is, but I know something else." Harrison glanced at his daughter for a moment before he said, "Your child is alive."

August let go of Theo's hair, clicked the straight razor shut.

"You mention my daughter again, I'll cut the tongue out of your head."

"No. Your other kid."

August scoffed. "I only had one child."

"Lucas told me he can't have kids."

"He was lying," August said.

"Did you or didn't you have an affair with Maureen?"

"You don't get to speak on that. You got the story from a man who took everything from me, including the life of my three-month-old daughter, all because he was *jealous*."

"You slaughtered your own wife just because she loved Lucas and not you."

August laughed. "Is that the story he's tellin'?"

Theo's father coughed painfully into the earth and had no retort.

"Blacksmith is a con artist, Creed. You fell for it same as my whore wife, so—"

"Do you *hear* yourself?" Harrison said. "*Your child is alive.* Haven't you listened to a single thing I've told you? Your first-born child is *alive*."

August Gaines went still. His fingers twitched at his side. He looked over his shoulder at Theo, who had blood dripping down her eyelid and across her nose. She didn't bother to wipe it away.

There was a loud ringing in Theo's ears. She saw her father's lips moving, but she didn't hear anything after *your child is alive*.

The child in dispute—she knew who it was.

CHAPTER

29

Billy Boone was posted outside Bladestay.

It was his responsibility to hold the southern perimeter. His horse was tied to a nearby tree, and Billy paced mellowly nearby, scanning the surroundings as he fiddled with the cylinder of his revolver, clicking it open and flicking it back in place. It was partly nervous habit, partly deepening of intimacy a soldier should have with their weapon. He could load and unload the chambers without looking. He could draw it from its holster with the grace and prowess of a true gunslinger. Flea may be the most accurate shot this side of the Mississippi, but Billy was on his way to being the quickest in the entire Union. He had a natural athleticism, was uncommonly nimble, his mind never decelerated by drink, and he had great motivation: one day, he would challenge August Gaines to a duel. As far as he could tell, it was the only way to take the tyrant down. His gang was knit too tightly, too blindly loyal, and even if Billy did manage to take the life of Gaines, he doubted he would survive the following retribution. So, he decided, he would slowly sharpen and hone his skill until he was ready to take on August Gaines in a way that was true in accordance to the law and accepted by outlaws both.

He saw the flaws in his own plan, but he had been making things up as he went for about six years now, and although his choices had their own collateral, he had also gone too far, too deep, to turn back and return home empty-handed. As he saw it, the collateral he'd caused wasn't worth it until he had relieved August Gaines's body of its head. Simply put, he'd committed to the long con the moment he'd truly realized what he was up against.

After Brody Boone lay slaughtered, Billy had heard something spoken between August and his silhouetted crew.

We win the war, August Gaines had said, *and the Mexicans still lay claim to land on this soil. Fuck'em all.*

Billy didn't think he'd ever have the chance or ability to get close to Gaines based solely on the color of his skin, so he'd planned to track him down, to walk right up to him and put a bullet in his skull, consequences be damned. The early phases of his revenge plot were shaky and problematic, mostly because he had no idea the kind of precise monster Gaines turned out to be, partly because every idea he had would surely leave him dead alongside Gaines.

He had a lot of time on the trail, alone, to ponder this. Time makes a man look his deeds in the face. He didn't like what Time was reflecting, so by the time he caught up to Gaines (in Carson City), the August Gaines he'd witnessed just outside Ruidoso was so opposite of Billy's understanding of the man that Billy's gears began to switch in another direction.

August Gaines was surrounded by outcasts. His closest ally, a man he called Spartan, was a runaway slave. Rook was Indigenous. Pathfinder was a brown-skinned man from New Mexico, just like Billy, and Pathfinder was far from the only one in the gang. Billy didn't understand how these men followed a white man with an ideology such as his, but he was immediately and overwhelmingly curious to find out.

When curiosity meets caution, they tend to draw things out.

The complexities of the world messed with Billy. The contradictions of mankind screwed with his formative years. He was a perfect victim for grooming, and although August wasn't in the business of recruitment, he knew a ripe target when he saw one.

Billy didn't know when it happened. How it happened. He only knew that, somewhere along the way, it did happen. He had developed a warmth for August—a respect for him. August treated Billy so well that Billy had a difficult time resolving this man against the one who so effortlessly murdered Brody. Somewhere along the way, it made sense, felt right, to allow himself to be carried away by a group of people who treated him like an equal.

So, as he sat outside Bladestay, waiting for any residents who might try to escape, he didn't find it strange. He hardly thought about Brody with clarity anymore. He kept sharpening the tools he anticipated destroying Gaines with, but it had turned into a sort of rote obligation, an undercurrent he knew he had to answer to someday—a way to stay loyal to Brody—but Brody's death had turned into something nebulous, distant, and ultimately, something that used to have sharp edges but had now been dulled by years of the grinding of justification: Billy had slowly reduced the murder to a fluke in August Gaines's character. This wasn't emotional cowardice; this was mental survival. The mind creates walls, those walls are called justification, and those walls don't behave like normal ones because those walls are far easier to build than they are to tear down.

Billy saw a flash of something through the trees.

He pressed his shoulder to a tree trunk and peered through the collection of spruce.

He saw it again.

He yanked the quick-release tie of his horse and leaped on his back in a practiced, elegant maneuver. His gelding was weaving and galloping through trees before he even had his feet in the stirrups. He took his rifle from the holster attached to the saddle at the horse's shoulder, sat hard, and pressed the butt of the rifle against his own shoulder. The horse rocked back on his hind end and slid on his back hooves to an obedient halt, placing them purposefully close to the large girth of a tree trunk. Billy pressed his left knuckles against the tree, elevated his elbow up to create a level line with his forearm. He swung the barrel of the rifle down to rest atop the straight line of his arm and found his target fleeing about fifty yards away and counting.

Billy took a deep breath, wrapped his finger around the trigger, and moved the end of his aim in steady tandem with the movement of the fleeing rider.

"*Whoa,*" he muttered lightly to his horse, then continued to let out his breath steadily as he increased the pressure on the trigger. The rifle kicked him in the shoulder and his horse hardly flinched.

Billy saw the rider tumble from his horse.

He jammed his feet in the stirrups as he returned the rifle to its holster. His horse leaped forward, from standstill to canter, from canter to gallop in the matter of four strides. When he reached the rider's mount, the horse was carelessly munching on vibrant, knee-high grass, the reins caught behind his ears.

Billy opted for one of the six-shooters, thumbing the hammer back carefully as he picked his way through the forest where the rider had been thrown by Billy's bullets. Billy had strict no-kill orders on any man until August could determine whether that man was Lucas Haas or not, but shooting a moving target from over fifty yards away was a beggar's choice.

A blur caught the corner of Billy's eye, but not quick enough.

A body slammed into his, and together they tumbled from the height of the horse and to the ground.

Billy landed with the loss of the upper hand. His attacker had him pinned quickly, the revolver knocked from Billy's hand. Billy twisted and jerked his body, swinging a free hand, grazing his attacker's jaw. The man on top of him hit him back, and his knuckles did more than graze Billy's temple.

It jolted and doubled his vision.

The man had all his fingers around Billy's neck. Blood was blocked from entering his brain, and his vision went from double to blurred beyond numbers in horrifying rapidity.

Numbly, Billy's hand searched for the knife in an inconspicuous holster that sat perpendicular against his spine. He wiggled his fingers between his back and the matted grass, vision going from gray to black by the time he unbuckled the holster. He didn't remember closing the gap between holster to his opponent's neck, only came to an awareness capable of recalling after the blade had disappeared into the man's throat. Billy pulled the knife out, releasing a geyser of the carotid, covering Billy in a hot, coppery shower.

He pulled the knife out and stabbed again.

It didn't take long for the body to go limp, and Billy kicked and shoved it off him. He rolled on his side and coughed, spitting out someone else's blood.

Dragging himself onto his hands and knees, he caught his breath as he looked down at the man.

The man was young, shockingly so, not even old enough yet to be called a man—couldn't be older than fifteen. The boy had auburn hair, a straight nose, and a bold jawline. He was holding his erupting neck. His eyes were a dark blue. Billy knew this because they were looking directly into his.

Billy sat back, tenderly rubbing his own throat as he watched the light dim from the boy's eyes. He had killed men before, but never one who was younger than him. It didn't feel as devastating as he thought it might, but Billy didn't yet understand that these things stay with you, that his mind was already constructing a wall around this, shock acting as a cocoon around trauma. He didn't yet comprehend how a single thing can layer upon itself, only to weigh something impossible years later.

He only knew that he was wearing the paint of victory and he had no intentions of washing it away, not until it had dried on his skin and everyone was looking at him like the madman he felt he had finally become.

CHAPTER

30

A ugust was saying something, but Theo couldn't stop thinking about another thing, and when she forced herself to hear the words coming out of August, she discovered that those things were the same.

"Elliot," August was saying. "He was *my* boy?"

Harrison: "He wasn't Lucas's."

August's glance snagged on Theo's.

"I'm sure," August said, unconvinced. "Then where's this supposed kid of mine?"

Harrison's lips spread into a grin, and Theo's insides churned at the glum victory that she had never known her father to possess. "I reckon," Harrison said, "that your kid is on his way back to Bladestay as we speak, with the complete force of the US Marshals."

Theo's eyes were scanning the ground in front of her. Her mind was on the brink of figuring it out. A syrupy drop of blood landed on a thick blade of grass. She watched it crawl downward, leaving a trail of crimson in its wake. Then understanding came. Her chest ached so deeply, and she knew that kind of pain was unique to a heart breaking.

"Daddy," Theo said. "Elliot was the one who went for Clayton Creek?"

Her father nodded. "It's going to be okay, honey."

"*No*," she whispered. Nothing was going to be okay. She lifted her eyes to Billy.

His face was pale. His eyes were unblinking. He knew it too, knew he had entered Bladestay showered in the blood of her best friend, of August Gaines's son, blood of which Theo held no denominator, but how could that matter when she and Elliot had so many more important things in common, such as how both of them inherited sins that weren't theirs to reconcile.

Theo pushed herself to her feet, holding her side.

Pathfinder and Flea appraised their guns on her, but August held up a don't-you-dare hand.

August noticed the horrified trance that Billy had fallen into.

His hand hovered there in the air, his gaze on Billy.

"Sixer," August said.

"August," Theo said.

August took the revolver from its holster but didn't raise it from a resting place against his leg.

"Was that Elliot's blood you'd bathed yourself in?" He pulled back the hammer.

"What?" Harrison said, rolling onto his back to get a better view of Billy.

Theo didn't have the stomach to stand up to August right now, but she saw no other way to diffuse this.

"I—he—" Billy tried.

August raised the gun to Billy. "You had *one* job with *one* rule, you goddamn—"

"August!" Theo yelled as she limped heavily to him. "What are you doing?"

"This don't concern you, Youngblood."

"How?" She hollered. "*How?* Elliot was *my* kin no less than he was yours." She took her hands, placed them on August's chest, and shoved. He stepped back more in surprise than lack of balance. "I loved him and you hardly even *knew* him! You said we were a *family.* That makes Brody your son more than Elliot ever was." She shoved him again, and August gave her a shocked appraisal. "Elliot died because Brody Boone was doing what August Gaines *said* to do! How don't you get that, you son of a bitch! My best friend—your son—he's dead because of *you!*"

That did the trick.

August snarled and grabbed her by the throat. He put the barrel of the gun against her forehead. "Family doesn't betray family."

She clutched his arm. "I know where the diamond is."

He yelled, "Liar!"

"No, August, *no!*" Harrison begged.

"Shut *up!*" August roared.

She adjusted her fingers to wrap around his wrist, touching the back of his hand, reaching for his humanity. At the same time, she said, "Do it then." She leaned into the pressure with a challenging snarl. "Go on, August," she said. "Pull that trigger and never find your diamond."

August started dragging her across the camp and into the woods.

Behind them, Harrison screamed pleas for his daughter.

August yanked her to the same place she'd held her razor to his neck and tossed her onto the ground. She landed in the soft earth, crying out in pain from the way her melted skin yanked and pulled against itself.

August paced nearby. He swiped a hand through his hair. The gun hung menacingly at his thigh, his huge, hunched shoulders heaving.

"You could have killed me," August said so quietly that Theo barely heard it.

"More than once." Theo scooted away from August until her back hit the thin width of a sapling. She leaned her weight against it, waiting for the pain in her side to subside.

August stopped pacing and turned to face her, a heavy scowl on his face. "Why didn't you?"

Theo winced as she adjusted her seat to take pressure off her side. She gauged her options to flee, but there was no cover thick enough she could run to, not that she was in any shape to move quickly anyway. She was still trying to get her father's voice out of her head, the one where he was begging, almost crying, for mercy, for her. If she was going to survive this moment, she was going to have to focus.

"I don't know," she said.

August cocked a half smile as he lowered himself onto the boulder where he'd sat with his life in her hands just the day before, dangling the revolver between his knees in a posture that was both menacing and casual. "You don't know," he repeated, a near mock.

"You don't believe me."

He looked amused. "What part?"

Although the muzzle was pointed at the ground, the gun remained primed to fire and his finger still hugged the trigger.

"That I know where the diamond is."

"Decidedly, no."

"Then why am I still alive?"

Amusement descended to malice. "You don't deserve the truth."

"Bullshit!" she yelled, impressed with her own ability to gather the courage. "You *owe* me."

He raised his eyebrows and took a look around them as if he were searching for someone else she could be disrespecting because it certainly wasn't him she was speaking to like that. "Why don't you skate on back to thicker ice, Youngblood."

"I'm not stupid," she spat out. "I know you're going to kill me."

"Oh so you've got me all figured out, then?"

"I've lost *everything*." She eased the snarl out of her words. "Let me have this one thing." She dropped the spite from her tone. "If I'm going to die, August, at least let it be with the truth."

He looked heavenward, grimly. He smoothed his eyebrow again. Then he nodded in a conceding sort of way. He scratched at the smooth part of his neck. He sniffed. Slowly, his finger uncurled from the trigger.

Finally, he admitted, "You remind me of her."

Theo felt something invisible catch in her throat. There it was again. That antithetical thing.

"Who?" She managed.

Hunched over with his face still pointed at the ground, he lifted his eyes to her.

Unsteadily, Theo said, "Your daughter?"

He frowned at the ground. Shook his head before he nodded. "I only had three months on this earth with her. But, over the years . . . whenever I imagined who she might've grown to become—" August pointed at her over the grip of his gun. He shook his head again.

"August," she said, imploring. "You have to understand. You have to see that I didn't know. I didn't know what Blacksmith was. I didn't think he was capable of—" She stopped abruptly and looked down at the grass. When she spoke, it was low and unsteady. "Somebody killed my baby girl? I'd burn the whole goddamn world just to make that man pay." She looked back up at him. "If I'd known, the story I told about slicing Blacksmith's neck wouldn't have been lie."

August looked down at the six-shooter in his hands. "You sure you ain't my kin, Youngblood?"

"I wonder that myself from time to time, Mr. Gaines."

He bowed his head. Then he shook it.

Theo glanced at the gun. His finger had relaxed downward, but the hammer was still depressed.

"Let me help you take Lucas down."

August let out a short laugh. "How did God fit so much ego into such a little thing?"

"He made space by leaving out all the self-preservation."

He chuckled. "Yeah, I reckon. But I know you ain't short on logic so it's wildly bewilderin' to me that that sharp thing in there," he tapped his temple with the barrel of his gun before tipping it at her, "could believe I'd trust you."

Theo wondered about the state of mind you had to be in to point a weapon at your own head while it was in its most impetuous condition. He was communicating something to her, whether he meant to or not. To threaten her life was as distressing to him as endangering his own.

An idea started to take shape in her head. She said, "When's the last time you needed to trust a worm on a hook in order to catch a trout?"

He sat upright, looking at her, puzzled. "You know, Youngblood, I don't know one person who wouldn't be bargaining for their own life right now."

Theo kept everything in her body contained. She focused on breathing, on simply looking up at him, on pushing through the burning pain in her side, the sting of the slice through her eyebrow, the throb of the bruise on her skull.

He unlatched the hammer.

Nobody watching would know the relief she felt. Not even August, who didn't notice she'd already won that bargain for her life.

"What are you proposing," he pointed at her again, "and what's in it for you?"

"If I help you get Lucas, you spare my family. You give me your word no harm comes to them."

He narrowed his eyes at nothing in particular. He nodded. Took his time with the following silence. "And supposin' I'm more concerned about the hooking of the worm than the catching of the trout?" His voice was tender. Soft.

She swallowed hard. Something sharp caught in her chest again. "Well, Mr. Gaines—"

A whistle interrupted her. August scowled in the direction of camp, held up a hand for her to stay quiet, then gave Theo a look she couldn't read.

She sent a desperate look toward camp even though it wasn't in their line of sight.

August popped the cylinder of his revolver and checked the chambers as if he could find the answers to all the questions in his head there. A nonsensical thought entered Theo's mind, of pulling petals off a flower, one by one, and in the same way, she imagined August touching each bullet in his revolver—*I trust her, I trust her not.*

"Shelve that thought for a minute," he said. "Because right now?" He clicked the cylinder back into place. "Wicked business, Young-blood." Then he stood, holstered his gun, and held his hand out to her.

CHAPTER

31

Pathfinder and Flea stepped back from Harrison when August brought Theo back into camp.

"What is it?" Theo asked. When Theo tried to move toward her father, August's hand clamped around her bicep and pulled her back.

"He's speaking nonsense," Billy said. He was next to his horse, messing with the holster that held his rifle.

Harrison was trying to look at Theo, but his aim was slightly off.

"Dad," Theo said. The grip on her arm didn't yield. Theo looked at Billy, an unconscious plea for help.

"Sixer," August said, beckoning him over. "Water."

Billy left the horses and walked over. He was unnervingly calm, impressively steeled.

"Hold her." He gripped Theo above her elbow and handed her to Billy, and in exchange, Billy gave the canteen to August.

"Sir," Billy said as he took her arm. His fingers were tight. He didn't look her in the eye. Theo had the sensation of things going bottomless beneath her feet again.

"It's too late now," Harrison said. "Damn it! Rats!"

She looked among the men. "What's he saying?"

August cradled the back of her father's head, tilted it back, and poured water over his lips. Harrison's eyes gazed at the sky. The water poured over a wide smile, dripping down his neck.

"Do you see that?" Harrison said, awed. The water gurgled his words.

August stopped pouring and followed Harrison's gaze upward, at the blue sky. They all did. There was nothing there.

August looked at Theo mournfully.

She gave the smallest shake of her head, denying his pity.

"I'm thirsty," Harrison said, suddenly sounding clearheaded.

August put the water to Harrison's lips again, and this time, he drank. Billy loosened his hold and gently ran a thumb over her arm.

She felt the ground beneath her return.

Harrison's face fell into a scowl when he noticed his daughter.

"Get your hands off her!" Harrison yelled with a renewed clarity. Water sprayed from his lips. August blinked and stood to his feet, wiping his face.

As August screwed the cap back on the canteen, he glanced at Theo and said to Billy, "Like a hawk, you hear me?"

Billy nodded and August stepped toward the horses, motioning for Flea and Pathfinder to follow. Harrison tilted his head back to the sky, staring in wonder, his mouth hanging open. His neck was colored in purples and reds the noose left behind.

"Dad?" Theo tried again.

Harrison smiled at the sound of her voice, but he didn't seem to otherwise know she was just a few feet away from him, let alone on the same planet as him.

"What's wrong with him?" Theo said, her voice strained.

"I think . . ." Billy didn't continue that thought, He dropped his voice real low and asked, "Did August hurt you? Are you okay?"

"No," she whispered. She didn't spare him a glance, for both the sake of optics and for not wanting to take her eyes off her father. "You?"

"You have *no* idea how hard that was for me to do nothing while he—"

"I do know," she whispered. "I do. But you did exactly the right thing."

"Theo—"

"Rook and Spartan," Theo said as she looked around camp for any sign of the missing men.

"Gone," Billy said.

"My brothers?" Theo asked in a small voice.

She saw him shake his head in her periphery. "I don't know about Jude, but the older one . . . Zeke?" He held her steady. "I'm sorry, Theo."

Her legs went weak. "*No*," she said. She looked over to her father. He was crying. Silent tears, quietly shaking shoulders. He was still staring at the sky. She'd never seen him cry before.

"I'm so sorry," Billy whispered again.

Theo glared at Flea and Pathfinder, who were holding council with August, standing closely, speaking quietly. "Who killed him?" she asked.

"I don't know."

"Where—" her voice cracked. "Where is he?"

Billy sent a strained glance over the cliffs.

She ripped her arm from Billy. "How *could* you!" she sobbed. The men glanced at her outburst but continued talking.

She once again had the urge to run, but instead she fell to her knees.

Billy crouched in front of her as she sat back onto her ankles.

Her body was limp in defeat, everything dulled, even the pain in her side. She held on to the seared bullet wound to remind herself of it.

"Billy?" she said cautiously, checking to see if he was still with her.

His face cracked slightly, and the way he darted his eyes to the remnants of the gang to see if they'd noticed, told Theo he still was. He nodded and sniffed and tried to return the mask to his face, the one that told everyone he was Sixer. He pulled out his gun for good measure. "I'm not going to let anything happen to you," he whispered. He leaned forward, placing his hand next to her knee. Out of sight from the gang, he touched his fingers against her leg.

She put her hand over his. He held her hand tight.

Her father started quivering, his eyes rolled nearly to whites.

"Daddy," she said, rising to her feet.

His body slipped askew against the tree he was tied to.

"*Dad*," she said again. Nobody tried to stop her as she went to her father's side. His cheek fell into her palm, white foam beginning to bubble through his lips.

"Hey!" she said to him, to August, to Billy, to *any*one. "Dad—hey, help me!" She pulled at his rope but couldn't get it free. "August, *help me*!" she pleaded.

August appeared at her side, knelt gently there. He had his revolver drawn again, the muzzle pressed into the grass.

"He's seizing," August said. "He won't survive this."

She heard him cock the hammer and she screamed *no* at August.

"I'm sorry, Youngblood," he rumbled quietly. "Mercy is all we can offer at this point."

Theo turned her head to look August in the face. "And what do you know about mercy, August Gaines."

The gunshot made her startle. The involuntary jolt broke her tears free, but she never took her eyes from August, even as he put a bullet in her father's head, not when August replied, "Everything there is to know, Youngblood."

"Sixer," she heard August say over the high-pitched whine in her ears.

He gave Billy the two-finger beckon, and a moment later, Billy took August's place at her side. He helped her to her feet and began to guide her away from her dead daddy. Theo knew she shouldn't look, but she also knew she couldn't not, but it didn't make it any better when she did. She slammed her eyes shut the second she did, allowed Billy to guide her steps because she wasn't sure she ever wanted to open her eyes again.

Then there was another gunshot. Her mental chaos didn't register the start of another descent into the physical kind. And for a moment, nobody did. Not until a third and fourth and fifth—*pop, pop, pop*—echoed in quick succession.

"The horses!" Pathfinder hollered.

The horses? Theo thought.

Pathfinder yelled a curse foul and frightening as he sprinted into the woods.

Two more shots, quick and lethal.

August made a noise of despair.

Billy was dragging her backward. Five horses lay slain.

Flea was pressed against a tree, his rifle scanning the ones above.

Another shot popped through the scatter.

Billy had Theo by the hand, pulling her through the labyrinth of trees, running as fast as she could keep up. He held a gun in his other hand, pointed at nothing as he ducked and wove every time there was the sound of gunfire.

Two shots sounded in frightening succession.

He stopped at an old, thick tree and pressed her back against it. She caved her body to be as narrow as possible, holding her hands over her ears as Billy shielded her, wedging her body between his and the tree. He aimed over her shoulder, around the tree. He fired. The loudness was obscene and disorienting. He aimed and fired, thumbed the hammer and fired again. He did so until the chambers were empty.

Yanking his gun back, he caged his arms over her head, cocooning around her. The roughness of his stubble pressed against the short shear of her scalp. Bark sprayed around them, on one side, then the other, accompanied by the *crack* of the frightening onslaught of Lucas's ambush.

Billy said something in her ear, but she couldn't hear it. Everything was echoes and ringing.

He said something again, this time loud enough for her to hear. "*Point!*" he said.

She shook her head. "My dad . . . Zeke . . ." Nothing felt real.

Grabbing her by the side of her head in one hand, the heat of the pistol against the other, he leaned out just enough for her to see his face. He was so close to her. His face was almost touching hers. "*Which way's east?*"

She looked to the left, then to the right. Skyward, past the tops of the trees.

Billy dumped the spent shells and reloaded the chambers.

"Point." He thumbed back both revolvers. "*East.*"

She looked up at him. He was no longer wearing his hat. She realized it had been a while since he had it. The last time she saw him wearing it was the night she threw bullets into the fire.

Come to think of it, that was the last time she had hers. The most absurd thoughts could run through a person's head when their world was imploding.

Theo pointed at Billy, through him: east.

He nodded, stepped back, and said, "Now run."

He must have seen the terror in her eyes because Billy reminded her, "I'm not going to let anything happen to you."

She was clutching his coat at his chest. Her instinct was to draw him back to her, close, not run in the opposite direction. Again, as if to read on her face what was going through her head, he said, "I won't let you out of my sight. I'm right behind you. *Go.*"

She ducked under and around him. Immediately, the symphony of Billy's guns chorused behind her.

As she found herself once again running for her life, it finally clicked for Theo. It finally made sense how Lucas had evaded August for so long. Even if she could anticipate his next move, an architect of stratagem will always be confounded by the face of mayhem.

CHAPTER

32

The air smelled like gunpowder.

Theo felt caged. Her body was balled as small as she could make it. She had her hands over her ears even though the gunfire had quit minutes ago.

Billy was pressed against her in the hollowed crevice of an old tree.

"Deep breaths," he said quietly. Scanning, his eyes on everything all at once—the heights of the trees, the floor of the forest, to the right, to the left, and back around again—he pulled a hand off her ear and repeated what he'd said. The muzzle of his gun followed the sweep of his eyes.

"You put everything out of your mind," he continued. "It's no different than what you've been doing."

Her eyes were wide. "He killed all the horses," Theo said. "*Why?*"

A bird somewhere nearby sang a cautious melody, the first sign of wildlife recovering from the violence.

Billy adjusted his body in the small hollow and lowered his revolver to rest upon a knee, but he never stopped surveying their vantage.

Theo raked her hands through her short hair, feeling like she was losing her mind. "He could have killed August or me or you or *anyone*. He—" She couldn't do this. She couldn't outsmart madness. "We should run," she whispered.

"Maybe." She didn't like the way he said that. That was a placating maybe. That was a maybe that was waiting for her to get to a conclusion he'd already drawn. "But not yet," he added.

She pressed the heels of her hands against her eyes, shaking her head.

"Tell me what you need."

"A minute." She wrapped her fingers over his free hand, and for the first time since they wedged themselves into their hiding spot, he looked at her. He tightened his hand over hers. Their faces were close. His eyes were a deep brown, almost indistinguishable against pupils. He had a total of three freckles, two above one eyebrow, one just below the same eye.

"Maybe two," she said.

He nodded and angled his body slightly, lifting his arm over her head. She rotated and curled against him, knees drawn to her chest.

Her heart slowed. "An argument could be made for three," she said into the collar of his coat.

"Take as long as you need," he said softly into the top of her head. "We should stay hidden for a while anyway."

She nodded and held on to him. For a long time, they said nothing.

Billy finally broke the silence. "Theo."

The barbs that twisted inside her softened and went pliable but twisted all the same when he said her name.

"Please don't," Theo replied just as quietly.

"Don't what?"

"Apologize. You don't owe me anything."

"It ain't about owing." He paused. "I'm sorry for what I did to Elliot. I'll—" He swallowed. "I'll carry it with me to my grave."

They were still and quiet in Theo's uncertainty what to say next.

"Was it over fast?" she whispered.

He took a breath. "I—"

"Don't answer that."

"It's never over fast enough," Billy muttered.

Theo swallowed the uncomfortable pressure of anguish in her throat.

"If I could change it, Theo—"

Theo wanted to tell him to stop talking, but she kept quiet until he finished the thought.

"I wish he'd killed me instead."

"I don't," Theo said, not because it was the right thing to say, but because it was the truth. "It shouldn't have been you or him. That's not a choice you should have had to make." She swiped a tear away. "It's not your fault, and I don't blame you for it."

"I'm not deserving of that."

No, you aren't, Theo wanted to say. But it wouldn't have been out of malice, it would have been from her growing ideology that nobody deserves anything because deserve and receive are constantly engaging in an unethical warfare, but that was a conversation for another time. Right now, all she could think about was the mindless circles that Billy was sketching on her arm, such a small, thoughtless tic that was completely and utterly wrecking her ability to have any negative thoughts about him or the careless ways of the Universe.

"Do you think we should cut our losses?" she asked him.

His fingers went still. "Did you hear how fast his bullets fired?" The uneasiness in Billy's voice finally gave reason to why that particular ambush felt specifically terrifying, why that *maybe* was so uncertain.

"Haas has a weapon I've never seen before," Billy continued. "He shot eight horses with eight rounds without a single pause to reload. In order to make those shots, he'd have to have a long-distance, high-capacity weapon. Any rifle I've ever seen is single-load. He's got this kind of firepower? And now he's the only one who's got horses."

In the chaos and its aftermath, Theo hadn't been able to put words to it. But now that he defined it, she saw how single-handed carnage of that magnitude could elevate terror into something bigger.

"He's trapped us up here," she said.

To punctuate that, a gunshot shouted somewhere in the woods. Theo jolted and pressed her free hand over her mouth, silencing things that wanted to escape her.

Billy pressed them against the curve of the hollow even though they were already as deep as they could go.

The trees went silent again.

"Shh—shh," Billy said as if he could feel the scream that was rising in her chest. He had raised his gun again, holding it at the edge of the opening.

There was another gunshot, and this time it was answered with two quick ones, a deadly conversation that Theo hoped didn't involve Jude.

Theo squeezed her cheeks harder, clenching her teeth.

"He's picking them off," Billy whispered.

She pressed closer and felt the hammer of Billy's pulse matching her own, but when she looked down at the gun in his hand, she couldn't believe the steadiness there. It was an art form that Billy had mastered, to disagree with his panic.

There was one more *crack* that sounded like it might be a little closer, and then, silence again.

They were frozen in place, not daring to speak, not daring to move, and only when Billy finally lowered the gun to rest his arm across his knee did Theo lower her hand from her mouth.

The hammering of their hearts slowed.

"We should stay hidden until sundown," Theo whispered.

"Agreed."

"And then—"

She stopped.

"I'll think of something," she said.

"I know you will."

They were quiet for a while after that, listening to the noises of the woods return. Chirps and melodies resumed. Small scurries in the leaves and underbrush became bold. As Theo came down from adrenaline, she felt heavy with fatigue. She didn't know how long they sat in silence—an hour, maybe two—holding on to one another, listening for danger, waiting for it. But in that span of time, it surprised Theo how quickly unrest could return. Not quite boredom, but something close to it.

In it, Theo's mind began to work on something.

"He's going to find us." Her words sounded loud after the long stretch of silence even though she spoke in a whisper.

Billy didn't say anything. She didn't blame him. To disagree would be a lie; to agree would admit their death sentence. But the truth was that Lucas could outlast their hiding just as easily as he could outrun their attempt on foot.

Running wasn't an option and hiding was delaying inevitability.

"I need you to promise me something," she said.

"Promise you what?"

"Take the shot," she said. "The moment you have it, you take it."

"Haas?" Billy said.

Theo nodded.

"I can't make that promise."

"Why?"

"Because if I could keep it without risking your life, you wouldn't ask me to make it."

"He killed all the horses instead of taking August out. Why would he do that?"

Billy just shook his head.

"*Why, Billy?*" She needed to hear him say it. She needed to know that he understood what they were up against.

Reluctantly: "Because this is a game to him."

"We either play it, or we don't. Two choices. That's it."

She felt his throat bob when he took a hard swallow.

Finally, he said, "What's the option that gets you out of this alive?"

She shook her head. She didn't want to tell him that option, not really. There were too many unknowns, and she didn't like those very much.

In the end, Theo told him.

He was quiet for a while after that. Then he whispered, "That's not much of a choice either."

"No. It's not." She hugged her arm over his chest. "Just take the shot, Billy."

Another stretch of quiet passed, and fatigue returned, weighing heavier. Theo had the urge to give in to sleep as equally as she felt like bursting out of their hiding spot and running as fast as she could. She closed her eyes and saw death. She opened them and the peace made her homicidal.

This restlessness took hold and wouldn't let go.

Billy breathed steadily. He continued to sketch her arm, seemingly deep in thought.

Although there were layers between them, her skin felt hot where his fingers traced.

Theo's voice was small when she asked, "Do you trust me?"

He leaned back a little and she tilted her head to look up at him.

"Yes," he said.

She moved her hand up his chest and touched his chin, looking at his lips.

Carefully, Billy set his revolver in the crook of the soil and decaying trunk as his eyes danced slowly across her face.

He placed his palm over her cheek so his fingertips touched the length of her neckline. When he brushed his thumb under her eye, her skin flushed.

"I ain't sure this is a good idea," he said.

"I think we ran out of those a while ago."

He smiled and then his lips were touching hers.

She snaked her hand up until it was clutching the back of his head and her fingers were tangled in his hair. She kissed him deeper, and he inhaled slowly, tracing her eyebrow with his thumb, then her jawline with his fingertips.

An urgency built quickly, an agreement that they'd both been wanting to do this for a while. But underneath, Theo could feel his hesitation, the invisible things between them and around them, things that had already happened and things they had yet to face that made the thought of yielding to this, to the notion of *them*, nearly unbearable.

She pulled back. "Where do you stand on that sureness now?"

"Well," he said. He felt along her short hair, gently touching the knife-scrape on her scalp as he inspected it. It gave her chills when his hold settled back on her neck. "I still ain't sure if it's a good idea. But I *am* sure I don't care."

Billy put another kiss on the smile he'd bidden, and she tilted her head back, leaning into the cradle his fingers created, hypnotized by the way his lips danced with hers, the way his touch seemed to be trying to memorize every piece of exposed skin.

Billy broke off abruptly and had his gun outstretched through the wide opening of the hollow before Theo could register any threat.

The birdsong had quieted again.

"I wouldn't." The voice that was unmistakably Blacksmith/Haas/Mansford sounded out of place to Theo's ears. It brought back countless good memories and conjured unfair feelings of security. She had a flash of her confrontation with Patrick in the street, how seeing

Blacksmith up on those steps made her believe that nothing bad was going to happen to her as long as he was there. She didn't realize just how unafraid she'd truly been of August until she turned and saw Blacksmith aiming his rifle at her head.

Billy's thumb rested on the hammer.

"You press that hammer down," Lucas said, "then I pull this trigger."

"Brody," Theo whispered.

Billy swallowed. The bed of his fingernail turned white, but he didn't apply enough pressure to depress the hammer. Speed in a standoff doesn't only rely on movement and mechanism, it's equal parts reading a person, telling whether or not the other person will hesitate.

"Put it down, son." The tranquility on Blacksmith's face wasn't calmness, it was madness. "Nobody needs to get hurt."

Take the shot, Billy. TAKE THE SHOT.

But Theo didn't think he would.

CHAPTER

33

Lucas closed the distance between them and pressed the end of the long barrel against Theo's temple. When Lucas reached down and wrapped his hand around Billy's gun, Billy didn't fight him.

No no no no no Billy, she wanted to holler. But it was too late.

Lucas stepped back and swung his rifle onto his back.

"You first, hon," Lucas said to Theo, aiming the revolver at Billy.

For a moment, Billy's grip on her went firm and desperate, but then he let go.

"Nice and slow," he said when it was Billy's turn to leave the hollow.

Billy complied.

"Come on, boy, don't give me a reason to shoot you. Hands in a safe place now."

Billy interlocked his fingers behind his head.

"Stop right there," Lucas told him. "You," he told Theo, "disarm him."

She went to him, paused, then reached for the buckle of the holster slung low on his hips.

"Shh—*quiet*," Lucas said suddenly.

In Lucas's brief distraction as he strained to listen for a threat, peering past them into the woods, Theo looked up at Billy and he flicked his eyes downward, ever so slightly bowing his left hip toward her. She slipped her hand into the front pocket that his hip indicated and found the long bone handle of her straight razor.

She confiscated it.

"Okay, quickly now," Lucas said.

Theo unlatched the leather strap, rolled it back on its tongue, and let the holster drop to the ground.

Billy kicked it away and Lucas said, "Let's move."

Thirty minutes later, they came to a tree with two horses tied. Likely the last two up on this mountain.

"Did August tell you how many men I killed in the war?" Lucas asked as he pulled something out of his pocket.

"Forty-three confirmed kills, sir," Billy answered.

"You know how?" Lucas asked as he came close to Billy and pressed the revolver into his throat.

"Lucas—" Theo tried.

"Everyone behaves, everyone stays alive. Yeah?" Lucas said.

Theo nodded.

"You're a sniper," Billy said calmly as if there were no threat to his life.

Satisfied with that answer, Lucas conducted a thorough search of Billy's person, running his hand down one leg, up the inseam, his crotch, up and down the other leg; then along his torso, squeezing the lining of his jacket and emptying the pockets; he felt along the hems, going slow over the rivets. The only other weapon Lucas found was the knife that intersected his spine.

"Get up on that mare," Lucas told him.

Billy's forehead creased, sending Theo an uneasy glance, but he complied. Lucas followed him, and after he'd mounted, Lucas pressed the revolver into the backside of Billy's knee.

Haas reached into one of his pockets and pulled out a pair of state-of-the-art round bow shackles. "Cuff yourself to the pommel," he instructed.

Billy did as he was told, every compliance a little more hesitant than the last.

Haas mounted the other and tied the mare's lead line to the gelding's saddle horn. "Try to keep up, little Creed," he called over his shoulder.

Billy gave Theo a look of frightened concern.

"She's injured, Mr. Haas. Let me be on foot."

"I aim to shoot the person on the horse if the person on foot can't keep up," Haas said. "And I'd much rather shoot you."

"We haven't eaten in two days. Please, Mr. Haas. The mare can handle the weight of the both of us."

"Yeah, you'd like that, wouldn't you?" Haas clicked his horse into a trot, tugging the mare up to pace.

Theo muttered a curse and began to jog after them.

Two hours later, the sun was about halfway through the sky. Theo's lungs were rattling and burning from gasping at frigid air. She stumbled to a resting lean against a tree, doubled over and clutching the wound at her side. Theo had never felt true hunger before, the kind that feels like it's burning a hole in your stomach, like a monster was in there eating you from the inside. Those pangs were becoming as loud as the pain of the seared bullet wound. Her stomach was starting to cramp, and she knew her legs were next.

"Lucas!" she called after him.

He turned the horses around and trotted back to Theo. In the bright midday light, she could finally get a good look at the man she had grown up knowing as Bram Blacksmith. There was no Blacksmith left there. His usually clean-shaven face was lost in an emerging tangle of a heavily salted beard. His countenance was cruel, as sometimes happens when one no longer needs to heed to the accountability of civilization.

If August Gaines was the man preaching anarchy while brutally enforcing his dictatorship, Lucas Haas was the man who would kick you off a cliff and, watching you fall, he would shake his head and criticize gravity.

Lucas regarded Theo. "The day's only just begun, Theodora." He leaned down and grabbed the gold around her neck, yanking it off. Tossing it onto the trail behind them, he said, "You disappoint me." He pulled out his gun and leveled it at Billy.

"If you shoot him, Lucas," Theo panted, "I will scream and scream and I will never stop fighting you."

Haas snorted a laugh. "I should hope so."

Theo felt her mind racing, scrambling to come up with something.

He smiled at her silence. Reveled in her obvious uncertainty.

"I'll tell you what, darling," Lucas said. He popped out the cylinder of his revolver and emptied the bullets. "We'll do this fairly." He pocketed the bullets. All except one. That one, he thumbed back into one of the six chambers.

"Lucas—" Theo said.

He spun the cylinder and snapped it back into place. It happened so fast. Too fast. Billy watched with a heaving chest.

"*Please!*" she cried.

Lucas aimed his gun back at Billy's head, cocked the hammer, and pulled the trigger.

Theo fell to her knees. A noise came out of her that may have been a scream if she hadn't already been robbed of all the air in her lungs.

Blacksmith holstered his pistol.

Theo looked up at Billy. His jaw was set tight. She wanted to reach out to him. To tell him it was going to be okay.

But Lucas was already moving on, tugging the mare to catch up.

"The odds get worse every time, little Creed," Lucas said as he trotted down the trail.

For a while after that, Theo kept up. She didn't let Billy out of her sight.

Around noon, Theo collapsed.

"Get up," Blacksmith said. He stopped their horses. He took his gun out and aimed at Billy. "Get up, Creed."

She tried and she failed.

He pulled back the hammer.

She screamed more pleas.

He pulled the trigger.

On hands and knees, she sobbed.

"Get up, Creed."

When she looked up, she found that Lucas hadn't lowered the gun. He pulled the hammer back again.

She clawed her way to her feet.

He holstered and kept on.

The next time she collapsed, she retched. The muscles in her legs were seizing. Every breath felt like it was shredding her throat and lungs.

"Okay, little Creed." Haas swung down. "You lasted longer than I thought."

He rubbed her back gently as she dry heaved. He somehow made her grateful that he was no longer causing anguish. She felt discordantly comforted from the very terror he had cultivated.

She couldn't look at him. At either of them.

She stared at single spot on the ground in front of her, focusing on all the rage, all the pain, and all the things she was going to do about it.

Should've taken the shot, Billy.

CHAPTER 34

They didn't stop to rest until sundown.

For Theo, everything hurt. She was beginning to see things that weren't there. She was starting to lose gaps of time. More than once, after Lucas had given her the sweet relief of horseback, she had been jerked awake by slipping down the side of the horse, just in time to catch and right herself. She rode behind Lucas, her head frequently against his back and her arms around his waist. It was a unique kind of torture.

Lucas swung down first, then helped Theo off. Her legs refused to work, and Lucas left her on the ground where she landed. He told Billy to dismount, then took the saddle off the mare and secured it to the tree, leaving Billy cuffed to it.

He armed himself with all the weapons.

"Eat," he said, dropping a saddlebag full of food on the ground in front of her.

Theo frowned at him as he hiked up a steep incline, leaving them to their own devices. Theo didn't wait to tear through the saddle bags. She guzzled water as she slung the pack over her shoulder, pushing painfully to her feet, and tripped her way over to Billy. Crumpling aside him, she put the water to his lips, and he finished the water in several huge pulls.

He shoved his wet chin across his shoulder, rested his head back against the tree, and closed his eyes briefly. Theo found packages of dried, salted beef, rolls of hard biscuits, dried apricots, cans of peaches and beans, and a foil of broken chocolate.

She fed them mouthfuls, trying to remember to not go too fast.

"How's your side, troublemaker?"

"It's fine."

"It hurt?"

"Constantly." Her voice was low and her eyes were shifty toward the woods where Lucas had disappeared into. "We could run."

Billy pointed upward, his eyes going skyward. Then he shook his head.

"He won't miss."

"What's he doing?" Theo whispered. "Where did he go?"

"Getting eyes on August."

"What if August isn't alive?" Theo asked with a thin desperation.

"Look at me," Billy said.

She did.

"Lucas wouldn't be doing this if August were dead," he said.

She pressed her palm to her forehead, angry with herself. She was spent. Her mind was scrambled.

"He's doing this on purpose, you know. He's running you ragged so you can't think straight. Trying to keep you scared so that's all you're thinking about." He paused, then added softly, "Stop letting him use me for that."

"I don't know if I can do that."

"Yes. You can. August is coming for us, just like you said. Remember the plan. Outsmart this asshole."

"*Plan*?" Theo laughed thinly, feeling delirious.

"Theo." He waited until she was looking at him again. "Be patient."

Her eyes stung.

The cost of patience was uncertainty, and Theo didn't know how to pay that price when it was roulette with Billy's life.

"Come here," he said.

Theo crawled under his elbow and curled and settled there, enveloped in his long limbs, the beat of his heart in her ear.

"Wait for that final card," he whispered. "And then you tell me when it's time to play it."

She nodded. "I—" She didn't continue.

"What is it, Theo?"

"I think it's going to cost a lot."

He was quiet for a little. She listened to his steady breathing. "That's okay," he finally whispered back. "I owe a lot."

Then he made his body snug around hers and moments later, they didn't fall asleep so much as they couldn't stay conscious.

Theo awoke to something wrenching on her ankle.

Lucas had his claws around her leg, yanked her from the illusion of comfort, and was dragging her across the carpet of pines and cones and pebbles.

Theo twisted her body, clawed at the earth, and kicked at Lucas.

He dropped her leg and she scrambled backward slightly.

"Get up. Time to go."

She glared at him for a moment. She gave Billy a glance. His eyes shot back and forth between Lucas and Theo, his body strained against his constraints.

Then she pushed to her feet, fishing for the razor up her sleeve as she did. She slung the blade open as she leaped forward, and sliced at Lucas.

He dodged backward, avoiding a deadly blow. Instead, the blade fell across his cheek, carving a straight line from his ear down to his jaw. Lucas made a noise of surprised pain but didn't hesitate for a moment. He caught her wrist and kicked her legs out from under her. He stepped on her neck as he twisted the razor out of her hand.

Theo clawed on his leg as she gasped for breath.

"Shut up," Lucas hollered at Billy.

Lucas touched the opening in his face. "Fuck's sake," he muttered. His beard was drenched red. "Okay, little Creed." He took his boot off her neck. "All right then." He beckoned her to her feet and said, "We'll do it your way."

"Lucas—" Billy said.

"One more word out of your mouth, boy. Go on. One more."

"Please," he said.

"That's the one." He took hold of Theo's arm and pulled her to her feet. But her lungs still refused to draw air, breath knocked out.

"Lucas!" Billy yelled. "Listen to me—"

Lucas stopped, put a finger up to Theo. "Give me a second."

"If you do anything to hurt—"

He walked back to Billy and landed a blow to his head. "You'll what, boy?" He hit him again. "What are you going to do?" He kicked him in the ribs.

Billy wheezed and coughed, blood pouring from his lip.

Lucas cupped a palm behind his ear mockingly. "What's that? That's right. You'll bleed, that's what you'll do, because that's all you can do."

Billy drew his knees to the splintering pain in his side.

Theo's breath returned with a gasp. Billy made a helpless noise when Lucas dragged her out of sight.

They didn't go far.

Lucas lowered himself onto a rock, rested the revolver on a knee, and said, "Undress."

She did, and as she stood there, arms crossed protectively over her chest, Lucas went through her clothes. Finding nothing else, he studied the straight razor. He turned it over in his hand, admiring his own craftsmanship. He slid the razor from the scales, ran the edge across his thumb, smearing his own blood against it, and smiled.

Clicking it shut, he said, "Turn."

After he was satisfied she had no other weapons on her person, he gave her clothes one more inspection, then said, "Why did you do it, Theodora?" The scruff on his cheek was dripping blood, but he completely ignored it. He stood and held the razor up. "You had this at his throat and you let him live."

He saw. Again, she didn't need the confirmation, but it was good to have it.

"What are you smiling about?" Lucas snapped.

"You've had his head in your sites. Why did you?"

He clicked the razor shut. "Call out for August."

She glared at him. *August must be close. Close enough to fluster him into making poor decisions, but not close enough to make him a threat.*

"You can do it or I can make you," Lucas said.

She gave him a taunting laugh as tears tracked down her face. "You can give it your best shot."

He stood, walked to her, and reached down to the mess at her waist. "Do you know why I picked up the forging trade?" He squeezed, his thumb gouging at the tender skin. Her face twisted and she gritted her teeth, her body caving and buckling under the piercing pressure. "I like taking something hard and immovable and watching it turn red in the fire before I bang it into whatever shape I please."

Theo didn't make a sound.

Lucas removed his hand with an air of irritation and admiration both.

"And how many times, Mr. Blacksmith," she said, snarling through the pain, "have you been burned by the fire of your own forge?"

"Do you understand that I was trying to give you the benefit of the doubt—you brought this on yourself."

"It would be a mistake, Mr. Haas, to give me any benefit amid any doubt."

"God," he laughed. "You're him. No wonder he likes you so much."

"If you got in the same room with him, he'd crush you. *I'd* crush you if I weren't a fraction your size."

He smiled softly. "Get dressed," he said.

She did, maneuvering around the renewed pain in her side.

When they came back into view, relief washed over Billy.

"Sit," Lucas told Theo with a shove. He walked over to Billy and flicked open the razor.

Theo's eyes bounced in panic. "Wait—Lucas, please."

He crouched next to Billy and said, "Let's soften that steel, little Creed."

"I'll do whatever you want, Lucas," she said as she caught Billy's eye, who was keeping his composure like a statue.

"I know you will, honey." Lucas pressed the edge against Billy's jaw. "But you've just really provoked me," he said.

Billy tensed but made no movements otherwise.

"No—don't—*please,*" she said.

"Call out for him."

Her eyes filled as she nodded. "August," she tried, but she had no air in her chest.

Lucas dragged the blade down, slicing the edge of Billy's face open.

Billy choked out a sob, slamming his eyes shut.

"*August!*" Her voice echoed through the hillsides.

"That should do it." He wiped the blood on the buckskin at Billy's shoulder. "Let's go."

Theo's thoughts raced with wrath. Her body rattled with exhaustion.

Billy wouldn't look at her.

His chest shrank and expanded rapidly, eyebrows pulled tight, and mouth pressed tightly shut. Blood dripped down his jaw and landed on his shoulder.

This anguish was an impossible thing to hold with clarity. In that moment, she figured she'd sacrifice just about anything to make Lucas pay for the things he'd done.

REFERENDUM

PRIDE IS A SHORT GAME;
SURVIVAL IS THE LONG CON.

CHAPTER
35

The inn was a single open space: on the left side, a giant fireplace took up much of the wall, a centerpiece to the rectangular dining table and grizzly hide spread on the ground. On the right side of the structure, eight bunks lined the wall. In the center, a straight island bar framed the stone oven behind it. Polished iron poles that stretched from bar top to ceiling, one on either side of the island, glimmered in the sunlight they let in.

Lucas cased the place, dead-bolting the front and rear doors. He paused before the fireplace as if admiring it. He touched the stone masonry and ran his hand along the oak mantel. He stopped. Metal scraped against wood when Lucas dragged something across it. He picked it up and held it in front of him. It was an iron poker. He felt the sharpness of its tip.

As he did so, Theo saw that it was time to play her final card. She may only have a single club to Lucas's aces, but she still had the turn and the river to consider, and maybe, just maybe, those would turn up flush.

She rose to the tips of her toes and kissed Billy like it was the last time she ever would—two birds, one stone, and all that.

Lucas came over and yanked her away, muttering, "Insufferable teenagers."

"Sit," he told her, shoving her into a chair. "Hands flat on the table." She obeyed.

"And you," he said to Billy. "There." He pointed at a stool at the end of the bar.

Billy sat and Lucas cuffed him to the iron pole.

"What will you do after?" Theo asked. And when Lucas didn't respond, she continued. "After you've killed us and made August suffer and once you're the big bad jackass of the mountain, then what will you do with your life?"

Lucas smiled idly as he peeked through the windows again. Then he came up behind Theo, grabbed her under her armpit, and dragged her out of the chair. He placed his hand against her collar, pushing her against the log wall as he kept an eye out the window.

"Be still," he said.

He left her there and kicked the chair back so he could stand at the head of the table, putting Theo on his left, and farther across the room, Billy on his right. He set the iron rod on the table and switched out revolvers. He popped open the cylinder.

"Huh," Lucas said. "Look at that." He angled so Theo could see the chambers. She saw that one more round of Russian roulette would have been the death of Billy.

Billy and Theo exchanged a quiet glance from across the room.

Lucas dropped the bullet into his hand and set it upright on the table.

Dark red plastered the side of Billy's face. He kept his hands still and calm. His shoulders curled menacingly over his body and his legs were drawn to the top rung of the barstool. Theo thought he looked like a loaded weapon, a coiled viper, a crouching wolf. His hair fell down his forehead and over his eyes, a glower that was downright palpable when he cast it at Lucas.

She shook her head at him.

His jawline flared but he remained otherwise motionless.

Lucas snapped the empty cylinder back into place. He picked up the poker as he went back over to Theo.

His attention was momentarily drawn outside. He pressed her against the wall as he stared out the window.

"Impeccable," Lucas said, presumably about the approach of August.

Then he drew the iron rod behind him and drove the apexed end through Theo's shoulder.

Theo screamed.

"Theo!" Billy yelled.

"While you wait," Lucas said to Theo. "You can ponder the defiance that led you to this moment." He flipped the gun to hold it by its barrel.

Theo was gasping at breath, her bound hands touching around the impale.

He stepped back up to her, shoved her hands away, and placed his own hand there, and then, as if to steady a nail for a hammer, he swung the hilt of the gun against the head of the rod that he'd impaled in the triangle of her armpit and collarbone. He hammered, driving the poker deeper through her flesh and into a groove of the log wall on the other side.

"Lucas—Jesus Christ—STOP!" Billy yelled.

She screamed again, clutching the poker in an attempt to counteract it. Every time she tried to reach for it, Lucas swatted her hands away and hammered again. She didn't realize she was screaming August's name until Lucas returned to the table and sat heavily back into his chair to reload his revolver.

"Theo," Billy was saying. "Theo. Look at me. Look at me."

She let out a screaming breath, gasped one in, and screamed one out again.

"It's okay," Billy said calmly. "We are going to get out of this. Do you hear me? You're going to be okay."

Theo nodded, weeping. Her hands hovered shakily around the rod, fingertips brushing the iron.

Lucas ignored the commotion, only stared out the window, guns ready.

"You are going to be okay," Billy repeated. "I promise. I *promise*."

She kept nodding, trying to convince herself of the same thing.

"Shut up," Lucas said.

Billy kicked his chair away. "I'm going to kill you!" He yanked and pulled, his back arched and his arms strained as he set all of his weight against the futile effort of resisting his constraints. Billy hopped up onto the bar top and began stomping the pole and shoving his shoulder into it.

"Hey," Lucas said. "*Hey!*" He yelled at Billy. "Calm down. *Sit* down!"

Billy slid to his knees and pressed his forehead against the pole, gripping it until his fingers turned white. The handle to the back door slid downward and Lucas laid one gun across his chest, the barrel pointed at Theo, and the other he appraised at the rattling door.

"Things are bound to get emotional," Lucas said as he watched the door. "Keep it down and let the adults speak."

"*Lucas!*" August bellowed from outside.

"Come on in, friend," Lucas called back.

Thuds began to shudder the door, and after about four heavy stomps, the nails on the deadbolt gave and the door splintered and gave, exploding inward with a cloud of swirling dust. August stood in the doorway, his gun aimed at Lucas's head the moment he found it.

Lucas pulled the trigger, and a spray of splinters burst just inches from Theo's head.

She cringed away from it, clutching the impale and squinting her eyes shut.

"August, please!" Billy yelled.

Lucas cocked the hammer again, inching his gun to the right so if he pulled the trigger again, it would splinter bone too.

August took a step forward, holding the gun in both his hands as he glanced across the room at Billy before he swept his gaze over to Theo. His mouth turned into a grim line as he assessed Theo, then his face turned homicidal as he regripped the weapon aimed at Lucas.

They said nothing to each other as they silently appraised the other. August, wondering if he could put a bullet in Lucas's brain before Lucas put one in Theo's; Lucas, pondering the same thing.

"You won't shoot her," August said, taking another step forward.

"You won't take that wager," Lucas said.

August sent her another glance and she let out a sob.

That's all it took. The tip of August's gun dropped slightly, and Lucas didn't let the moment pass. He pulled the trigger and August's gun flew from his grip. It clattered onto the floor and spun into the wall.

August growled and clutched his hand, the index finger mangled.

Lucas said: "Let's talk, you and I."

CHAPTER

36

The facts are as follows.

August met Lucas in 1830 at West Point Military Academy. Their friendship fast-tracked to a bond akin to brothers that sprouted from many similar ideals, specifically from their love of country and unwavering patriotism, coincidentally from the proximity of their respective hometowns in Texas. Four years later, they graduated and when they returned home, they traveled together. It was a hard journey home with many trials and conflicts along the way, but it was always the two of them against the world, in which the they occasionally emerged bloody but always unscathed and feeling invincible.

Upon their return home, Lucas met and fell in love with an English immigrant, but the woman had eyes for August, and so began the first plank that was wedged in the center of their friendship. Lucas conceded quietly, and after August married the Englishwoman, Lucas didn't see him or his wife until the 1844 presidential election, almost six years after the wedding that Lucas didn't attend. Neither August nor Lucas considered themselves petty men, and Lucas liked to think he held no ill will toward the man until he saw August in the Austin saloon which doubled as a polling location. At some point, Lucas had caught word that August's English wife couldn't hold a pregnancy, which softened Lucas's heart further on the matter. He had all but let it go until he saw August getting handsy with a local woman who was most certainly not the Englishwoman he'd married. Vowing to take the high road, Lucas greeted August with warmth and went to cast his vote. Like mostly everyone else who came to vote, he stayed to drink. And like it has always been and always will be, alcohol and politics blend very poorly together. Debates rose and Lucas kept drinking.

Lucas was an obnoxious man when he drank socially, the kind of person who liked to draw lines in the sand just to argue with people on the other side.

August voted for Henry Clay.

Lucas voted for James Polk.

At that polling station, the wedge between Lucas and August that started with the Englishwoman wedged deeper over political disagreements. August tried to subdue a very belligerent Lucas, which turned into flying fists and ended with August's knee on Lucas's neck. Lucas was humiliated. By the next morning, August and Lucas shook hands and shook off the scuffle as a drunken blip. They decided to put it behind them.

Two years later, President James Polk sent eighty men to the southernmost tip of Texas, near Brownsville, which sits on the western edge of the Gulf Coast. The sitting president had no intention of winning the battle, but he did intend to start a war. The destiny of America included the annexation of the southwest, and Polk would be damned if the Mexicans were going to encroach on the land that God had deemed the Union's.

August and Lucas were both a part of those eighty men.

Those eighty men ended up walking into an ambush. Of those eighty, fifteen were killed. Of the sixty-five, six were greatly wounded. The remaining fifty-nine were captured.

August was one of those six.

Lucas was one of the fifty-nine.

The American soldiers of what would later be called the Thornton Affair had been told they were being sent on a scouting mission, to report about the presence of Mexican soldiers in a long-disputed territory along the Texas border. When they were met with sixteen hundred Mexican soldiers, Polk went straight to Congress with his declaration of war, citing that American blood had been spilled on American soil. A provocation that left blood on boundary lines in the desert because one man said so, and that same man recommended international war as response. The direct result of the Mexican-American War was the ceding of what would become Texas, New Mexico, Arizona, Utah, Nevada, California, and parts of Colorado, Kansas, and Oklahoma.

The Mexican army had no interest in tending to the wounded of the conflict, so they sent them home.

As August returned home an American hero, Lucas remained imprisoned in Mexico. During that near two-year gap between Polk's inauguration and the Thornton Affair, Lucas had married a cattle rancher's daughter by the name of Maureen. When Lucas finally returned home after eleven months of being a POW, he found that August had wormed his way into the deep pockets of his family, left his English wife, and married Maureen. Lucas discovered that August had told his family that Lucas had died in battle.

Disillusioned, furious, and betrayed by both family and country, Lucas dug his heels into what would soon be the Confederacy as August began to pay attention to a congressman who was gaining notoriety.

Whig party congressman Abraham Lincoln fervidly condemned the war, disputed Polk's claims of the Thornton Affair, and called the conflict immoral and proslavery, which was both factual and damaging to Lincoln's reputation, an ironic reality that would prove to be not unique to the time period. The Mexican-American War was the passive-aggressive prelude to its far more violent progeny, and Polk was a prolific enslaver whose empire and wealth, like every other enslaver, was mostly, if not strictly, because the law said colored folks were not really people. The sitting president understood that bolstering the South with slave states could tip the scales in favor of the democrats. Polk had a personal, *financial* interest in leading the nation into a conflict with Mexico, which in turn aggravated domestic tension, ultimately detonating the deadliest war—by far—in American history.

Throughout this time, countless feuds were borne. It was an era when it was common for brother to turn on brother.

Upon Lucas's return, Maureen returned to her husband—the husband she was told had died.

August didn't understand how a woman who had once chosen him over Lucas, even when Lucas *wasn't* at war, would now choose to go back to Lucas now that he was home. August confronted Maureen, and when she held her ground, he lost his temper and killed her.

For Lucas, this all felt painfully familiar. First, with Elana the Englishwoman. Then, the affair with Maureen. August just couldn't let Lucas have something for himself, it seemed. So, Lucas decided to take the tide in his own hands and turn it himself. In retaliation, Lucas murdered August's three-month-old daughter.

On his way out of Texas, Lucas burned the Gaines plantation, vanishing with Elliot and a translucent little rock.

CHAPTER

37

August lowered himself into a chair, holding his mangled hand in his lap. "Why don't we let the kids go, Haas. You and me. Come on."

"Hand where I can see it," Lucas said.

August raised his broken and bleeding hand off his lap and placed it on the table.

"Why did you join the North, Gaines?" Lucas asked.

August looked heavenward, settling deeper into his chair. "Lucas . . ." He sighed deeply, shaking his head as he pulled out his pipe. "The South is doomed, that's why. But I ain't a soldier anymore and neither are you, so that ain't what this is about, is it?" He stuck the pipe in the corner of his mouth, lit a match—with difficulty—with one hand. He puffed the tobacco to life.

"Why did you kill her?" Lucas asked.

"*Nah*," came the enormous eruption of a growl from August's chest. "You ain't gonna do that. Her death's on you."

"Your turn—go ahead, ask," Lucas said.

"She was just a baby," August said. There was a slight tremble to his lips; he tightened them around the pipe and took a puff.

"She didn't belong to you any more than Maureen did."

"Belong," Theo scoffed quietly. Nobody heard her.

"You took my wife from me not just once. You had to kill her too," Lucas said.

"You said Lucas killed her," Theo said angrily, this time loud enough for them to hear.

"It was an accident," August said, barely audible.

Lucas was motionless.

"What are you talking about?" Theo asked, gripping the rod with bloodied fingerprints.

August was silent.

Lucas said, "When I came home, Maureen was completely destroyed. She told me she married August only because he could take care of her. She decided to stay with me and when August found out, he beat her to death."

"God," Theo whimpered.

"That's not what happened," August said, sending an imploring look at Theo.

"No?" Lucas snapped.

"I did hit her. But just once."

"Oh good, just once," Theo spat out, glaring at August.

"You hit her so hard, August—is this what you're telling me? You hit her so hard that she died? How do you hit someone, *once*, and have it *kill* them? That was a kind of rage that meant to be lethal. Don't say you didn't mean to. You meant to hit her that hard."

The room hung silent.

Theo caught Billy's eye, to whom she shook her head once again. She glanced back at August to see if he'd witnessed the exchange, and of course, he had.

The corner of his lip curled slightly, and there is where he shoved his pipe.

"Let me see if I've got this straight," Theo said, wincing as she readjusted her fingers around the impale. "You both went to war. While you got the short end of the stick," she pointed at Lucas while holding on to the rod in her chest before she turned her finger toward August: "you went home and married his wife. What ever happened to your *first* wife?" Theo asked in a bewildered, just-occurred-to-her sort of way. "Did she actually survive the two of you? Make it back to England?"

Lucas answered for August: "She returned home when she found out he was having an affair with Maureen."

"If Elana's dead, it has nothing to do with me," August muttered.

Theo shook her head, then to August: "Then, when you found out Maureen—shocker—actually wanted her husband back, the husband that *you* said was dead, you killed her?" Back to Lucas: "Then, in retaliation, you murdered an infant? To get back at him?" Back to August.

"I'll burn down the whole goddamn world if just to see August in a little bit of pain," Lucas said.

Theo leaned her head back onto the log wall and began to laugh. She couldn't believe Lucas just said, almost verbatim, the same thing she'd told August. Maniacal and delirious, she gasped at a laughing sob, shaking her head.

"This funny to you?" Lucas said.

Nodding, tears tracked down her face as laughter hitched out of her chest, then she shook her head. "Yeah, Mr. Blacksmith. It's a roaring *riot*. You like funny stories? Well, I got one of those too." She sent an aggrieved look to Billy. "Almost two weeks ago, I got put behind bars for stabbing an eighteen-year-old boy. His name was Patrick."

August settled into his chair, the creases in his forehead deepening.

Theo winced against the pain in her side, her shoulder, her face, *everywhere*, before continuing. "Two years ago, I had just turned fifteen. Patrick was a late bloomer, didn't hit a real growth streak until he turned sixteen, and by the time he was seventeen, he was thick with muscle, too. Around the same time, I became sexually appealing to him. Isn't that something? The same time a boy turns into a man, that's the same time he grows stronger than the thing he wants. What kind of joke does the Almighty think that is?" Theo sniffed an inhale and cried out an exhale, her face twisting in anguish as she held the skewer.

Billy leaned his forehead off the pipe he was chained to.

This time when their eyes met, Theo nodded at him.

Billy swiped his hand down his mouth, scowling.

"Sometimes," Theo continued, "in the summer months on nights when it was warm enough to look at the stars without a blanket, I would go to the stables. I always loved the smell of horses and straw. There was a loft in the stable and it had a hatch that you could open and just look at the sky." She leaned her head back and looked at a random spot in the ceiling as if to look out of a window there. "Sometimes I'd bring a book, sometimes I'd knit, sometimes I'd practice loading and unloading my gun, sometimes I'd bring nothing at all and just look at the stars. The first time Patrick laid hands on me was on one of those nights. It was late and I couldn't sleep. I grabbed a blanket to lie on and a lantern to see by, and as I was about to walk up the stairs, Patrick said, 'I thought that was you.' My heart dropped, you know? Like it always does every time I hear his voice." She gave a pointed look to Lucas. "Unfortunately, it wasn't one of the nights I brought a gun"—she lifted her unimpaired shoulder in a half shrug—"but what Patrick *didn't* know is that sometimes Elliot would meet me out there." This time, she managed a small, grimacing smile at Lucas. "Elliot never tried to kiss me or anything; it wasn't like that—we just always talked. We talked about books, we talked about philosophy, about politics and war, this girl he liked, and I remember he even once warned me about Patrick. 'He has eyes for you and the look in them aren't kind,' he'd said. I laughed him off even though I felt it too." Theo looked up at August, pausing. "I loved your son. He was the kindest person I'd ever met."

Theo paused again after that, turning to look at Billy who was watching her sternly and steadily. "That night when Patrick followed me out there, he had me cornered so fast I don't even remember how he did it. He kissed me on the mouth. He tasted like whiskey. I pushed him off me and I said, '*Please stop,*' and he took the lantern from my hand and shoved me into the wall."

"Youngblood," August said quietly.

Lucas watched her intently, but somehow blankly too.

"Didn't you want to know why I was in the Bladestay jail that morning? Well, Mr. Gaines, it wasn't because I tried to steal a horse." She looked around mockingly, then settled her gaze at Lucas. "And you wanted me to ponder the *defiance* that led me to this moment?" She spit out the word bitterly. "Well, it's a real damn *hoot.*" She sobbed out more laughter. She sent a look at Billy. The corners of his mouth were starting to tug downwards.

"He kissed me again," she said. "I hit him and he threw me onto the stairs. It was about that time that Elliot got the jump on Patrick and beat the snot out of him. I told my mom. She told my father. They went and talked to Patrick's parents, but we all knew the reason Patrick thought it was okay to throw women on stairs and shove them into walls was because that's how Patrick sees his father treating his mother. And on and on it goes. Patrick left me alone for a long time after that. But months later, he came after me again.

"This time, he caught me alone. And this time, Elliot wasn't on his way. The more I fought him the angrier he got. He said, 'You're going to be my wife someday, Theodora. Why are you fighting me? I don't know why you're fighting me.' When he's finished, he tells me he loves me."

Theo glanced at Billy, whose face had grown more stern, more hardened, less readable.

"I should have shot him," Billy said.

"I'm thinking somebody should have," Theo said. "I never told anybody that happened. I stopped going anywhere by myself. And the *second* I did, he—" She took a regulating breath. "When Patrick grabbed my arm that morning, when he sliced at my head with a knife, I I don't really remember much of what I did, but I do remember that I would have stabbed him to death if it hadn't been for Blacksmith." She paused. "Isn't that true, Haas?"

"Not a doubt in my mind."

"Funny," Theo said, still glaring at Lucas. "Isn't it?"

"It's a hard world, kid," Lucas said as he got up.

"That's all you got to say about it? Your son is dead and the only thing you can say about his memory is *It's a hard world*?"

"Honey. That boy? *That* kid? He wasn't my kin. For if he was?" He approached her slowly. "He wouldn't have stopped. He would have cracked Patty's skull open that first time, and do you know what that means, little Creed? That means that if Elliot was *my* blood, my *son*, then what Patty-boy did to you wouldn't have ever happened to you and right now? You'd be sitting pretty with all the other fair maidens back at Bladestay." He stopped in front of her. "I have *plenty* to say about it." He tilted his head over his shoulder to send Billy a nefarious glower. "That boy's going to get what's coming to him and not a fraction less. I'm just a one-thing-at-a-time kind of man."

Theo couldn't take her eyes off Billy even though the devastation on his face was wrecking her.

"Just let the kids go, Haas," August rumbled again.

"There's a noose on that gelding out there," Lucas replied. "Go fetch it. You do that, and I'll let her go."

August scowled but rose to his feet.

"Kick that gun over to me on your way," Lucas said.

August did and Lucas caught it under his foot. As soon as August was out the door, Lucas bent down and picked up August's revolver and holstered it. Theo watched him, her chest heaving, nearing hyperventilation. Lucas stayed close to her as he tracked August's progress outside.

When August returned, Lucas told him to sling the rope over the rafter that ran down the center of the ceiling.

August did.

"Get a chair, get up on it, then tighten that sucker around your neck."

August gave Theo a reassuring nod as he did as he was told, and when he was standing on the chair with a noose around his neck, Lucas finally moved from Theo and secured the end of the rope to the other pole on the bar. August held on to the rope around his neck until Lucas came back to him and took his hands and bound them behind his broad back.

Lucas rounded August and stepped out of his leg span. He considered August, watched him as he said to Theo, "Okay, honey." He took out his hunting knife. "You first."

August struggled in a frustrated sort of way.

Billy gripped the pole powerfully—powerless.

But Theo just stood there, waiting, for she never had a single misapprehension.

CHAPTER

38

"He's going to find us."

Theo's words had sounded loud in the hollow of that tree after their long stretch of silence.

Billy hadn't said anything.

To disagree would have been a lie; to agree would've acknowledged their death sentence.

"I need you to promise me something," she said.

"Promise you what?"

"Take the shot," she said. "The moment you have it, you take it."

"Haas?" Billy said.

Theo nodded.

"I can't make that promise."

"Why?"

"Because if I could keep it without risking your life, you wouldn't ask me to make it."

"He killed all the horses instead of taking August out. Why would he do that?" She needed to hear him say it. "*Why*, Billy?" She needed to know that he understood what they were up against.

Reluctantly: "Because this is a game to him."

"We either play his game, or we don't. Two choices. That's it."

Finally, he said, "What's the option that gets you out of this alive?"

Theo didn't want to tell him this option, not really, but in the end, she did.

"Haas isn't going to kill me," she said.

"He don't care about you, Theo."

"I know," she said. "But August does."

"Okay, Theo? Let me stop you right there—"

"Do you know what a brown recluse is?"

He sighed. "Sure."

"I used to keep one in a jar."

"Of course you did," Billy said.

"Well I was just trying to one-up my brother. Jude had a scorpion."

"Your family are freaks."

She smiled against his chest. "We'd argue about whose would win. One day, we finally put them together."

"Who won?"

Theo didn't answer right away.

She listened to his heartbeat carefully, wanting to memorize its rhythm. "Both. Neither."

He paused. "Theo . . ."

"I know."

"And if their prey was trapped in there with 'em?"

"Haas'll keep you alive too," Theo said.

"I ain't talking about me, Theo," he said gruffly.

She looked up at him. "You asked. This is the answer. Play his game. Maybe . . . *maybe* we get dealt a good card."

Billy was quiet for a while after she said that.

There had been a time where Theo could have cut Lucas's throat while he kept camp next to her brothers; could have done the same to August a little later.

Perhaps should is a better word. Could continues to prove more difficult than should.

Billy whispered, "That's not much of a choice either."

"No. It's not." She hugged her arm over his chest. "Just take the shot, Billy."

"Creed," August said.

Theo looked across the room at him.

"You're the bravest kid I've ever met."

She shook her head. "Not me." Her eyes traveled farther across the room to land on Billy. "It's easier to be the one in pain than to watch the person you care about be in it."

Billy held her gaze, resting his temple against the pole; his body had crumpled from coiled and poised to slack and resigned. His face was grim, his jawline a stone. Purple bruising clustered around his left eye. His split lip was swollen and held a line of dried blood across it.

"Truer words, Youngblood."

"You don't really believe that," Lucas said as he leaned on the edge of the table, facing Theo.

"You don't know a goddamn thing about pain," Theo said, her lip curling as she adjusted herself.

"I know *every*thing there is to know about pain," Lucas said as he ran his thumb along the edge of his blade.

"You know a lot about loss," Theo said. "That's not the same thing. Not for a man like you." She made a terrifyingly menacing face and inched her hands down the rod, away from her body. She cried out against the pull of her pierced muscle.

Lucas watched with enthralled fascination.

She gripped and pulled, sobbing as she did.

Lucas frowned lightly, amused.

She wept as she slid her body down the rod.

"Dear god," he said in delighted amazement, leaning forward.

She inched herself toward the end of the impale.

Lucas got to his feet, pressed a hand on her chest, and shoved her back into place.

She screamed.

"You're insane," he said.

She pressed her head back into the wall, then she began to laugh again. She nodded as she gasped for air. "And *you*—" She let out another maniacal burst of laughter, her body shaking. She gasped in more air. "*You*—" She shook her head back and forth against the wall, and when she spoke again, it was in a whisper. "You are so *predictable*."

Lucas saw the movement, but it was a fraction too late.

Billy dropped his hands over Lucas's face, hooked the links of his chain under his chin, and yanked, eliciting a strangled noise of shock from Haas's lungs before cutting off all noise altogether.

Lucas's hand went to the iron at his hip, but Theo raised her foot and smashed her heel into his hand.

A noise strangled in his throat.

Billy had a look of menace on his face, something that was both dark and tranquil.

Lucas tried to elbow Billy.

Billy put the open ratchet in his other hand, the one that was still cuffed, and continued to choke Lucas as he began to pummel the side of his head with his closed fist.

Lucas crumpled to the ground and Billy followed him there, maneuvered over him to jam his knee into Lucas's throat. "Give me a second, would you, troublemaker?"

Theo closed her eyes and nodded.

"Take your time," she muttered.

She heard knuckles colliding with flesh, over and over. There was a shuffle and then a dull thump that sounded like Billy might have picked up Lucas's head and slammed it into the floor. Billy continued hitting him. Then, the only thing Theo heard was Billy's rapid breathing and the wet, choking sound of Lucas trying to.

When she opened her eyes, Lucas was face down and Billy was cuffing his hands behind his back.

Billy shoved himself to his feet, blood dripping from his fingertips.

Behind him, August chuckled darkly.

Billy stood in front of Theo, his eyes bouncing around all the problems before him. His hands reached cautiously, unsure where he could touch her without hurting her. The placid anger on his face was fracturing, slipping into anguish as he bent down and picked up Lucas's hunting knife.

She watched him with relief and agony as he gently took hold of her wrist and sliced her bindings free. He struggled to keep his composure as he settled really close to her, the knife clattering at their feet when he abandoned it to place his hands lightly on either side of her face.

Hitching jerky breaths, she said, "You've got something in your teeth, partner."

He grinned, tears breaking free and sliding down previously laid tracks. Through the grin, his tongue pushed the little brown hairpin out between his teeth. He spit it away and pressed his lips against her forehead. His movements were slow as his fingers gathered and tightened around a fistful of shirt at her chest.

She placed both her hands over his forearm, clutching.

"Are you just going to stand there," she said, "or are we going to do this damn thing?"

He planted a palm on the wall behind her, steadied his grip on her clothes, then yanked with everything he had.

Theo collapsed into him, weeping exhaustedly. He wrapped his arms around her, held her closely, then lowered her into a chair. She refused to let go of him, which was fine with Billy because he had no intentions of going anywhere. He quickly put pressure on the hole in her shoulder.

"I got you," he said as he reached out to grip the side of her head. "I got you."

"I know you do." Her bloodied fingers trembled as she touched his hand where he was pressing on her shoulder.

He took her hand and placed it over her wound. "Keep pressure on it."

She nodded.

He stripped Lucas of his guns and his belt, then tore Lucas's shirt from his body. With it, he padded her wound and tied it in place, tightening until Theo made a little noise that further cracked the mask of calm that Billy was struggling to keep in place.

With the belt, he slung it over her head and buckled it diagonally across her chest, a makeshift sling. Lastly, Billy strapped the guns to his hips.

"I would applaud," August drawled, "if my hands weren't predisposed."

Theo reached her free hand up and Billy took it, pulling her to her feet. She had plans to go to August, but Billy instead encased her back in his arms. He rested his lips on the top of her head, holding her tightly, and although she was trembling, she said, "I'm okay."

"I know you are," he said into her hair as he held her a little tighter. "I ain't."

Lucas began to stir at their feet, a hoarse groan coming out of him. Billy said, "You good?"

Theo nodded.

Billy stooped down and dragged Lucas around the table. He squirmed and kicked as Billy hoisted him off the ground and shoved him into a chair. Billy pulled back the hammer and pressed one of the revolvers against Lucas's skull.

August chuckled again. "Little help," he rasped.

With her arm held carefully in the makeshift sling, Theo limped to August and stood before him.

"Is that what you think?" she asked. "That we're going to help you?"

A sad confusion drew his face before heavy understanding dragged it downward. "Theo—"

Behind her, fists collided with torn flesh. Lucas wheezed, and Billy swung at Lucas again, righting the dense body in the chair before he flexed his hand and hit Lucas again. Theo didn't try to stop him when he hit him once more.

August watched with grim satisfaction.

Billy stepped back from Lucas, sweeping hair out of his face as he came to stand at Theo's side.

"Is there anything you'd like to say to each other before you meet your maker?" Theo asked.

Lucas let out a garble of maybe-words, spitting blood from his mouth. His face was nearly unrecognizable.

"What'd you say?" August said. "What'd he say?"

"How'd you find me?" Lucas managed.

"What do you mean?" August asked.

"Santa Fe." It sounded like Lucas had a mouth full of pebbles.

August cocked his half smile. "You had me chasin' my own tail for two goddamn years. I really thought you'd show up there. It took me a long time to figure you'd bought the land just to throw me off."

Lucas made a noise that sounded like it was meant to be a laugh.

"You changed your name, Haas, but you didn't change the way you wrote it. It took me four years to catch your scent again. I almost had you in Reno. Lost you again in Denver." August snorted a scoff. "Almost for good that time. It was pure luck that I overheard someone say something about a man who dressed like a king and had a big ol' gold ring on his pinky finger. A tiger can't change his stripes, Haas, but I don't think you ever even tried to."

Lucas looked at Theo. "Can you believe this bitch—"

Billy punched him in the mouth and pushed his gun against Lucas's forehead. "Anything else?"

Lucas dazedly tried to shake it off, shouting a growl with an agape, bleeding mouth. He spit more blood and said, "I still got it," he slurred. "The diamond."

"Congratulations," Theo said.

"You really don't want to know?" Lucas asked.

Theo and Billy looked at each other.

"I want to hear what he has to say," August said.

Billy cocked the revolver. "I bet you do."

"Wait," Theo said. She took the gun off Billy's thigh.

He took a step back, out of her way, bloodied knuckles limp at his side, the gun in his hand now pointed at the ground.

Lucas darted a swollen glance to August and said to Theo, "Kill him first and I'll tell you where the diamond is."

She looked over her shoulder at Billy.

"Don't make no difference far's I'm concerned."

"You can still make the right choice here, Youngblood. You don't have to go down this path—"

The gunshot was deafening in the enclosed space, and it was over so fast and all she wanted was to see him suffer but that was vengeance and that wasn't what this was.

August made a noise that sounded like someone had knocked all the air out of him.

"*Fools*," August whispered.

Theo watched the blood drain from the hole in the back of Lucas's skull, land flat on the ground below until there was a puddle full of it and then she finally looked away, gratified and horrified at the gratification.

If you're evil, and you know you are, but you direct it for the greater good, does that then make you, ultimately, good?

Theo hoped so.

"Fools!" August yelled.

Billy and Theo turned toward him.

"This diamond is the biggest thing you've ever *seen*," August said.

Billy scoffed a laugh. "You're a piece of work, Mr. Gaines. It's *over*."

"I ain't lying," he drawled.

"We ain't caring," Billy retorted.

August looked back and forth between them, shook his head, then nodded. "All these things," he said. "All these things I've done, all this time I've spent, and you don't even care."

"How did you come upon this diamond?" Theo asked.

"A group of runaways, they—"

"Slaves?" Billy asked.

August nodded.

"What happened to them?" Theo asked.

August opened his mouth to respond, then he shut it as soon as he understood that the question was rhetorical. His shoulders heaved with a deep sigh.

"Jesus, August."

There was a long silence in which August contemplated before, finally, he said, "Thank you, Youngblood."

"You ain't going free, Gaines," Billy said.

"That's not what he was thanking me for," Theo said softly while she kept her gaze on August.

"Maybe you go through with it. Maybe you let me hang. But for letting me watch him die, I'm forever grateful."

"There's no maybe here, Mr. Gaines."

August gave her an irritated snarl. "We're the *same*, Creed. And you're gonna stand there and tell me I deserve to die and you don't?"

"I killed Shiner," she admitted.

August frowned.

"Shot him," she said. "Once in the chest; once in the head." She winced, but not at the physical pain. "And I'd shoot him again just to watch him die."

Understanding eased onto August's face. He darted his eyes to Billy, whose face remained neutral.

"You goddamn weasel," August said, chuckling. "Don't forget about Jester," August scolded.

"Oh, I won't," she said.

"You're unbelievable." He adjusted his stance and lifted his chin, indicating his discomfort. "Your admittance sabotages your own argument."

She nodded. "I think there might be something wrong with me, Mr. Gaines." She sniffed, ignoring a tear that sprinted down her cheek.

"We're the *same*, Youngblood."

"No, August." Theo shook her head. It had taken her a long time to draw the line in her own head. "For you, rage is a motive; for me, rage is a tool."

For the first time, August was looking at her with a measure of fear. "I gave up Lucas for you," he said, almost in a whisper. "I had the shot, I had the upper hand and I gave it up to save your *life*."

"Mr. Gaines, you haven't had the upper hand since you let me out of that Bladestay jail."

August let out a disbelieving chuckle. "You cocky little shit." Then, in a sudden outburst: "I SAVED YOUR *LIFE*!"

"Where's my father, August?"

August's lip twitched.

"And my brothers? Did you kill them both?"

"Their deaths ain't on me," August said.

Theo closed her eyes momentarily, fighting another crushing wave of grief. "Jude was barely twenty-two. Zeke was supposed to get married next fall." She swiped a tear from her cheek. "They were good people, August." She sniffed angrily and wiped her face again. "But good people don't stand a single chance against your rage."

He snarled, turning his attention to Billy. "And what about you? Huh, Brody Boone? What the hell is your excuse?" He flicked his eyes to Theo when he added, "He rode into your town covered in my son's blood."

"That's not Brody," Theo said.

"What?" August said. He looked at Billy, studying him from head to toe. "*What*?"

When Billy was done holding a mirror to the things August had done to his brother that night, August paused. "Your brother . . ." he said. "He shouldn't have been out there that night."

"*You* shouldn't have been," Billy said.

August nodded slowly, and Theo could see the gears turning in his mind, the way he was switching them, repurposing his circumstance, altering his approach.

"May I make one request?" August asked.

"They're your final words, Mr. Gaines," Theo said. "You can choose any that you'd like, in any order that suits you."

August cut her a look. "I challenge you to a duel, Billy Boone."

Theo snorted. "Oh? And in what way has *he* offended *you*?"

"His lack of loyalty is offensive."

"Your view of the world is offensive," Billy said.

"You're not getting out of this, August," Theo said.

Neither Theo nor August saw Billy's hand go to his hip.

It had been a slow, inconspicuous crawl, where his thumb nudged the strap off the hilt, his fingers settling into the worn grooves of the walnut grip.

Theo might be able to maneuver through stratagem, but Billy could read body language like words on a page.

He could see the way August subtly rolled his shoulders from time to time, the way he seemed to shift from discomfort.

"And what are your plans, children, upon your return to Bladestay?" August asked.

"We'll defeat them too," Theo said.

"You will then? My eighteen strong to your two?"

"The same reason you find yourself in a noose is the same thing that's going to give me back my town, August."

"And what's that, Youngblood?"

Billy drew his gun and pulled the trigger, his gun back in his holster before August's body went limp in the noose.

"*Billy,*" Theo said. "*Why?*"

"Check his bindings," Billy said, looking at the hole in August's face where his eye should be.

But she didn't have to. As August's body swayed slightly, his arms went limp and tumbled around his body to dangle at his side. The ropes were loose around his mangled hand, and in the other one was a small, compact switchblade. A moment longer, and those three inches of steel could have been lodged in one of their necks.

Theo kept her eyes on August's face. How peaceful a man could look when he dies with the absolute belief he won't. Even in his final breath, with a rope around his neck and standing before an armed man, August had evaded death too many times to believe that this, right here, was the way he was going out.

Cheat death too many times, cheat others out of life an equal amount, and eventually you confuse yourself for the one with the hooded cloak and sharpened scythe.

She stumbled around his dangling body and landed against the door. She struggled with the deadbolt, her hands shaking with pain and urgency. Billy's quiet footsteps came up behind her, and he reached over and unlatched the bolt with nimble finesse. He swung the door open, and she stumbled through it, landing against a pillar of the porch.

He stepped through the threshold after her, closing the door behind him.

"There's nothing wrong with you, Theo, you hear me?" Billy said as he reached for the revolver in her hand. She relinquished it without a glance at him and he dropped it back against his thigh. Then he stepped back until he could lean against the wall, wrapping his hand around one of his guns. When he did, the tremors in his fingers quieted.

She nodded, then shook her head. "I wouldn't have been able to do it."

"Not a lick of shame in that."

"Then why do I feel so much of it?"

"Because if you don't, Theo? Then there *would* be something wrong with you."

She closed her eyes, tears streaming.

They stood in the silence of shock, the kind that follows a horrendous sort of victory. Billy's hands were trembling. A murder of crows circled above, cawing playfully. The damage to Theo's shoulder was agonizing. The sun was inching above the eastern mountainside, flushing the sky with pinks and shading the mountains purple. August's body swayed behind them. The river continued to flow over its rocky bed.

Finally, Billy asked her: "What were you going to say to him?"

"I'm . . ." She turned her face to look up at the sky. "I'm not sure," she said. "I seem to have lost my train of thought."

CHAPTER
39

They galloped for eight hours straight. They slept for four. They ran their horses for another eight hours. They slept for six.

Underneath Theo's makeshift bandages, red lines were beginning to spread across her skin from the hole in her shoulder.

She developed a fever. She struggled to keep what little food they had down.

About halfway down the mountain, on their third sprint, Theo was struggling to stay balanced and upright on her mount. Their horses were soaked and lathered and as Theo's slump went severe, Billy kicked his horse to catch up, to press his horse against hers. Theo's horse was running aimlessly, but Billy's was struggling to stay in gait. Theo's horse scooted away from his attempts to match her stride, so Billy quickly got a heel under himself and into the seat of the saddle, curled his body into a brief crouch, then stepped onto his mount's neck, using the horse's withers like a stepping stone, and landed on the mare's rear in a single stride, immediately dropping onto the horse's back right behind the saddle

Theo crumpled.

He caught her, his arm outlined under hers in the sling, and righted her as he reached his other arm past her and snatched the reins, demoting them to a walk.

"I got you," he said into her ear as she leaned back into his chest. He glanced back at the gelding he'd abandoned and found him at a dead halt, head low, pawing at the ground with trembling, buckling legs.

"I know," she said, allowing her weight to be anchored by his. She layered her uninjured arm over his, holding him tight to her. "I know you do."

He pulled out his revolver, stretched his arm out behind him, and put his horse out of his misery. Theo jolted. He holstered his gun and returned his other arm around her.

By the time night fell, they were out of horses.

They took a brief rest, ate the remainder of their provisions, and when Theo couldn't hold on to her consciousness, Billy scooped her up, abandoned any hope of rest, and proceeded on foot. He carried her through the night and by morning the next day, Bladestay was in sight.

A thick, acrid stench drifted from the valley, and it put Billy on edge. He set Theo on the ground and she moaned in pain.

From behind him, Theo asked in a small voice, "What's that smell?"

Dropping to a knee, Billy unslung Lucas's rifle from his back and lined up the scope on the town. The whole valley was ghostly. In the field behind the stables, a black tendril of smoke reached into the sky. He adjusted the magnification, trying to steady his breath and his hands. When he saw the source of the smoke, he let the barrel of the rifle dip as he squinted his eyes shut.

"We have to get out of here," Billy said.

"What *is* that?" she asked as she pushed herself painfully off the ground, her eyes now on the tendril.

"There's nothing left for you here." He rose to his feet, blocking her.

She pushed him out of her line of site, shaking her head as she desperately searched her town for life. Her chest was beginning to move rapidly, her hand clutching her throbbing shoulder. "Are those bodies, Billy? Did they kill everyone?"

"I'm sorry, Theo," Billy said.

"No!" She whimpered as she hit him weakly in his chest. "*No!*" she screamed.

"You have to keep your voice down."

"Get out of my way!" she yelled, her voice broken and hoarse as she shoved him.

"*Theo,*" he said firmly as he took her arm gently.

She tried to shake free, her sobs getting louder.

He dropped the rifle and clapped a hand over her mouth and said, "*Sh.* You're going to get yourself *killed.*"

"I don't care!" she was trying to say through his hand.

"*Get your filthy hands off her.*"

Billy froze.

Consciousness was beginning to slip from Theo's grasp. She blinked at the woman holding a shotgun to the back of Billy's skull.

Billy took his hand from Theo's mouth, but when she tried to talk, to tell the woman to drop her gun, all that came out was a mumbled *no no no no.*

Billy laid her gently on the ground. She tried to grab at him, to pull him to safety, but her limbs weren't cooperating.

"Let's just talk about this," he said to the woman with the shotgun.

"The next conversation you're going to have," the woman said, "is going to be with God Almighty."

There was a *crack*, then Billy was falling to the ground, and then there was nothing at all.

It was full dark when Rose Creed stepped out of the root cellar. Shotgun snug in her shoulder, finger curled softly around the trigger, she swept the double barrels across the prairie of her yard and over the crackling embers of her house. The burned cedar and the thirty years it once housed smelled offensive.

Keeping her eyes sharp for any movements among the incompetent starlight, she let out a quiet, low whistle, disguised by the chirrups of the nocturnal collective. Behind her, the three youngest Creeds emerged from the cellar, the eldest of them holding a younger one in each hand.

As soon as they were free of the underground, the eldest boy guided his brothers across the prairie, loping toward the idealistic hide-and-seek grounds of their childhood. After the night swallowed the silhouettes of her three boys, Rose did another sweep toward the town as she began backstepping after them.

When Rose was confident she could turn her back on the threat of Bladestay, she did so, retreating into the cover of trees, boulders, creeks, and ravines.

There was a deeply carved wash with naked roots woven through the earth that had been the result of a destructive flash flood two years prior. Within this sandy hollow, blanketed by chokecherry brush and jailed in firs, was where Rose Creed sheltered with what would soon be the last of the Creed boys. They created a camp of sorts of their own, but instead of a fire they huddled together under the deepest crevice of the wash under thick furs and heirloom quilts, silently sharing provisions. They shared fractured sleep, Rose rotating watch with her fourteen-year-old son.

For three nights, Rose Creed waited for Theo, her husband or Blacksmith, her elder sons, or Elliot, to return. Held on to the belief that help was on the way. When the agonizing reality began to show its apparents, Rose spent daylight of the fourth day gathering supplies for a new plan.

Rose Creed crept down the wash, farther away from Bladestay, carefully harvesting what her family colloquially called killer onions. Killer onions, properly known as its equally self-evident name, death camas, look like miniature in-bloom yucca plants with beautiful white flowers that blossom at the end of a scallion-like stem. After harvesting hundreds of the subterranean bulbs, Rose painstakingly extracted the juice from the onion-like plant like juicing a rattlesnake's fangs for poison. It took her all day, refusing help from the boys who watched her process with grim, white-knuckle fascination.

With a repurposed vial of dandelion tincture, Rose armed herself with enough lethal doses for more than double the men she intended to infect. She waited until the horizon began to turn from black to steel gray, the time of day when most predators prefer to hunt. The men posted on guard were dozing, the rest in a whiskey coma, so navigating her way to the saloon wasn't difficult. She dropped a healthy dose of her camas extraction into every bottle of liquor she could find. Then she sneaked back to the sandy wash with a revival of provisions and invigoration of perspective. The day that followed was one of the longest of Rose's life. She had taken a large gamble, and it was with the lives of every resident of Bladestay. The bet she was willing to take was that the gang wouldn't share the whiskey reserves with the innocents.

By dawn the next day, the takeover of her town was more effortless than the one performed by August Gaines. Those who survived the drink were wishing they hadn't. Rose Creed fulfilled their wishes with bullets. Not a single resident was harmed.

Together, they gathered and piled the bodies in the meadow behind the stables, tossed the infectious spirits onto the corpses, doused the dead in kerosene, then set them ablaze.

It didn't take long for a group of volunteers to find the body of Elliot in the tall grass on the way to Clayton Creek. Rose Creed dug the grave herself, a sort of self-penance that she herself couldn't rightly articulate. She had an angry sort of stoicism that nobody dared interrupt as she dug a massive hole in the ground, but after she lowered the body of the teenager into it, after she returned the displaced soil, only then did she fall to her knees and weep. Fingernails black with dirt, face smeared with it too, hair refusing to stay pinned back, she rocked back and forth before the grave, crying out, mourning the loss before her, but deeper, the losses that transpired up on that mountain, losses she didn't have to witness to be certain that they had already happened.

Two days later, two of the six men who had gone to Clayton Creek returned with news that the sister town was in ashes. Four of the men continued on to Denver, to complete the job that Elliot had intended to do.

For the first time, Rose considered leaving her babies in the hands of the restored order of Bladestay to go after her family. The town was on high alert, expecting the return of August Gaines and his crew, but Rose just couldn't sit and wait any longer. Everybody advised her to stay, and although she knew they were right, that the best tactic was to lie in wait for the bandits' return—ambush them with the upper hand—Rose had reached her limit of patience alongside her limit of loss. The only person willing to go with Rose was Evangeline, and Evangeline just happened to be the only person Rose wasn't willing to take. Rose saddled her horse, packed her shotgun and her rations, but she didn't even make it a mile out of town when she found a lean, dark-skinned boy with his hands over her daughter's mouth.

"Let's just talk about this," the boy said when he felt the mouth of her shotgun pressed into his skull.

"The next conversation you're going to have," Rose told him, "is going to be with God Almighty." She wanted to take the kid's head off right then and there, but then she thought of Theo, thought how her little girl would like to see that boy hanging from a tree, thought that at the very least, if Theo survived this, she had earned that.

Theo was in the throes of a raging infection from a horrific wound in her shoulder. For the next two weeks, Rose questioned whether her daughter would ever open her eyes with clarity again. For two weeks, Rose Creed didn't sleep. Rose Creed didn't eat. She held Theo's damp, hot hand. She changed cooled cloths on her forehead. She changed bandages on her shoulder. She applied balm to the sear in her waist. She brewed oregano tea and poured it down Theo's throat.

Rose Creed cried, she prayed, and fifteen days later, her daughter opened her eyes with a tired but hardened clarity.

The first words out of Theo's mouth were: "Where is he?"

CHAPTER
41

Theo nudged the Bladestay jailhouse door open. The sling that held her arm was no longer makeshift and the balm on the cauterization was soothing.

Billy was on his feet in an instant, his fingers wrapped around the bars of the prison that had previously been hers. The bruising on his face had faded to patches of yellow, the swelling was all but gone, and the split in his lip was a thin line. The laceration that Lucas had gifted him on the left side of his jaw was sewn shut.

Theo vaguely registered that there was another person in the jail, but suddenly, her legs felt unsteady and the thoughts in her head vanished. She didn't remember crossing the room, was simply grateful that her legs were strong enough to get her there. When she pressed against him as much as confines allowed, Billy snaked his arms through the bars and held her. His embrace was almost frantic, his hand moving up her back to clutch the nape of her neck, fingers tight wherever they landed as if nothing, not even the iron bars between them, could keep them apart.

"What do you know," Patrick Holmes said. "You *weren't* lying."

Theo's stomach clenched, her heart sank, her jaw tightened. She turned and saw Patrick sitting in the same spot she'd left him.

Billy tugged her attention from the other prisoner. "Just a minute ago, Evangeline Creed burst in here and said the stables were on fire."

When Theo turned back to Billy, he tore a murderous glare from Patrick to give her an amused look. "You wouldn't happen to know anything about that, would you?"

She reached into the back pocket of her loose-fitting breaches and wiggled the ring of keys. "I'm sure I have no idea what you're talking about, Billy Boone."

He smiled at her as she began to unlock his cage.

"Hey, you can't do that!" Patrick said. "He's a *killer*!"

"Ain't he just," Theo responded coolly.

Billy stepped out of his prison, and as Theo went to unlock the mesh cage of the armory, he went straight up to Patrick's cell.

"Toss me them keys, troublemaker," Billy said, not taking his eyes from Patrick, who was beginning to cower deeper into his cot.

"Whoa whoa—" Patrick said as Theo underhanded the ring of keys.

Billy snatched them from the air and stuck a key in Patrick's door.

"Hey *hey*!" Patrick said.

From the arsenal, Theo grabbed Billy's belt and ammo and guns and walked them over to him.

"*Theo!*" Patrick said.

Billy exchanged the keys for his guns, strapped them across his hips, then kicked the door open. It banged with a loud clatter, making Patrick jolt and holler out the interim sheriff's name.

Billy stole a glance over his shoulder at Theo, who was leaning against the wall with her arms folded. She shrugged her answer to the question she saw on his face. He pulled out his gun. Closing the distance between them, Billy grabbed Patrick by the collar and shoved him flat on his back, pressing the muzzle of the gun against Patrick's lips.

Swinging a leg over to press his knee into Patrick's ribcage, Billy clutched the underside of Patrick's jaw and said, "Open your mouth."

Sobbing, Patrick did.

Billy hunched over him, his untamed hair dangling down his forehead. "Don't fight it." He slipped the gun between Patrick's teeth, and Patrick let out a guttural whimper. Billy leaned down closer to his face as he pulled back the hammer. "I don't know why you'd fight it."

Loudly and suddenly, Billy shouted, "*Bang!*"

Patrick screamed around the metal in his mouth, then Billy holstered his gun.

"You get that out of your system?" Theo asked as they walked out of the jailhouse.

Billy put his arm around her. "Little bit, yeah." Then he stopped them at the top of the stairs, pulling his gun out with a twirl to offer her the gun grip first. "You want to take a pass at him?"

She smiled. "If I put a gun in Patrick's mouth, he's eating a bullet."

He planted a kiss above her temple as he slid the gun safely back on his hip. "Fair enough." They trotted down off the raised deck to a pair of horses.

"Where to, troublemaker?" Billy asked as he bent down and interlocked his hands together below a stirrup of one of the horses.

She reached up and grabbed onto the horn with her hand not in a sling, and Billy hoisted her up.

"I want to show you something," Theo said as Billy swung onto the other horse. "Follow me?"

"Anywhere."

Before they galloped out of Bladestay, they stopped at a freshly disturbed mound of soil. *Elliot Blacksmith* was etched into the crude, wooden cross crookedly posted at the head of the grave. Billy swung down, his movements small and calcified, reminding Theo of the careful way he sat before her when August had sneaked up on him in the jailhouse. He kept his eyes on the grave in a terrified way as if he wasn't convinced the boy's ghost wouldn't pop up from the earth. Finally, he stepped over to Theo and looked up at her, offering her a hand down.

"I've already said my goodbyes," she said.

He was still a moment, then he gave a single nod and turned shamefully back toward the grave. As he took his slow strides toward the grave, his hand unconsciously going to the blade that intersected his spine, Theo hoped he could find the same thing she did when she visited the grave.

"When it comes to our wounds," Theo said softly, "I think we might be better at licking than we are with the sutures."

He knelt, drew the blade from its sheath, and wriggled the cross out of the ground. Etching out the incorrect surname, he recarved the proper one. Then he staked the cross back in place, ensuring it was proper and level. After, he set the weapon atop the grave. He held his hand there, said not a word—not out loud.

"Unless we're aiming to end up like them, I think we need to start stitching."

That's the hardest thing about closure: you have to choose it, you have to want it, but hardest of all, you have to believe you deserve it.

They loped through massive prairies, trotted up long inclines, and walked over rocky hillsides. Through their half-day journey, they avoided the topic of August and Lucas, and in that, found it was hard to say anything at all.

Yet, it was healing, to enjoy the ambivalence of nature without the backdrop of terror. Billy would often catch Theo in deep contemplation, like she was miles elsewhere, trying to mentally outmatch a player whom she'd already defeated, and whenever she found him studying her, she'd smile sadly. He didn't want to ask, and she didn't want to tell him and for now, that was okay. She had a plan, and in Billy's experience, that was good enough.

The two crested a hill, and the landscape gave way to a glass-top lake.

Billy halted his horse. He slipped off, distractedly tying his horse as he slowly drank in the view of the plateau. Theo watched him, for when you share with somebody something that makes your soul feel free, you no longer chase that soul-freeing feeling, for you seek a new feeling altogether, and that's witnessing someone else experience it.

She smiled at him when he'd finally shaken his gaze free of the bright blue waters and light brown sand and the thick forest in which it was framed. When she swung down, Billy tied her horse aside his and said, "I've traveled a fair bit in my days, but I ain't ever seen anything this magnificent."

"It's a special place," Theo agreed.

They walked to the water's edge, and as Billy hopped out of his shoes, he said, "How much time you reckon we got?"

"As long as we want."

He unbuckled the guns from his waist and dropped them atop his shoes. "You don't think they'll come after us?"

Theo looked up at the sky, a baby blue with puffy white clouds. "They wouldn't dare."

Finally, Billy broached: "You okay, troublemaker?"

"There's a problem that I've been trying to work out. And I just can't seem to solve it, Billy."

He came over to her, a playfulness on his face beginning to ease the painful sutures of closure. "Against you? Well that's just not fair to the problem."

She smiled at him again. "How did the straight razor end up in your hands after August took it from me?"

His face fell back into something more serious. He stepped close to her and touched the side of her head, running his hand across the shortest part, a slow, gentle finger underlining the small nick in her scalp. "And after you have all my secrets, what will I have left?"

"Peace?"

He smiled down at her as his fingers started to trace her ear. "Wouldn't that be something." Goosebumps flushed her skin. Then he brought his hand in front of her face, twirling the razor between his fingers.

Her hand went to the empty pocket he'd picked it from. Then she snatched it from him, her smile widening.

"Now what's the real problem, Theo?"

She turned the razor over in her fingers then slipped it back into her pocket. "I can't leave Bladestay. And you can't go back."

"Ah." He took a step back, reached behind his back, and yanked off his shirt. "*That* problem." He made his face turn playful again, and this time, it was unabashed. "I thought you were talking about the *other* problem."

"Which one's that?" Theo asked, pressing back another smile.

"The problem, Theo Creed, is that we rode four hours to a lake that we ain't in yet."

She angled a brow. "How *ever* are we going to solve that one?"

He stepped close again, placed his hands on either side of her head, and said, "I've spent the last two weeks wondering if I was ever going to see another sunrise again, let alone you. We barely made it off that mountain. We hardly survived our return. The future ain't got nothin' on us, not after what the past has put us through." Then he kissed her, making every thought in her head completely turn to vapor. She felt the way the skin on his back absorbed the warmth of the sun. The way he handled her that was both cautious and assertive. He didn't stop kissing her until the buttons down her blouse were undone, and even then, it was merely a hiatus.

Within this gap, Theo told him, "You keep kissing me like that, and I promise you that there won't be a single problem on my mind."

He gave her a smile that looked like it held all the secrets of the universe. "That is the plan."

The afternoon was cruel with the swiftness in which it passed.

As they lay in the spaces between the long shadows of evening on approach, sand clinging to their damp bodies, Theo reached over to her pile of clothes.

She said, "I found something."

Billy saw her hand that had closed into a fist.

She reached over to him and uncurled her fingers.

Billy sat up and picked up the translucent stone. It was raw, uncut, and although it wasn't nearly the size of a fist, it did catch the sunlight in spectacular ways.

"You won't believe where I found it," Theo said.

Transfixed, Billy held it up in front of his face. "Where?"

"In the ashes of my house," she said.

He looked at her in question.

"That nonsense my dad was saying . . ." She took a quick composing moment and Billy lowered the diamond. "He was trying to tell us where it was." She looked at Billy's hand and what was in it. "Everyone knew to not go down there because it was filled with rat poison," she added, almost to herself. "He was talking about the crawlspace beneath the floorboards where I pretended my family was."

He gazed out over the glass surface of the lake as he took that in, then he let out a singular laugh. "If I'd just let you pry it open—"

"Yeah."

Billy turned the diamond over in his fingers. "Crazy old world, ain't she?"

She nodded absently as she watched him fall into a further mesmeric state, beholding the rock in his hands.

"Any idea what it's worth?" he asked.

"Nary a one."

"What are you going to do with it?"

"Funny—I was going to ask you the same thing."

He cast a sideways look at her. "You're entrusting me with this?"

She nodded slowly.

"That's good."

He arched his hand over his shoulder and chucked the diamond as far as he could. It made a small, hollow splash when it collided with the surface of the water. "That thing has left buckets of blood in its wake. In my world, that's what we call cursed."

Overhead, clouds rode the current of the breeze, unanimously ushered toward each other to eventually turn into something gray and grumbling, until finally, they would no longer be able hold the weight of the things they'd gathered.

"I think I might love you, Billy Barba."

"Ain't no think nor might when it comes to the way I feel about you."

Theo took his hand and laced her fingers through his.

They watched the ripples the diamond made, watched the ringed ridges of the disturbance spread and grow and flatten until, finally, the surface returned to reflect the blue and white of its opposite with neither a blemish nor indication of the curse it apathetically ingested, a blameless object that had traveled so far for so long, only to be plunged back into darkness, forever a thing to be culpable, never again a thing to be accounted.

ACKNOWLEDGMENTS

Thank you foremost to you, the reader. This book is for you.

Next, to my friends and family who encouraged me during every hardship and cheered every victory. Yellie, the world doesn't deserve people like you, and I'm so lucky I get to call you my best friend. Thank you for your unshakable belief in my dreams and your unconditional support through every shift in my life. I could write pages about how grateful I am for you, about how much you mean to me, so I'll simply say: I love you very much.

Ray and Laverne, thank you for the countless times you called just to tell me how much you love my stories. You never let me forget how much you believe in me. Thank you for your ceaseless prayers.

Jen B, I'm so grateful for our mutual love of books and the magic that exists between us because of it. (Amaze.) You're the Harry to my Hugo, and you make me a better person.

Shayna, your eye for thematic detail is astounding. You always understand the truths I'm trying to tell, even when the concepts are raw. Thank you for buying me ice cream and telling me everything will be okay.

Jessie, you saw things in me long before I saw them, and believed them long before I did. You inspired me to pursue, and later, persevere. Thank you.

Jenn Archer, your feedback on an early draft of this book was precise and wise. This story wouldn't be what it is today without your insight. Thank you for lending me your brilliance and for supporting me from halfway across the country. I look forward to the day I can hug you in person.

Thank you to Spencer and Sara for generously donating your time and expertise. Madison and Kristen, you were there for the very first story idea for *Bladestay* and then you kindly proceeded to listen to all the ramblings about it that followed—you two have kept me sane and grounded and I love you both.

Gigi, you are a pillar in my writing journey and I'm deeply grateful for your unwavering support. Thank you to my mom and dad, who taught me how to ride horses and shoot guns and climb mountains.

Thank you to Sue for the most joyful welcome an author could ever hope for. Elana, your passion for this story and your patience with me as we worked to get it right—I am immeasurably grateful. Meredith, I feel so lucky to have you on my team, luckier still to have it turn into a friendship like ours. Thank you to Maryann for my gorgeous cover. To the rest of the CamCat team: thank you for bringing my story to life.

Most importantly, thank you to my husband, David. You are fearless and generous and I'm so grateful we get to spend our lives together. You are the noble parts of every good man I write. My children, you are bright lights in a dark world. I love you 3000.

Lastly, thank you to my Savior, the keeper of sparrows—and far more important things.

ABOUT THE AUTHOR

Jackie Johnson has a BA in history and a love for storytelling. To her, there's nothing better than discovering new worlds and meeting their heroes, their villains, and most of all, dissecting the ambiguity found in between. She's been riding horses for over twenty years and had her own real-life cowboy love story when she fell in love with and married a horse trainer. Jackie and her family live on a ranch in Southern California with a shared passion for animals, homesteading, community, and self-sufficiency. *Bladestay* is her first novel.

If you liked
Jackie Johnson's *Bladestay*,
please consider leaving a review
to help our authors.
And check out another great read from CamCat:
Andrea Lynn's *Dust Spells*.

CHAPTER ONE

The morning light on the dirt road was eerie, but that was nothing new. The sky was always sickly yellow and filthy just after dawn. The clear, blue skies and lush green fields of five years ago sometimes seemed a dream to Stella. It was hard to imagine her home had ever been anything but diseased and covered in dust, though she knew it had. She knew a lot of things she didn't want to know, like how the entire world could be upended overnight, forever changing not only her life, but the lives of millions, and none of them had the power to change it back again, not ever.

She pulled her family's Chevrolet pickup into Jane's driveway and put it in park. When she cut the ignition, the engine sighed, as if as tired as she was.

Don't you die on me now, she thought. *You're the last luxury we have.*

A harsh, discordant clanging met her ears when she stepped outside. Jane's neighbor, a widow named Mrs. Woodrow, had an ungodly number of wind chimes on her already cluttered porch. Stella cursed her silently as she hurried up Jane's drive. Why have even *one* wind chime in a place where the grimy, choking wind never let up? Where dust storms called Black Blizzards rose up and blotted out the sky, raining debris on cars and buildings, tearing through the cracks in the most well-sealed homes, and mutilating the Great Plains as thoroughly as they had mutilated Stella's life forever?

Stella opened Jane's back door and let herself in. She closed it behind her, muting the chimes, but then heard the equally irritating sound of a baby's cry.

"Morning, Stella," Jane called, rushing into the kitchen with Jasper in her arms. She sat down at the table and opened her blouse, baring her right breast. "Sorry. I meant to feed him before you got here, but he wasn't hungry."

"Not a problem," Stella replied, grateful no writhing parasite depended on her for its sustenance. She had too many people dependent on her as it was. "Is everything ready?"

"Yes," Jane said as Jasper found her nipple and quieted. "I filled the jars last night."

Grateful that part was already done, Stella turned and crept down the rickety stairs to Jane's basement. When she passed the large, copper still, she fought the urge to blow it a kiss.

When Jane's parents died, they left her two blessings: a house with a paid-off mortgage and her father's old moonshine still. President Roosevelt had repealed prohibition the previous year, but that didn't matter in Kansas, which had been dry since the last century, and Stella—who almost never prayed—prayed it would stay that way. With liquor outlawed, she and Jane could make fifty cents a pint.

The idea had been Stella's. Though Jane was four years older, the two of them had been friends since childhood. Jane married right out of high school, but her dirtbag husband abandoned her and Jasper after losing his job last winter. Jane made ends meet by taking in laundry, and when Stella remembered Jane's father's old still, she suggested they go into business. Jane brewed the moonshine, and Stella delivered it, hidden among the laundry.

Her heart thumped as she crouched down and picked up the crate. Sixteen beautiful jars. She held the equivalent of eight dollars in her hands. After three months, she and Jane had twelve consistent clients. And the demand was growing. Their only competition was the local drug store, where the owner sold malt whiskey smuggled in from Colorado, but most people couldn't afford it. Jane's moonshine wasn't cheap, but it wasn't so expensive it would break the average person. If they had a bigger still, or more people to help, Stella knew they could make their little sideline a real business.

But they didn't. And Stella knew enough to be grateful for what she did have. She started up the stairs, holding the crate that would bring her the only thing in the world that was hers alone. The thing that, once a week, brought her closer to her dreams.

Jane had finished feeding Jasper by the time Stella finished loading the crate and laundry into her truck. When she walked back inside, Jane was burping him over her shoulder.

"Do you ever want to murder Mrs. Woodrow?" Stella asked, closing the door behind her.

Jane laughed. "I hardly notice those wind chimes anymore."

"How? They're maddening."

"She thinks they ward off evil spirits."

"They're about to ward off my sanity."

Jane laughed again, and Stella wiped her brow.

"How are you on ingredients?"

"I have plenty of corn and yeast, but I'm running low on sugar."

"I'll pick some up and bring it by afterward with the money."

She smoothed her hair and checked to make sure the patches she'd sewn beneath the worn spots on her dress were well-concealed. "How do I look?"

Jane smiled, her dimples showing. "Like a sweet, eighteen-year-old girl."

"Wash your mouth out with soap. There is nothing sweet about me."

The last thing Stella wanted to be was sweet. Greta Garbo and Jean Harlow weren't sweet. They were vixens wrapped in diamonds and furs who consumed men like champagne. Jane was a sweet girl.

Sweet girls ended up alone with a baby.

"But sweet girls aren't bootleggers," Jane countered. "They'll never suspect."

"True," Stella agreed. "I'll be back with some sweet, sweet dough."

The sun had barely risen, but the inside of the truck already felt like an oven by the time Stella reached her first stop. She dabbed at her forehead with a handkerchief and checked her lipstick in the rearview. Just because she lived in a dusty prairie town didn't mean she had to look like it. The money she would earn today could buy her powder, blush, mascara, and maybe even a new dress, but it was going straight into her Folger's can in the attic, so lipstick alone had to do. The crimson stain was perfect, so she stepped out of the truck.

Her first client was a man named Lewis Johnston, who lived with his mother and preferred to take his deliveries at work. Stella always made his stop first because he worked at the train station, and the train-hopping bums who littered the place were mostly asleep in the morning. They camped in the hobo "jungle" in the nearby woods, and some of them liked to whistle and yell at the women who walked by.

That morning, the coast seemed clear as Stella clipped up the drive to the station, holding Lewis's shirts, with the mason jar between the folds. But then she heard shouts, and two men tumbled out from between the trees. The first one fell onto his back, and the second leaped on top of him and punched him square in the face. Stella shrieked and jumped back. With a savage groan, the first man shoved the other man off and scrambled back to his feet. Then, he gripped the man's shoulder and swung his fist deep into his stomach. The man doubled over, and the first seized his head and drove it down into his knee. Blood burst from his nose and splattered the pavement, as well as the other man's pants. He crumpled to the ground, and the other man spat on him, viciously.

"You bastards always make the same mistake. You go for the face."

"What's going on here?"

Both men looked in Stella's direction. She blinked and spun around. A police officer was jogging up the drive. She heard a scuffle and turned back around to see both men bolting toward the trees, the first moving like lightening, and the second stumbling and clutching his stomach.

"That's right, get out of here," the cop yelled, and Stella turned back to face him. He nodded and tipped his hat. "You okay, miss?"

Stella stared at him, suddenly very aware of the mason jar in her arms. "Oh, yes. They didn't hurt me. They were fighting with each other."

"Dirty bums," the cop grumbled. "Why can't they kill each other out in that jungle, away from decent folks?"

Stella nodded and started back toward the station.

"What's a young lady like you doing here so early anyway?"

She stopped. After closing her eyes and taking a deep breath, she turned back around.

"I'm delivering laundry. To a man who works at the station."

The cop stepped closer, glancing down at the shirts. "He doesn't want it delivered to his house?"

He looked back up, but before he met her gaze, his eyes lingered a few other places. Her crimson lips, her dark curls, the swell of her breasts beneath her dress.

Men.

"I guess so," Stella said with a laugh. She stepped closer, glad she'd taken the time to dab on a bit of her dwindling reserve of perfume. "You men can be so silly sometimes. I never know what you're thinking."

He smiled sheepishly and blushed. "I suppose we can be. Well, go ahead. I'll make sure no more of these hobos get in your way."

"Thank you, so much," Stella said, flashing a smile. Then, she turned and walked up the drive, thinking Jean Harlow couldn't have done any better.

Over the next hour, Stella made the rest of her deliveries. Not all were for moonshine; some were really laundry. When she'd finished, however, she cursed herself. She needed to get more sugar for Jane, but the general store was all the way back by the train station. She should have gotten it after her first delivery.

Now, she would have to go all the way back and risk arriving home late and angering her Aunt Elsa. She sped to the store, went in, and used two of the of the eight dollars she'd made to buy fifty pounds of sugar. Then, she hoisted the two, twenty-five-pound sacks over each of her shoulders and trudged out into the heat.

"That's a mighty amount of sugar."

She turned around and stifled a gasp. The man who'd beat up and spat on the other man at the train station was leaning against the wall. He was more of a boy than a man, she now saw, just a year or two older than she was. His lower lip had been split by the blow he'd taken to the face, and he was picking small chunks from a stale loaf of bread, eating carefully. There was a bakery next door, and Stella guessed the loaf had been thrown out with last night's trash. Her stomach turned, and she flopped the sacks onto the bed of her truck.

"What's it to you?"

"Just wondering if you might have the same amount of yeast and corn somewhere."

She froze, and then spun back to face him. He read the guilty look on her face and grinned.

"That's what I thought."

She stared at him. Besides the split lip, he had a yellowing bruise beneath one eye and a scar through his other eyebrow. His skin and clothes were filthy, and his hair was a rumpled mess beneath his flat cap. Her gaze slid down to the knee of his pants, stained with the other man's blood. He followed her gaze, popped a piece of bread in his mouth, and looked back up.

"Don't worry," he said as he chewed. "I'd never hit a woman. You could come at me with a knife, and I'd just let you stab me, sugar."

She flushed, determined not to let him know she'd been afraid. "How thoughtful. If you'll excuse me."

"Hold on." He stood up from the wall and stepped into the sunlight. "I'm interested in becoming a customer."

He had a backwoods, southern accent. Maybe Texas or Louisiana. Some desolate, nothing place even dustier than Kansas.

"I don't know what you're talking about."

"Come on, now. No girl in worn-out out heels is gonna spend that much money on sugar unless she expects some kind of return. And I watched you work that lawman this morning. Saw the fear on your face when he looked at those shirts. Saw the way you turned on the charm to fool him. Pretty impressive."

Stella's lips parted. Even the man who'd sold her the sugar hadn't questioned why she'd bought it. He was just happy to make the sale. This boy talked like a hick, but he was smart. She studied his face. It was pleasant. Beneath the dirt and scars anyway.

But then she remembered what he'd said about her shoes.

"You couldn't afford it."

She purposefully raked her eyes over his filthy clothes as she said it. But his grin only curled, and he stepped closer.

"Ain't you heard, sugar? We got a depression on. People trade and barter for the things all the time."

"Stop calling me that. And you have nothing I want."

He placed another chunk of bread in his mouth and looked her over. "We've only just met." He lifted his gaze. "You don't know what I got to offer."

She flushed again. "You're disgusting."

"Disgusting?" He cocked his head to the side. "My, what dirty thoughts you've got in that pretty head of yours."

Feeling a sudden kinship with the man who'd punched him in the face, she spat, "Don't flatter yourself," and turned away, tossing her curls.

"I see those patches in your skirt, sugar," he called. "Don't pretend you're better than me."

"At least I've taken a bath this century."

She didn't look back when she said it, but she caught sight of his face when she opened the door to the truck. His smile was gone. Guilt rose in her throat, but she swallowed it, got in her truck, and drove away.

She sped toward Jane's house, now certain she would be facing Aunt Elsa's wrath when she arrived home. There were six dollars in her pocket, three of which were hers, but she found herself too shaken to enjoy their comforting presence.

Because the boy had been right. Her family was barely hanging on by a thread, and though they weren't sleeping in hobo jungles and fishing stale bread out of the garbage, that could change at any moment.

Nothing was certain. No one was safe.

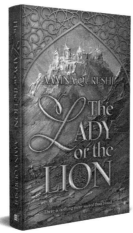

CamCat
Books

VISIT US ONLINE FOR MORE BOOKS TO LIVE IN:
CAMCATBOOKS.COM

SIGN UP FOR CAMCAT'S FICTION NEWSLETTER FOR
COVER REVEALS, EBOOK DEALS, AND MORE EXCLUSIVE CONTENT.

CamCatBooks   @CamCatBooks   @CamCat_Books   @CamCatBooks